Winner Takes All

by

Laurie Winter

Warriors of the Heart, Book 4

Winner Takes All

Contact Information: info@thewildrosepress.com

Cover Art by *Tina Lynn Stout*

The Wild Rose Press, Inc.
PO Box 708
Adams Basin, NY 14410-0708
Visit us at www.thewildrosepress.com

Publishing History
First Sweetheart Rose Edition, 2019
Print ISBN 978-1-5092-2408-1
Digital ISBN 978-1-5092-2409-8

Warriors of the Heart, Book 4
Published in the United States of America

He stared at Colleen. "This morning, the producers of the *Scavenger Hunt* show called. They want to cast me, and I told them I can't wait to beat all the other contestants."

Colleen raised her gaze to meet his.

Her large, china blue eyes still had the ability to steal his breath. His heart fluttered inside his chest.

"Well, Liberty Ridge hasn't seen something this exciting since George Quinn was drafted by the St. Louis Cardinals," Grace said with a smile. "Colleen's been cast, too."

Like his life wasn't difficult enough. "You sure you want to even bother, Colleen?" He crossed his arms across his chest. "A pampered princess with nothing but a pretty face has no shot at winning. I've spent the last five years traveling and living off the land."

"So…you admit I'm pretty?" Colleen narrowed her eyes and glared back. "You underestimate me. Good."

How could he keep his composure while competing against her? A simple answer, really. He'd make sure she was the first one eliminated.

Praise for Laurie Winter

"I loved watching these two discover each other, discover how their lives could be and how to be stronger individually…"

~*BrizzleLass Books*

~*~

"*HOME FIELD* is a real romance that will have you turning the pages and leaving the rest of the world behind. If you're a fan of good sweet romance, you'll enjoy this one."

~*My Reading Journeys blog*

~*~

"I just finished reading *AFTER ALL*, and I must say it was one of the most heart-warming and sweet romances I've read so far this year."

~*Ariel Book Blog*

~*~

"Another great romance from Ms. Winter! I really enjoyed *AFTER ALL*. I sense another story here! Looking forward to Colleen's story in the next book of the series!"

~*Stacey K.*

Dedication

To my readers.
Thank you for allowing me to share
my characters and their stories with you.
Words can't express my gratitude.
You are truly warriors of the heart.

Chapter One

A strong gust of wind ripped the sign from Colleen Gardner's festival booth and sent it soaring into the air. The park was filled with a large crowd, but unfortunately at that moment, no one was standing on the other side of her table to help.

"Shoot." She jumped to grab hold of a corner. The cursed thing had the nerve to slice her finger before the wind swept it up, out of reach. She stood on the ground, totally helpless, while the sheet of white cardstock rode an air current before starting its descent.

"You better hurry before our sign gets away." Grace sat behind the raffle booth, her baby son snug against her chest.

Colleen sprinted toward the wayward sign as it floated back to the earth before coming to rest at the base of a thick oak tree. She could barely make out the red printing spelling out—*Fifty/Fifty Raffle to Benefit Veterans' Retreat*. Two more steps and the sign would be within reach, but the wind picked up again and sent it flying toward the river.

Stupid wind. Her sign wasn't the only thing being tossed around at the Founders' Day Celebration. Food vendors waged their own battle, in an attempt to keep their plates, napkins, cups, and even their tents from blowing away.

Eventually, she accepted defeat and returned to the

welcome shade of a tent. Beads of sweat slithered down her back like rain on a windowpane. Oh well. She'd return to her booth and rustle up something to create another one. She had six more hours to sell raffle tickets. No way she'd accept defeat so easily.

The sound of a banjo and fiddle duet filled the air, along with the delicious scents drifting from the BBQ pit operating in the booth next-door. A heavyset man wearing striped denim overalls lifted one of the lids, sending up a cloud of thick, sweet smelling smoke. Her hungry stomach growled.

As she waved goodbye to her sign, which flew in the air toward the bank of the river, she observed a hand reached up out of the crowd and grabbed it. She glanced at the hand, and then lingered down a very muscular arm, which connected to a solidly male body. Finally, she looked at the man's face, and her breath hitched. He was gorgeous.

When their gazes met, the unexpected intimacy nudged her memory. But she didn't remember seeing him before. Liberty Ridge was the size of a town where, for better or worse, everyone knew one another. Once she'd totally taken in his handsome face, she noticed a little girl held in his other arm.

The girl reached her pudgy hands up toward the sign, causing the man to hide it behind his back.

With a scowl on his face, he took long strides toward Colleen and handed her the sign.

"Thanks." She gratefully accepted her runaway sign. "You have ninja reflexes."

His face didn't crack a smile.

Instead, he watched her with serious, dark brown eyes. A green baseball cap covered his head and shaded his face. The blond hair curling from under it only enhanced his rugged appeal. "I'm Colleen Gardner." She attempted to break the uncomfortable silence. "Who's the little princess?" She reached over to touch the girl's hand.

The man stepped back and scowled.

The little girl started wailing. Her pink face streaked with tears. "I want balloon." She tugged on the man's shirt and pointed to the person making balloon animals.

"I said later," he whispered. "We have to find Grandma first."

"Now," the girl cried. Her hair swung wildly as she shook her head back and forth. Her small cheeks burned red.

"Harper, once we find Grandma, then we can get you a balloon." He brushed back her hair with the palm of his hand. "But if you cry, we're going home."

"I want home. I want Momma." Harper howled and arched her back.

"Would you like me to stay with her here while you find your mom?" Colleen didn't have children of her own, but she'd learned a lot from helping Grace with baby John. "I promise I'm trustworthy. I'm from Liberty Ridge. Everybody here knows me. Your daughter will be safe until you get back."

"I don't think that's a good idea," he said over the crying child and started walking away.

"I'm sorry, but I never got your name?" She followed him, unable to help herself.

He spun to face her, a scowl on his face. "I'm surprised you don't remember me, Colleen. It's been a long time, but I thought I'd made a lasting impression."

Venom seeped through every word. The tone of his voice forced her to retreat a step. Uneasiness replaced her pleasant mood. Searching his face, she tried placing him in her memories of Liberty Ridge. She'd grown up here until at the age of eighteen, she'd moved away to attend college. This man didn't look familiar. Could he be a veteran she'd treated in the past?

He laughed.

For a second, Colleen thought she may have misinterpreted his anger.

"Colleen Gardner…you haven't changed a bit. Let me know once you've figured it out." With his little girl clinging onto his neck, her thumb stuck in her puckered mouth, he strode away.

Strange. She slowly walked back to her booth, sign in hand.

"Great, you got it," Grace said. Baby John started fussing, and Grace rocked back and forth in an attempt to calm him.

Why did her presence compel children to cry? "The weirdest thing just happened. This guy grabbed my sign before it flew into the river. When he gave it back, he acted like I should know him. He was really cute. If I'd met him before, I definitely would have remembered."

"Cute, huh?" Grace continued swaying with the whimpering baby.

"Very. If I see him again, I'll point him out." She scanned the crowd. "Maybe you'll recognize him."

Baby John tossed back his head and let out a scream, leaving little doubt of his current mood. He was only three months old but had a strong set of lungs

Grace picked up the diaper bag. "I need to find a

private place and feed him. Then Heath can take him home. The temp's too hot for a baby."

The temperature was too hot for her, too, but Colleen needed to work the booth. This raffle would only be a drop in the bucket toward the total she needed to open her veterans' retreat. Between the cost of land, building ADA compliant facilities, and hiring staff, the sum of money she had to raise seemed well out of reach.

Well, she wasn't giving up. Starting the retreat was the reason she'd moved back home. Through her practice, she'd seen too many veterans suffer with the consequences of their service in war zones. They deserved a safe place to come and heal. She only wished the financial aspect of the project wasn't holding her back. No telling when she'd finally open her doors. The nation's vets needed the retreat now. Every day, suicide rates continued to climb. "Go take care of the baby," she said to Grace. "I can work the booth myself. Come back when you can." Armed with a roll of masking tape, she went to work re-securing the sign to the front of her booth.

During the next hour, she sold almost four hundred dollars in 50/50 raffle tickets. The winner would be announced over the festival's loudspeaker at five o'clock. The people in her hometown were very supportive of what she wanted to accomplish. But most people weren't rich by any means. They did what they could to help.

A gust of wind made Colleen reach across the table and hold down her sign. Catty-corner from her own booth, flyers on an unoccupied one blew away like birds taking flight.

A young woman darted forward in an attempt to rescue a few sheets still nearby.

Colleen ran over to help wrangle the remaining flyers. "This wind is crazy." She handed the woman a small stack.

"Thanks. I should have known better than to leave these without weighing them down." She set the flyers back on her table and covered them with her laptop.

"What are you recruiting for?" Colleen read one of the flyers. "A reality TV show?"

"Yup." The young woman brushed off a few strands of brown hair stuck to her brow. "A new show called *The Great American Scavenger Hunt*. We're casting contestants from all over the country. You should send in an application video. The winner receives one million dollars."

Holy cannoli, that's a lot of money. "I'd never want to be on a reality show." Colleen imagined depositing a million dollars into her savings and how far the sum would go to fund her dream.

"Take the information." The woman handed Colleen a wrinkled flyer. "Look it over. You might change your mind. I'm sure you could find a way to spend one million dollars."

Duh. No one would turn away that kind of money. What demeaning things would she have to do on national TV in order to have a shot at winning it? No way. Instead of tossing away the flyer, she folded it up and slipped it inside her purse.

As she sat and sold raffle tickets, she continued to scan the crowd for her mystery man. She'd been racking her brain in an attempt to put a name to the face. Nothing. Why had he'd been so hostile toward her? Was he someone she'd known when she was much younger? Growing up, she certainly had not been a Pollyanna. Just the opposite, in fact. She'd been the school's resident mean girl.

If the mystery guy had attended school with her, he would have remembered Colleen. But if he had been that good-looking back then, she should remember him, too. Now, if she could just get another look, maybe she'd place him in her memories.

A glimpse of a green baseball cap above the crowds sent her heart leaping. Was that him? She craned her neck to get a better look. Oh, there he was. His little girl toddled alongside him with a firm hold on his hand.

She noticed a woman wearing a long, colorful skirt on his far side. His mother, maybe? She was too far away to get a good look.

Standing to stretch her legs, she watched as they passed. They were almost out of sight when he turned his head and looked straight at her. Under the shade of his baseball cap, she recognized contempt in his eyes. Despite the heat, her skin chilled. The scents of food cooking around her, which had smelled delicious before, turned her stomach sour.

Who was this man? And why did he hate her? She had a bad feeling he meant trouble for her fresh start in Liberty Ridge.

****

Just his luck to run into the one person in Liberty Ridge whom he didn't want to see. Storm Thompson had only been back for two days. He'd hoped to avoid seeing Colleen Gardner for as long as possible. He should have known she'd be here. The perfect citizen supporting her hometown community. *Blah*—the sight of her had made him sick.

Colleen still had the look of a princess. Her blonde hair had darkened slightly over the years, but those eyes were as distinct as a fingerprint. Ice blue, the color of a glacier, and just as cold. Of course, she hadn't recognized him. Storm had changed a lot since high school. If she'd known his name, she probably wouldn't have been so kind.

"Daddy." Harper pulled on his hand. "Up."

Now, here was a true princess. He lifted his daughter into his arms and gave her a kiss. Her lips tasted like peaches—the result of a few bites of pie she'd eaten earlier. Harper was one reason he'd returned to Liberty Ridge. His mother was the other.

Rose Petal Thompson sat on a park bench, staring blankly ahead. Most people classified his mom as an aging hippie. Her long hair was braided into two thick ropes, and she wore loose, colorful clothes made of hemp. Growing up, Storm had lived with her on a small commune on the outskirts of town. Her strange behavior had been chalked up to her lifestyle, but he knew the truth. Rose Petal had Schizoaffective disorder. As she aged, her condition grew worse.

"How do you feel, Mom? You ready to go?" He tapped on Rose's shoulder. "Mom, did you hear me? Are you ready to leave?"

"No, let's stay a little longer." Her voice was high and reedy. "The baby's having fun."

"Okay." Storm scanned the large crowd, which grew and became louder by the second. "How about we sit in the shade, and I'll get you some shaved ice? The weather's hotter than Hades out here."

They found a quiet spot, away from the noise of the crowds.

"Leave the baby with me," Rose said after she got seated. "You can't carry her and the cups of shaved ice at the same time."

He shook his head. "Harper's coming with me. You sit here and relax." After spending the past two days with his mom, he'd come to the conclusion she didn't have the attention span to safely watch an active toddler.

She wagged a finger. "Storm, I raised you, don't forget. I promise I won't let Harper out of my sight."

Yes, she'd raised him. Which was why he was so concerned. If not for the other members of the commune where he'd grown up, he might not have survived past childhood. He'd learned from an early age his mother was not someone to be counted on. If he needed something, he found a way to take care of things himself. His upbringing had made him very self-reliant, as well as being the source of many of the problems he carried into adulthood.

"Harper's staying with me. I won't argue with you." He adjusted the weight of the little girl in his arms, who became heavier as the day progressed. "I'll be right back. Don't leave this bench."

"Nana," Harper cried and reached out.

Storm continued walking, ignoring both his daughter's and his mother's shouts of protest.

Valerie had trusted him with the care of their daughter for the week. No way would he take the chance of losing Harper in the crowd. Normally, he saw his daughter every other weekend. Not nearly enough time. Now that he'd moved back to Liberty Ridge, he'd see her even less.

Litter blew across his path. Other people would blame the mess on the strong wind, but he found the weather no excuse to dump garbage on the ground. He reached down to pick up a few sheets of paper, doing his part to keep the planet clean, when the writing on one caught his eye.

Send in your application video for a chance to win one million dollars!

He read a bit farther. A production company from LA was sending out a casting call for a new reality TV show called *The Great American Scavenger Hunt*. The winner would receive one million dollars. That amount of money was incomprehensible. One million dollars would definitely breathe life into his dreams.

But he never wanted to be on a reality show. Even so, he stuffed the ad into his back pocket instead of the recycle bin. After a short walk, he approached a very long line for shaved ice. Of course it was long. The temperature had to be in the mid-nineties.

"Down." Harper wiggled in his arms.

Up, down, up, down—the playlist of his day. "Stand next to me," he instructed the two year old as he set down her small feet onto the grass.

"No way," a man's deep voice sounded. "Storm Thompson. I don't believe it."

Storm turned to see a familiar face. Rocky gained weight since the last time he'd seen his friend on graduation day. The same day Storm had packed a small bag and left town. "Rocky Diaz," he said with a laugh. "I should have known you'd grow up to be an accountant."

The men embraced in a quick hug.

"How did you know I was an accountant?" Rocky cocked an eyebrow.

"Dude, you're wearing socks with sandals." Storm's only friend in high school had been a math genius. The nerdy attire only confirmed his assumption.

"What brings you back to town?" Rocky pushed his wire-rim glasses up his nose. "Must be twelve years since I saw you last. You've changed so much I almost didn't recognize you. Actually, the sound of your voice was what jogged my memory."

"I'm here for my mom. Her friend from the commune called a few weeks ago and said they asked her to leave. Her behavior became too disruptive."

Rocky nodded. "Sorry to hear that. So, you back for good?"

He'd been the only person Storm had trusted with the truth about his mother's illness. "Maybe." He grabbed hold of Harper's hand to keep her from following the clown walking past. "I hope to convince my mom to continue seeing her psychiatrist. Of course, she's resisting. I'm also looking at buying a piece of local farmland to start an organic farm."

"Plenty of available farmland around here." Rocky glanced down at the small girl attached to Storm's side. "And who is this little one?"

"My daughter, Harper." As he introduced his daughter, pride radiated off Storm. After all the crap he'd been dealt in his life, Harper was the one bright star. Being her father was the only thing he cared about getting right.

"She's a cutie. About my own daughter's age. Anyways, let me know if I can help with a loan to buy land. I'm an accountant, as you've already figured out, and can help put together a business plan for the bank."

"Thanks. I'm not sure you can work enough magic to get a bank to approve me for a loan. My work history is not solid." To say the least. Storm had worked for the past five years as an organic farm consultant. He'd traveled around Northern California, from farm to farm, and was usually paid in cash. Besides a small savings and the joy of doing what he loved, he had little to show for his work.

"Let's find a time to sit together and discuss the matter," Rocky said as they made their way to the front of the line. "You see anyone else from high school here? There're a lot of us still hanging around town."

As Storm ordered three shaved ices, Colleen's pretty face came to mind. The ringleader of his tormentors. Where was she now? He'd love to drop this cherry ice all over her expensive haircut. "No." The memory of her 'Judas kiss' at their graduation party left him physically sick. That night had been his last in Liberty Ridge, and the last time he'd seen Colleen Gardner. "No one here I care to see. You know how they treated me…treated us."

"People change, you know." Rocky raised his hand and pointed around at the crowd. "Some of my good friends are people I never would have talked to in high school."

Rocky had grown up in a normal family, with a mom and dad who weren't crazy. Rocky was capable of forgiveness. Storm was not.

Chapter Two

Jenny Murray held up her cell phone and pointed it at Colleen. "Action," she announced with flourish.

Colleen sat behind the large, mahogany desk in her office, surrounded by the imagery of her profession. Her medical degrees hung on the wall behind her, and a large bookcase held various books most people would only read to help with insomnia.

Jenny, her good friend and mom to two great little girls, agreed to film an audition video for a new reality TV show. The idea was crazy, and Colleen had serious doubts about her sanity. But if she was cast for *The Great American Scavenger Hunt*, she'd be in the running to win one million dollars. Her veterans' retreat was important enough she'd do anything to open the doors ASAP. Colleen smoothed back her hair, which she'd wrapped in a tight bun, and then straightened her spine. "Do I look okay?"

"You look beautiful." Jenny raised her hand. "Now, let's do this…in five, four, three, two, one, go."

"Hello, my name is Doctor Colleen Gardner. I'm a Clinical Psychiatrist, practicing in Liberty Ridge, Texas. After working with many soldiers and veterans suffering with PTSD, I've made it my mission to build a place of recovery and healing."

Jenny pressed Pause and lowered her phone. "You sound as stiff as Pinocchio. Come on, loosen up. The producers want people who will be fun to watch."

She stood and paced next to her desk. "So, you're saying I'm not coming off as fun?"

"Not exactly." Jenny grinned, which caused the clef in her chin to deepen. She blew a curly strand of golden blonde hair out of her face. "Maybe you should do your video somewhere more natural. Your office feels too uptight."

Colleen figured this video wouldn't be a big deal. Just tell a little bit about herself and why they should cast her. But her friend was right. She'd be competing with thousands of other people for one of only twenty spots. Her video had to stand out from the crowd. "What I need is to channel my inner Elle Woods from *Legally Blonde.* I think I have a sparkly bikini in my dresser at home, and we could use Grace's pool."

Jenny burst out with laughter. "Perfect. The smart and sexy look got her into Harvard Law School."

Flopping down in her office chair, she sighed. "This video is hopeless. They'll never pick me."

"Why not? You're cute and smart, and the cause you're raising money for is solid. We just need to show them you're more than a tailored suit."

Colleen glanced at the expensive black suit coat, pencil skirt, and designer heels. What she wore wasn't the outfit of an adventurer ready to scour the country for clues. "You're right. The office isn't working. Would you mind meeting me at Grace's ranch in an hour?"

Looking at her phone, Jenny nodded. "Sure. Let me go pick up the girls, and I'll bring them along. They love visiting the ranch."

"You're the best." Her anxiety and doubt eased,

sending her body into a more relaxed state. Colleen crossed her fingers all this effort would pay off. Not only did she have to make a memorable video, but if she did get picked, she'd fly out to LA for a live audition. Only after jumping through all their hoops would she know if she'd be cast for the show.

Slipping her cell phone into her purse, Jenny walked toward the door. "Oh, I forgot to tell you." She spun to face Colleen. "You'll never guess who moved back into town."

Could he be her mystery man? Since the festival, she'd become obsessed with placing him. She'd even gotten out her old yearbook, but nobody matched the good-looking man at the park. "Spill, Jenny. Who?"

Jenny grinned.

Her friend looked as excited as a kid on Christmas morning. "Alex said when he was at the grocery store, he ran into Rocky Diaz. Rocky said he was at the Founders Day Festival on Saturday—"

"Get to the point. Who is it?" Colleen's curiosity built to the point of combustion.

"Storm Thompson. Can you believe it?" Her hazel eyes widened. "That's not the best part. Alex saw him at the restaurant and barely recognized him. I guess he's bulked up and looks really good. He had a little girl with him. His daughter, Harper."

Colleen's vision whirled so she held onto the desk for support. Storm Thompson was her mystery man. Why hadn't she put those details together? A car horn sounded from outside, drawing her attention to the large picture window facing the downtown street. She knew why. Because the man she'd met at the park was an altogether different person than the boy she'd known growing up. No wonder his eyes held so much hate. She didn't blame him.

"Colleen, are you okay? You look like you're getting sick." Jenny, a frown forming, stood beside her and held her arm.

"Yeah, I'm just surprised. I didn't recognize him at the festival."

"Well, don't feel bad. Most people didn't. I guess his mom is having some problems, so he's here to help."

Memories of events she'd rather forget flooded her mind. Young Storm missed school for a week at a time then returned looking like a street urchin. Once they got into high school, his attendance improved, but he still was a social misfit. Not many teens wanted to be friends with the kid who lived with a strange mom on a hippy commune, including her.

She thought back to all the pranks she'd been a part of, especially that last one. Why had she ever agreed with their plan? She could blame her choice on social pressures or wanting to please her then-boyfriend, but deep down, she'd known what she did was wrong. Yet, she invited Storm to the graduation party, gotten him alone, and then handed him over to bullies. During their graduation ceremony, shame and guilt left her physically ill, especially when she hadn't seen Storm at the ceremony then learned he'd skipped town.

The saddest part was Colleen had been best friends with Storm up until fourth grade. She'd understood too well the pain in his eyes, which he hid behind a shaggy head of hair. "Where is he living now?"

"Sounds like he's rented an apartment in town. He must plan to stay for a while."

Great. Her stomach constricted, and the chicken salad sandwich she'd eaten earlier churned in her gut. Just when she'd finally made amends for past bad behavior, another victim stepped forward to pick up the baton of hate.

Jenny patted her shoulder. "Alex talked to Storm at the restaurant. He seems not to hold any grudges. People change. You know that better than most."

Bull's-eye. "People do change, but Storm didn't seem very happy to see me at the festival." *Likely, he hates my guts.* "Next time I see him, I'll do a better job of making him feel welcome."

"Okay, enough gossip." Jenny turned to leave. "I'll see you in an hour at the ranch."

After Jenny left her office, Colleen sat in a chair by the window and stared down at the activity on Main Street. She needed to get her mind off Storm Thompson and back onto her audition video.

As she locked her office to go home and change, she was haunted by Storm's brown eyes. She should have put the puzzle together on her own. Maybe he'd changed on the outside, but his eyes looked exactly the same—filled with hurt and betrayal.

****

Storm had just settled into a downward dog pose when Harper crawled under him and settled onto the yoga mat set in the middle of his small living room. She lay on her back, feet kicking in the air. One connected with his ribs. He shifted his body weight forward into a high plank and slowly lowered himself so he hovered over the wiggly girl.

"Daddy," she said with a giggle. "Off."

He kissed her soft cheek and raised himself to a

17

sitting position on the floor. Hearing her say "daddy" was the sweetest sound in the entire world. He had Harper for another two days and planned to make the most of this visit. Before he knew it, Valerie would arrive and take her back to California. He hated living so far from his daughter, but hopefully, someday soon, Harper would wake up at his house for more than just a few mornings a month. He'd get his act together so he could properly care for his family.

Running his own farm had always been his dream. If he could get the business off the ground, he'd win on all fronts. Now, if only the money could magically appear in his bank account to purchase the land. Maybe, he'd find a pirate's chest hidden at the end of a rainbow. Unfortunately, the only rainbow on the horizon was a reality TV show.

Storm wanted to finish his morning yoga routine, but his little girl had different ideas. He sniffed her backside, and his stomach turned queasy. "Do you have a messy diaper?" He didn't have to ask. The smell of poop drifting through the air was undeniable proof.

She peeked out from behind her light red hair. "I sorry."

"No worries, princess. Let's get you changed." He grabbed a diaper and wipes from the diaper bag set in the corner of the room. Had Valerie started potty training, yet? Changing diapers was something he'd never get used to. If Harper came to stay for longer periods of time, he'd make sure she learned to use the potty ASAP.

In the middle of wiping Harper's messy bottom, his mom exited from her bedroom.

She shook her head as she approached. "Those

wipes are full of dangerous chemicals. I can help you make some natural ones. And cotton diapers would be better for the baby's skin."

Storm bit his tongue. His mom meant well. She made most of her personal body care products out of natural oils, dried flowers, and herbs. But right now, he had too much on his plate to think about using anything other than what he could pick up at the store. "Maybe next time Harper's here we can make some."

She waved her hand in the air. "I was lying in bed, thinking about the little video you have to make. The commune's garden would make a good backdrop."

"I don't think the commune will work." For a number of reasons. First and foremost being, Rose had been asked to leave the commune and not return. She'd lived there for thirty years and the place had been her home. If she returned, she'd cause a scene. With Harper as his primary concern, he didn't want to do anything that would upset his daughter.

Rose looked around the small apartment before taking a seat on the one upholstered chair in the room. "You know. I want to help. I hate thinking I'm a burden to you."

"You're not a burden, Mom. I'm doing what's best for all of us. If I can get on this show, I'll have a chance at winning enough money to take care of you and Harper. So, how about you grab my cell phone, and I'll show you how to record a video. We can shoot my audition video right here, with Harper on my lap."

Rose smiled so brightly, her face glowed. Since her official diagnosis twenty years ago, she'd lived with the knowledge of her mental illness. When Storm was a teenager, he'd convinced her to get treatment. For a few years, she'd been good about taking her medication. But then she heard she could treat herself with herbal supplements and all the prescription drugs went into the trash.

She experienced severe mood swings and often talked to people who weren't there. Some days, Storm thought he'd go crazy. When he'd left town at eighteen, he'd turned his back on her. Now, the time had come to heal their wounds.

He gave his mom a tutorial on how to use his cell phone, and then dressed Harper in a pink sundress. Not bothering to change out of his yoga gear, he sat wearing a ripped superhero T-shirt and gym shorts. Storm settled Harper on his lap.

Here goes nothing.

They got a good video after only two takes. Harper looked so sweet. How would anyone deny her? His pitch was quick and to the point. He wanted to compete in *The Great American Scavenger Hunt* not only for the adventure but to provide a safe place for his daughter to grow up—a place where she could learn and be healthy. He wanted to share his love of growing food with Harper and to see her dig in the dirt and eat what they grew.

While Harper played with her favorite doll, Storm transferred the video to his laptop. He watched it one last time, said a little prayer, and uploaded it to the show's submission link. If he was chosen, he'd have to leave for three weeks—a small cost for a shot at his dream.

One million dollars. The amount of money swum around his head. If he won, he could flat out buy the farmland, plus seeds and enough equipment to get started. He'd probably still need a small loan from the bank to really flourish. But the prize money was the key to opening doors that until now had been slammed closed in his face.

Harper walked close and handed him her doll. "My baby." She brushed the doll's yarn hair with a pudgy hand.

His throat tightened. He gazed at his precious daughter and smiled. "Yes…my baby." He'd go to the ends of the earth to make sure she knew how much he loved her.

****

Colleen stood by the gate to a cattle pasture, self-conscious nerves fluttered in her chest. She was sure she looked like an idiot. Good thing True Horizon Ranch made a perfect backdrop for her audition video. The scenery would serve as a good distraction. Texas Longhorn cattle grazing on sweet grass spotted the hills behind her. This serene environment was what she wanted for the retreat. Texas prairie country was God's gift of peace through nature.

She'd decided to change out of her power suit into something more casual. More sexy would be a better description. Colleen wore cut-off jean shorts and a plaid shirt tied at the waist, which showed off a hint of abs—the same part of her body now twisted into knots.

"Here, put this one on." Grace handed her a straw cowgirl hat. "You need to look the part."

Colleen set the hat on her head then swept her hair behind her shoulders. *Hope I don't look like a city girl trying to play country.*

The baby monitor attached to Grace's hip squawked. "John's up." Grace lowered the volume button. "He'll want to eat. I'll send out Heath to help you."

With Grace on her way back to the white farm house, Jenny smiled at Colleen. "Relax, you'll be great." She lifted her cell phone and swirled her finger, the signal to begin.

Colleen inhaled the scents of grass and damp earth. As she shifted her weight, the ground underneath her boots squished. After one last deep breath, she began her pitch.

Halfway through, Heath appeared beside her. "Let me give it to you straight." He looked into the camera and smiled. "This girl's the real MVP. She reached out when no one would touch me with a ten-foot pole. She guided me back to the light. This veteran's retreat she has planned will be a lifesaver. And I'm not saying that to be overdramatic. Vets and their families need a place like this."

Colleen's heart grew about ten sizes during Heath's speech. When she'd first opened her practice in Liberty Ridge, Heath had been one of her first patients. He'd been a tough nut—angry with himself and the world. And with his healing, he'd become the motivation behind the urgency to start her retreat.

Wiping a tear from the corner of her eye, she faced Jenny and finished her audition spiel. Afterward, she replayed the video to watch the results. Her performance was cringe-worthy, but she had to admit the pitch turned out pretty good—mostly due to Heath.

"I love it." Jenny twirled in a little dance.

Her twin girls appeared from the horse stables and ran across the yard. They were covered in dirt and hay and didn't waste a second before jumping on Heath.

Colleen laughed and stepped out of the way. "I'll take it home and upload it. Tomorrow's the cutoff date."

"They'd be crazy not to pick you." Heath shook one leg and then the other in an attempt to remove his nieces, who had both wrapped themselves around his legs. "Hey, you little barnacles. I need these to walk."

They giggled and held on tighter.

While watching the sweet interaction between the heavily tattooed, former soldier with PTSD, and the little girls, she hardened her resolve. She would get the retreat off the ground. So many veterans and their families needed her help. She had to win.

Chapter Three

Two weeks later, Colleen parked her car in the driveway of her parents' house. Well, her dad's house to be exact. Clive Gardner had lost his wife, Colleen's mother, in a car accident when Colleen was six years old. After Colleen had moved away to attend college, Clive resided in the large Spanish Colonial home alone with only a bottle of scotch for company.

She'd been so young when her mom suddenly disappeared from her life. Memories of her were worn and faded. Smells seemed to be the strongest connection between Colleen and her late mother. A breeze blowing the scent of honeysuckle or a woman walking past wearing her mother's favorite perfume would arouse a longing for someone she loved but couldn't remember.

"Dad," Colleen called out as she entered the house. Her voice echoed off the tile floors. Her childhood home had been the envy of all her classmates. The Spanish-style house was beautifully decorated and spacious, boasting a large pool and guesthouse in the backyard. No one else saw the ghosts roaming the empty halls.

She entered her dad's study and sighed. Clive sat behind his desk, a highball glass of amber liquid in his hand. By the telltale flush on his face, the drink wasn't his first of the day. "Hey, Dad. You still up for going out to dinner?"

He looked up from the papers on his desk and blinked. After several seconds, he straightened. "Oh, yes…give me about another twenty minutes to finish up these reports."

"I'll wait out on the back portico." She left the stuffy office and headed toward the sliding glass doors leading outside. The fresh air blew away the anxiety that took over whenever she was around her father. The water in the in-ground pool sparkled under the late afternoon sunshine, and she regretted not bringing her swimsuit. A quick dip in the pool would have refreshed her body and mind.

Earlier that day, Colleen had received a call from *The Great American Scavenger Hunt* producers. They'd loved her video and asked her to travel to LA for a live audition in two weeks.

By the time the phone call ended, she'd been wired with nervous excitement. If she made a good impression on the producers, in two months, she'd be competing for one million dollars. Ideas of how she would use the money for the veterans' retreat swam through her head. Through all her fundraising so far, she'd raised a decent sum. Heath donated a portion of his grandparents' inheritance, and she reluctantly accepted a very small donation from her father. The town rallied to her aid, between raffles and bake sales.

Given time, she could raise the remaining money, but she didn't want to wait. Approximately twenty-two veterans committed suicide every day—one every sixty-five minutes. That statistic drove her to do whatever she could to help the struggling. She'd even go on a silly reality adventure show because she couldn't afford to wait.

An hour later, sitting across from her dad at the Desert Rose Restaurant, Colleen watched him order another drink. Luckily, she'd be driving them both home. She often wondered if deep down he really wanted to kill himself. After twenty years of heavy drinking, he was well on his way. Clive Gardner was a classic example of a high-functioning alcoholic. From the outside, he seemed like the all-American dad, a successful business owner, and good guy. No one else saw what Colleen had to endure as a child. No one felt sorry for the rich, pretty little girl who seemed to have everything.

"How about you have an ice water instead?" Colleen said. "I have something I need to talk to you about and want you to remember our conversation."

Her dad's cheeks flushed red, and he narrowed his eyes. "You might be my daughter but that doesn't give you the right to be disrespectful. Now, what do you need to tell me?"

No one talked down to Clive Gardner, not even his own daughter. "You know I'm raising money to open a veterans' retreat. I have an opportunity to win the rest of the money."

"Win?" Her dad took a sip of the newly furnished glass of scotch. "What do you mean *win*?"

"A new reality show was advertising an open casting call. The participants travel the country in a variation of a scavenger hunt, and the show films the whole thing. The winner gets one million dollars. They want me to come out and audition. Isn't that great?" Ignoring the jitters swelling in her body, she leaned forward and rested her arms on the table.

"Really, Colleen." His mouth twisted in a sneer. "Traipsing around the country for money. Don't you think that behavior's beneath you?"

In an attempt to push away disappointment, she closed her eyes. Of course, he'd consider the show beneath her, because she was a reflection of him, and Clive would never do anything demeaning. "Beneath me? After everything our military has done to protect us, I don't see appearing on a reality show too much of an inconvenience."

Thankfully, they were spared the impending argument by the arrival of Alex Murray, the restaurant's owner and Colleen's good friend.

"Hello, Mr. Gardner, Colleen." He glanced between the two and smiled. "How's your meal?"

"Very good, Alex," Clive said. "My steak is cooked to perfection." He picked up his fork and pressed down on the meat. Red juice puddled onto the plate. "Or should I say undercooked to perfection."

"Glad to hear." Alex folded his hands and rocked back on his heels. "Have you heard back from that show yet, Colleen? Jenny told me you sent in your video a few weeks ago."

To her dad's credit, he maintained an impassive expression. He'd had years to perfect his many illusions. He hid his sharp temper just as well as he did his alcoholism. Colleen faked a smile. She'd learned from the best. "I did. They want me to audition in LA soon. Tell Jenny thanks for being a killer videographer."

"That's great!" Alex patted her shoulder. "Well, I'll let you get back to dinner. Enjoy." He walked away.

Colleen was left to finish an uncomfortable dinner

with her father.

Clive drained the rest of his drink, set down his glass on the table, and picked up his steak knife. "You're not doing that show. I'll give you whatever money you need for your little retreat thing. No daughter of mine will humiliate herself on national television."

Frustration brewed. She leaned an elbow on the table and pinched the bridge of her nose. A tsunami of a headache washed away her previous good mood. Taking her dad's money would be easy but attached to those dollars were strings. Clive was a master puppeteer, and she refused to be yanked around.

****

Storm ran his fingers over Harper's fabric doll. The doll's soft felt face snagged on the rough patches on his hand. He tossed the doll in the basket of toys set off in the corner of the room. The apartment he rented month-to-month was adequate. The small space had a tiny living room, galley kitchen, one bathroom, and two bedrooms. Right now, this place was all he could afford. But a rundown apartment with peeling wallpaper was no place to raise his little girl.

Every day away from Harper made the hole in Storm's chest grow a little larger. Last weekend, Valerie met him in Austin to take Harper back to Sacramento. His life would have been so much easier if he and Valerie stayed together. They broke up before she found out she was pregnant. Storm tried to make the relationship work. In the end, they just didn't love each other enough to commit to forever. "Mom, I'm meeting the realtor about the farmland for sale," he called down the hall. One nice thing about their tight quarters was he never had to raise his voice in order to be heard. "Do you want to come with?"

"You really starting your own farm?" Rose stood at the doorway to her room, wearing a loose, colorful sundress.

"I don't know. I need the money first. But I drove by this piece of land for sale the other day, and I want to go check it out." His first choice would be to buy land in Northern California to be close to Valerie and Harper, but the region was ridiculously expensive. Plus, he had his mom to consider. She might need more time before she was ready to relocate.

"You win on that show, and you'll have more than enough money to buy that land. You can show the people in this town that a Thompson is just as good as the rest of them." She brushed the palm of her hand over his scruffy cheek. "I'm sorry I wasn't a better mother. I want to help you now, however I can."

"You can help by taking care of yourself. I'm flying to LA next weekend for the live audition. I need to know you'll stay on your medication while I'm gone." He'd dragged her to see her doctor the day after Harper left. If she wanted to be a part of his and Harper's life, she needed to start back on her prescription meds. No more excuses. No more lying to convince him she was doing fine. He wasn't subjecting his daughter to the dangerous roller coaster ride he'd endured growing up.

"I promise to take my pills. I want you to go and get on that show. They'll pick you for sure. You've grown into such a handsome man."

Every time he looked in the mirror, he wondered what his father looked like. Rose had met him at the commune—a dashing stranger traveling across the country. After a few nights together, he'd moved on, never to be seen or heard from again. Nine months later, Storm was born. Rose never even learned the man's last name.

"So, are you coming?" Storm asked. "My meeting with the realtor is in fifteen minutes." After a short car ride out of the city limits, Storm pulled off on a dirt road. About a quarter of a mile down was the realtor's beige sedan.

The property was perfect. Off in the distance, he could see a pond edged by tall trees. The realtor, a woman with a hairstyle that would have made the 80s proud, greeted them.

"Hi, Rose. So nice to see you again." Nicole Evans gave his mom a stiff smile before turning her attention. "Well, Storm…here's the property. What do you think?"

Before he could answer, another car approached, dust kicking up behind its tires. Just his luck, another potential buyer. Best case scenario, he was still months out from having the funds to buy this land—and only if he was cast for the show, and then won. By the time he'd be ready to purchase, this farmland would probably be long gone.

A silver luxury car parked behind his old clunker. Two women exited and began walking his way. Storm's blood pressure immediately soared like the red-caped superhero—up, up, and away. He couldn't believe his eyes. What was Colleen Gardner doing out here? On his farmland?

When she saw him, her eyes widened.

So, she'd finally figured out his identity. Was she

disappointed he wasn't the short, underweight boy who she'd loved to make fun of? He'd never make the mistake of trusting her again. If she thought she had any chance of belittling him now, she'd be very disappointed.

The woman walking with Colleen approached his realtor.

Colleen came to stand by his mother. "Hi, Ms. Thompson." She smiled at Rose. "You look lovely today."

Storm stepped between them.

Rose moved around Storm and took Colleen's hand. "Hello, dear. What are you doing out here?"

"Mom, let's take a walk and check out the pond." Storm took hold of Rose's elbow and started to lead her away.

She shook out of his grasp. "Don't be rude, Storm. Surely, you remember Colleen Gardner from school."

Colleen stared back with wide, ice blue eyes, which were framed with thick, dark lashes. If she wanted to look pure and innocent, she'd have to try harder. "Oh, I remember Colleen all right. She made sure she was pretty unforgettable." Storm stood with his arms crossed over his chest and a scowl on his face. He would have growled but decided that immature act would earn a slap from his mom.

"Storm." Colleen's knuckles paled as she gripped the handles of her purse. "Nice to see you again. I'm happy you're back in town."

"From what I remember, you were only happy flying around on your broom."

Rose elbowed him in the ribs. "Storm, what's gotten into you?"

"It's fine, Ms. Thompson. I deserve his scorn." Colleen's smile faltered.

"Call me Rose. Did you know Storm is looking to start his organic farm? He thinks this land would be perfect." Her hand swept over the rolling landscape. "Why are you here? Are you looking to start farming, too?"

Colleen's eyes really met his for the first time.

"Oh, no. I'm opening a retreat for veterans suffering from mental and physical trauma as a result of their service. My friend, Michelle, found this property for sale and thought it's the perfect location. She's right. It is amazing."

He suppressed his eager temper. No way he'd lose this land to Colleen. "That's right, you're a shrink now."

Colleen stepped forward and jammed a finger into his chest. "You've been gone for a long time, so I'll cut you some slack, but don't you ever discredit my practice." She tipped her head to meet his gaze. "I serve men and women who have given more to our country than we should ever ask. My mission is to help them make the transition into civilian life. The retreat I plan on opening is a tool to facilitate that."

"Too many fancy words for my simple farmer brain." Storm glanced down and imagined snatching her ridiculous-looking shoes and throwing them into the pond. Who wore high heels while walking around out in a field?

"So I've gathered." Colleen's blue eyes flashed.

He and Colleen mixed up a toxic potion.

Rose stepped between them. "I don't understand half of what you two are saying to each other. Colleen,

I'm glad to see you again. Storm, let's look at that pond."

Grabbing the hem of his shirt, she pulled him away from the impending eruption. For a middle-aged woman, Rose was quite strong.

"If you plan on living in Liberty Ridge, you'll have to learn to be nice to Colleen."

His mom's green eyes pierced his conscience. "Why? Because her dad's the richest man in town?"

"No. Clive Gardner has nothing to do with your behavior toward Colleen."

They stopped beside the pond. He imagined his livestock bending their necks for a cool drink. He relaxed, and the tension in his neck and shoulders fell away.

Rose lost her balance on the uneven ground and took hold of his hand to steady herself. "Colleen has done a lot of good for the town. She's helped people, myself included. She used to come out to the commune and talk with me. Colleen is one of the few people whom I've ever felt comfortable talking to about my…you know, condition."

He couldn't have been more stunned if his mom had grown wings and flown away. Meany Colleeny had visited his mom? She'd taken the time to help Rose, even without payment.

Okay, he'd conceded Colleen had grown up over the years. She'd gotten prettier since high school. Back then, he wouldn't have thought she could get more beautiful. But a cute body and a few good deeds didn't erase all the hurt she'd caused. And now, she might be after his dream piece of farmland.

Six years ago, he started yoga. Through daily

practice, he'd flushed out many toxins. During meditation, he'd learned the art of healing. He'd forgiven his mother for his upbringing and problems outside her control.

Storm had let go of what made him unhappy. Instead, he focused his energy on his dreams. Now that he was home, where bad memories resided, he slipped back into old habits. Even after so many years, forgetting his feelings for Colleen seemed impossible.

Chapter Four

At least one hundred people must be stuffed into this room. Colleen lost count after sixty. Her rear had gone numb from sitting on a hard plastic chair for the last two hours, and she wiggled her toes in an effort to rejuvenate circulation in her legs. When she'd flown to LA for the live audition for *The Great American Scavenger Hunt*, she'd pictured a small, intimate affair. Not the cattle-loaded-into-a-semitrailer scenario playing out before her.

While she waited, she'd tried talking to a few people. None were friendly. Everyone who did engage in conversation mentioned they were from the Los Angeles area and aspiring actors. Most people seemed to be looking for a break into the entertainment industry. Merely getting on TV was their goal. The prize money was a nice perk.

According to the digital number displayed on the wall, she had two more auditions to go before her number was called. *Ugh*. She just wanted to get out of this claustrophobic room and breathe some fresh air. Once she checked into her hotel, she'd take a long walk on the beach. The Pacific Ocean was calling her name.

While her mind wandered to the point where she could almost feel the sand between her toes, she caught a glimpse of a familiar face in the crowd. His hair drew her gaze. A tingling sensation traveled over her skin at the sight of Storm Thompson. The room, which had seemed matchbox small before, closed in.

She blinked a few times to clear her vision. Maybe the man was only someone who resembled Storm. Colleen looked again. Nope, the man really was him. Why would he be at this audition? The answer hit her like a sucker punch. Storm wanted to buy the same land she'd been looking at. He needed the prize money to start his farm.

When their gazes met, she had the slight satisfaction of watching recognition dawn on his face. He appeared to be just as unhappy as she was. Colleen smirked. Very immature, she'd admit, but Storm brought out an adolescent side. Since he'd returned to town, he treated her like the black plague. The nice, quiet boy she'd known grew up to be a world-class jerk.

He reclined in his chair, putting himself out of her line of sight.

She noticed an empty seat to his left. She'd go over and play nice. What's the worst that could happen? "Hey, Storm," she said as she approached. "Seems like we can't get away from each other."

He gazed up and sat with his foot resting on his knee, arms crossed over his broad chest. His strong chin pushed up in a defiant pose. Bicep muscles rippled as he tensed his arms. "If I didn't know any better, I would say you're following me."

Even with the unpleasant expression, he looked enticing. Colleen sat in the empty chair. "You're not that interesting. I have plenty to do without adding stalker to my list."

"How long has it been, Colleen?" He looked her up and down.

"Over twelve years. You've changed since high school. So have I." Storm's face appeared relaxed, but she could detect a hint of anger behind the facade. She cleared her throat. The room now felt uncomfortably hot and dry. Was the air conditioning shut off?

"Did you go to 'mean girl' rehab?" He narrowed his eyes." Or did you wake up one day and realize how evil you were?"

She twisted her body to face him. "For crying out loud, Storm, we're thirty years old. Back then, we were a couple of kids. How long will you hold a grudge?"

"You think what I feel for you is a little grudge?" He laughed, causing several other people in the room to turn in their direction. "You grew up privileged and had everything handed to you on a silver platter. And what did you do with your privilege?" A sneer curled one side of his mouth. "You made the lives miserable of those of us who didn't have the blessing of your approval. After what happened the last time we were together, I never wanted to see you again."

She hadn't wanted to face herself at times. The crack in her heart widened. Nausea built behind her forced smile. "I'm sorry. How can I make things right with you?" If making amends with a man with Storm's long-held animosity was even possible?

A female voice over the loudspeaker called Colleen's number.

She stood and ran hands down the front of her floral dress, smoothing out the wrinkles. "I'd like a chance to finish our conversation. Are you staying at the Sea View Inn? The show's producers booked my room there."

"I have nothing more to say. I'm not falling for

your sweetheart act like everyone else in Liberty Ridge." Storm turned his head to glare straight ahead. "You better get a move on, or you might miss your audition. Oh…and don't choke."

An evil grin pulled on his lips, telling her he wanted her to do just that. By the time she stepped into the audition room, she was completely flustered. The gentle Storm she'd known back in grade school was replaced by a bitter man. She'd been so tempted to kick him on the shin on her way out of the waiting room.

At the front of the room, four of the show's producers sat at a long table.

She took a seat on the lone chair in the center of the room.

A man stepped toward a video camera. Seconds later, a red light glowed above the camera's lens.

Her audition started with a few simple questions about her hometown, education, and profession. Before long, she forgot about the camera and talked from the heart. She explained her plan for starting the retreat and her commitment to helping the country's veterans. When she completed her interview, she stood to leave.

A male producer with long, black hair raised his hand. "Before you go. I see we have another audition for someone else from Liberty Ridge." He glanced back at his notes. "Storm Thompson. Do you two know one another?"

Great. Her audition had been going so well. "We went to school together but didn't hang out in the same circles. Storm moved away after high school. Until recently, I hadn't seen him in a very long time.

"So, you're not friendly?" A female producer tapped the eraser end of a pencil on the wood tabletop.

The opposite of friendly. Contentious was a better word to describe her and Storm's relationship. "We left town after high school and both recently moved back home, so I have no idea what his life is like now."

The producer smiled. "One of the casting agents saw you two talking in the waiting room and that your conversation looked heated."

All her dreams of winning evaporated. The prize money floated away, up into the blue sky and forever out of reach. "Storm and I have a difference of opinion on how we view our past. He's not my biggest fan."

"So, we shouldn't worry about you teaming up if you were both cast?" The producer with the long, black hair pressed his lips together and furrowed his brow.

Colleen wanted to burst out with laughter. "Storm would rather poke out his own eyes than help me. I can assure you that he wants nothing to do with me, whether we're on a TV show or not." What were the odds they'd both be chosen?

"Perfect," the long-haired man said. "Well, that's a wrap. Thank you, Dr. Gardner for your interest in *The Great American Scavenger Race*. We'll make our final casting decision within the next two weeks. You'll hear from us soon."

On shaky legs, Colleen approached the table and shook each producer's hand. The back of her shirt was damp with perspiration. Her armpits felt sticky and gross. A cool shower was first on her to-do list once she checked into the hotel.

As she entered the hallway, Storm was led toward the audition room. He didn't look her way as he passed. What would happen if they both were selected? He'd make sure her life was miserable the entire time on the road. They'd compete for the same prize money and only one of them would walk away the winner. If she won, and she planned to, he'd hate her even more.

Storm disappeared into the audition room.

Along with him went Colleen's desire to make amends. So what if he still held a grudge? Let him stew in a bath of his own hostility. What did she care? Storm Thompson would eat her road dust.

****

Colleen Gardner sightings were as welcome as a pinched nerve, always popping up at the worst moments. Despite Colleen's presence, Storm finished the audition interview feeling optimistic. Now back at the hotel, he stripped and took a long shower. Between the flight, and then sitting in the waiting room all afternoon, he was left with a strong desire to scrub himself clean.

He wasn't naive enough not to think Colleen was the kind of contestant the show wanted. Who could resist her—a blonde bombshell with blue eyes, a pretty smile, and a smart brain. Even after years apart, he hated himself for his lingering attraction. Every time he saw her, his body burned with desire. He was no better now than the love-struck fool he'd been in high school.

After his shower, Storm tossed on a pair of shorts, grabbed his yoga mat, and headed to the beach. He found a quiet strip of grass along the sand and unrolled his mat. The familiar routine calmed his nerves. Salty sea air filled his lungs and tickled his nose. A few seagulls stood on the beach, squawking and fighting over a piece of left behind food.

He settled into the Warrior II pose. His quad stretched as he pushed his knee toward the ocean. With a soft diaphragm, he breathed deeply. He focused on his *drishti*, or meditation focal point—a sailboat bobbing atop the waves. The sound of approaching footfalls disrupted his concentration.

"Mind if I join you? This patch is the only level grass." Colleen wore a tight tank top and slim yoga pants. Under her arm was tucked a pink yoga mat with Sea View Inn written on its surface with black marker. She bent over to unroll her mat.

Storm was gifted with a good look at her backside. His ankles wobbled under him, and he lost his balance. "I do mind."

"Eat sand," she muttered as she knelt down and settled into the child's pose.

A fragile restraint was the only thing keeping him from dumping a handful of sand over her blonde head.

They spent the next fifteen minutes side-by-side in a temporary treaty of silence. His gaze continually was drawn to Colleen. The sound of her deep breathing filled the air around them, and he remembered the little girl he'd once loved. She was a ray of sunshine in his dark life. His mom never forced him to attend school, but he had gone because of Colleen.

Had she known how much her friendship meant? No, she couldn't have. Or maybe she did and had used his feelings to inflict pain later on. Sorrow pressed on his chest, and he shook off the bad memories. He long ago mended his broken child's heart.

With a deep exhale, Colleen lowered to her mat and sat cross legged. With her eyes closed, she tipped her head toward the sky. "How did your audition go?"

The reflection of the setting sun turned her long, golden hair a copper red. "Fine." He wouldn't give her any more information than that.

"What if we both are selected? Do you think we'd end up killing each other?"

She smiled softly, full lips tilting up like a crescent moon. The skin on her shoulders glowed with the warmth of the fading sun. He wondered what she'd do if he reached over and ran his finger along the jut of her collar bone. Would she welcome his touch or slap his face? "I wouldn't waste my energy on fighting with you. Besides, you'd be too far behind to be serious competition."

Colleen's thin arms crossed over her chest, and one eyebrow arched. "You know nothing about me, Storm. If I get cast for the show, I plan to win."

"I do know you." He grinned at the years of knowledge he'd collected. Years he spent studying her while she, for the most part, had ignored him. "I know how much you hate snakes, and you have a fear of tight spaces. You never leave your house without doing your hair and makeup. No way would you survive two days competing on the road, let alone win."

"You have me all figured out, don't you?" Her ice blue eyes narrowed. "Your knowledge is long past its expiration date."

His body warmed with a strong attraction. The smell of her coconut lotion clouded his reasoning. *Don't forget, you don't like this woman.* "People like you don't really change. You only became good at hiding your ugliness."

"Grow up." Her voice carried away in the ocean breeze. "What right do you have to be my judge and jury? Do you even remember the good times between us? Like in kindergarten, when I'd rub your back at naptime."

The ghost feeling of her soft hand running across his back drained the anger from his body. During his first few weeks of school, he'd been afraid to fall asleep during naptime. Every afternoon, Colleen sat on the floor by his cot and worked her soothing magic.

"Or have you forgotten the books I brought you when you had a hard time learning to read? How I'd sit during recess and listen to you struggling to pronounce the words?"

"I remember." He clenched his fists. "I also remember the day you turned from someone I trusted to someone who mocked me like every other kid in school."

Frowning, Colleen choked back a sob. "I'm sorry. I was young and stupid. I should have never treated you the way I did."

Reaching for her hand, he pressed the warmth to his chest. "You used to sneak me candy," he whispered in her ear. "Strawberry candies from your dad's office. You would give me one almost every day after lunch." His lips swept across her smooth-as-glass cheekbone. If he kissed her, would she still taste like a strawberry?

His lips lowered onto her mouth, and she didn't fight his kiss. She did taste sweet, but different than he remembered—like honey and cinnamon. He'd only been a boy when their chaste kiss left him breathless. The soft yield of Colleen's lips rekindled feelings he'd worked hard to expel.

Her hands rested on his shoulders then wrapped around his neck. She sank into him.

"Remember our first kiss?" His voice came out raspy and strained. His body and mind fought for control.

Colleen trembled. Stepping back, she widened her eyes. "Storm, don't—"

He pressed a finger over her lips. "I was ready to tell you everything in my young heart."

"We were only in fourth grade." Her eyes shone with unshed tears.

"To me, our age didn't matter. I cared about you and wanted our first kiss to be something special." He fought his longing for her with his well-seasoned bitterness. "I'll never forgive you for what you did."

Fat tears trickled down her flushed cheeks. "You have to…believe me. I…didn't know those other kids followed me. I didn't know…what to do." Her words came out in a broken rush.

"You could have stood up for me." Storm let his hand fall from her waist. Touching her left him with a strange mix of repulsion and longing. "You didn't have to join in. You were my only friend." He grabbed his yoga mat off the ground and marched around her, heading back to the hotel. Anger flowed through his veins so hard and fast he was afraid his arteries would burst.

As he walked away, he could hear the sound of Colleen's cry mixed with the evening songs of the seagulls—a haunting melody.

Chapter Five

Still standing on the beach, Colleen thought back to that fateful day in the fourth grade. She'd been working on a picture to give her teacher when a white piece of paper appeared on her desk.

Meet me by the tall tree at recess. I have a secret.—Storm

When the bell rang for recess, she peeked back at Storm, who always sat in the back of the room. His head lay on his desk, with his curly hair falling over his forehead to cover his face.

He looked up and smiled.

No one else had a smile like Storm. Butterflies fluttered inside her chest. She was too busy watching Storm to notice Tyler grab the note off her desk.

"*Oooohhh*, Storm has a secret." Tyler held the note high in the air. "Maybe he's really a freaky alien."

Colleen leaped up to grab at the note, but she wasn't tall enough. "Give that back, Tyler. Now."

"Fine." He let the note drop onto the vinyl tile floor. "Why do you want to be around Stinky Storm anyway? He wears the same shirt to school every day and smells like old food."

"Shut up." She picked Storm's note off the ground. "Leave him alone."

Tyler walked away, laughing.

Colleen shoved the note into the pocket of her

shorts and headed outside for recess. She hated the way Tyler talked about other people, especially Storm. All the other kids in class followed his lead. Skipping under the bright sun, she found Storm hiding behind a tall tree.

He looked down at his dirty sneakers, kicking up small stones.

"I'm here." She hopped over and landed at his side. Standing next to a large oak tree, they were hidden from the rest of the playground. "So, what's your secret?"

Storm raised his head and gazed back with wide eyes. He stood silent for a long time. Then, he took a deep breath and leaned in.

Colleen wanted to close her eyes but couldn't. She watched Storm's puckered lips move toward her in slow motion. He was about to kiss her. When their lips connected, she felt a static electricity shock and jumped.

Their kiss only lasted a few seconds. Colleen wanted to try kissing again, until the sound of teasing voices broke the spell. Practically their whole class now gathered around the tree, laughing.

"Colleen kissed Stinky Storm," one girl taunted. "I bet she has lip fungus."

Tyler reached out and pushed Storm. "You think she likes you? Colleen told us to come over so you'd leave her alone."

"That's not true. I didn't tell them," Colleen pleaded. "I promise."

"Storm and Colleen, sitting by a tree, k-i-s-s-i-n-g," a redheaded boy with a missing front tooth sang.

Finally, their teacher strode over and put a stilling

hand on Colleen's shoulder. "What is happening over here?"

"Colleen and Storm were kissing." Tyler pushed back a lock of blond hair. "It looked so gross I think I'm sick."

Her face and body grew hot, and her stomach threatened to heave. Why couldn't everyone just leave her alone?

Their teacher grabbed Colleen's hand. "Go sit on the bench by the door. Your father will not be happy about your behavior."

While she walked away, Storm took off running in the other direction.

Their teacher yelled for him to come back, but he didn't. He left the playground and sprinted down the road.

For the rest of the day, Colleen felt like vomiting. She wanted to go home and get away from the other kids who teased her. But she did not want to see her dad. She could almost hear him scolding her for being a disappointment to the Gardner name.

After that day, Storm was absent from school for several weeks. When he finally returned to their classroom, she had to show the other kids she wasn't his girlfriend like they'd been teasing. To her shame, she no longer treated him like a friend. His note and their kiss caused her trouble with her dad, and she became the laughing stock of the entire Liberty Ridge Elementary School.

As they progressed through each grade, their ill will turned into outright hostility. She used her words as weapons, and Storm purposely did things to make her squirm, like the time in eighth grade when he'd changed the school's outdoor sign to read, *Congratulations Colleen Gardner on your pregnancy*.

When she learned Storm was behind the fake message, she plotted her revenge. A little laxative snuck inside his hot lunch had gone a long way.

Now, years later, Colleen stood facing the cool wind blowing off the water and shivered. Why did memories of Storm still rip out her heart? Until their fourth grade kiss on the playground, Storm had been a small bird under the shelter of her wing. Colleen rolled her yoga mat, and guilt rose to choke her.

With the fading daylight, the rolling ocean turned a steel gray, mirroring her own melancholy mood. She licked her lips and tasted the salt of her tears mixed with the spicy aftertaste of Storm. Earlier, when he'd leaned in to kiss her, the earth tipped underneath her feet. She'd thought he offered a chance to renew their friendship. Colleen was a naïve twit to believe Storm held anything but contempt. And why shouldn't he? After the way she betrayed him, just when he'd needed her friendship the most.

Looking back on the situation as an adult, she mentally berated herself. She had a choice—to stand by Storm or keep her other friends. Unfortunately, she'd chosen the wrong side.

Their first kiss broke their friendship. Their second kiss, here on the beach, asserted she had no hope of ever getting it back.

****

Back home, Storm tossed his bag onto the floor of his apartment and walked into the kitchen to get a drink of water. After a whirlwind trip to California and back, he was tired of airports and planes.

He swore he wouldn't let Colleen occupy any more of his thoughts, but the look in her eyes last night still pricked at his conscience. Throwing their first kiss in her face had been a low blow. Back then, they were both young and acted like children. Now as an adult, he held himself to a higher standard.

His mom sat in the rocking chair, knitting something resembling a snake that barfed up a rainbow. "Hey, there." He gave her a peck on the cheek. "You stay out of trouble while I was gone?"

The knitting needles in her hands trembled. "I was a good girl. I took my medicine, even though it makes me sick."

"Your medicine makes you sick?" Storm knelt before her on the carpeted floor, pushing aside a few skeins of colorful yarn.

"I just don't feel like myself." Rose shrugged. "I don't feel like eating, not even my vegetables. And you know how much I love my vegetables."

Worry for her health grew. "Your body might need more time to adjust. When we see your doctor on Wednesday, you can ask him about it."

Rose scoffed and waved a hand. "Those doctors use their prescription pad as a magic wand. I don't think he listens to half the things I say. He didn't even want to discuss my natural supplements."

Everything she said was true, but at least her doctor and the medication kept her stable—which was a sharp contrast to her behavior before he came home. "I know modern medicine isn't perfect, but you need to keep seeing him."

"Colleen's a doctor, and she actually takes the time to listen to me. No one ever listens. Can I go see her, instead?" Rose's chin trembled, and her knitting needles fell from her hands onto the floor. "You hate me, don't you? I was a bad mom."

He knew this song and dance well—guilt and reassurance. Storm knelt and took hold of her hands. They were cold to the touch, like frost on a flower petal. "Why do you think I hate you? Aren't I here to help?"

"Colleen said holding onto anger is like drinking poison."

He smirked. "I believe Buddha said that."

"*Humph*. Well, I heard the saying from Colleen." She patted his cheek. "Storm, I love you. I see the poison of anger inside you. You do a good job of hiding your feelings, but I'm your mother. I can tell."

How could he explain the deep-seated resentment still germinating in his heart? Maybe he didn't have to. His mom might not have been mother of the year, but she had a witch's talent for peering into a person's soul. "I want to make things right between us. Being back in Liberty Ridge stirs up a lot of bad memories."

"The people in this town are generally good. I know you were teased a lot growing up, and the teasing was because of my neglect. I'm so sorry." Her shoulders sagged. "I hope you can start seeing the positive energy flowing around you and stop letting the negative have control."

"I'm dripping in positive energy." He wouldn't debate his mom. Despite, or maybe as a result of, her mental illness, she was one of the most generous and loyal people he'd ever met. "What do you want for dinner? I need to go to the grocery store."

"Go to Nature's Harvest Market. Their produce is

to die for." Rose's blue eyes sparkled. "I never asked you how your audition went. Did they pick you?"

"I'll know in two weeks." Should he mention Colleen had been there, as well? Probably let that sleeping dog lie. For some reason, his mom had elevated Colleen to saint status.

"You know, I was at the park yesterday doing tai chi and heard the funniest thing. Colleen went to LA, too. Did you see her?"

Why did he think he could keep anything from his mom? "LA is a big town."

"I thought maybe she was doing the same thing you were. I saw the advertisement for the show at the Founders' Day Celebration."

He shivered at the notion his mom really did have psychic powers. She could always sniff out his bull. Once in his junior year, he'd snuck off the commune to meet up with some pothead guys from school. That night had been the one night his mom paid attention to where he was going. She caught him before he stepped foot off the commune, and he spent the next month pulling weeds—the real kind—out of the community garden. "Colleen was at the audition." He shook his head. "Knowing my luck, she'll be chosen, and I won't."

"What if they picked you both?" Smiling, she clapped her hands. "How wonderful."

Yeah, not wonderful. He broke out into a sweat simply thinking about spending time with her. "I think the chances arc pretty low."

"If they were smart, they would pick you both. Oh, imagine the fireworks. You've always carried a flame for that sweet girl."

What girl was she referring to? Colleen was not sweet. "I've never carried a flame for Colleen. She's a rich brat."

"I remember you coming home from school and all you talked about was Colleen this and Colleen that." Rose gave him a pat on the shoulder and kissed his cheek. "When I moved, I found a stack of letters hidden under your old mattress. They were all made out to her. You were too young to understand that you loved her."

Storm jumped to his feet. "What you found were letters written by a silly boy. I didn't love her then and definitely don't love her now. I wouldn't be shocked if she has horns and a tail tucked beneath her couture clothes."

Rose closed her eyes and inhaled deeply. "Colleen was right. Anger is like drinking poison."

"Again…I'm pretty sure she stole that saying from Buddha. And for crying out loud, the woman is far from a saint." Pressure built behind Storm's eyes. His temples pounded with a growing headache.

Rose huffed then picked her knitting needles off the floor and resumed her work.

Why did he always come out the bad guy? His own mother would side with Colleen if push came to shove. Was there something in Liberty Ridge's water that made people totally oblivious to her true nature? Maybe he was on a reality show right now, and everybody else in town was in on the joke, even his own mother.

Forget *The Great American Scavenger Hunt*. He was already starring in a remake of *The Truman Show*.

****

"I feel like I'm on freaking *Days of our Lives*," Colleen said to Grace as they stood in the main aisle of the ranch's horse stable. "I'm the evil vixen ruining his life."

"Give him more time." Grace nuzzled a gray-colored mare, who hung her head over the stall door. "He hasn't gotten reacquainted with the reformed you, yet. The fact you and I are now good friends should testify to how much we've all grown up since we were teenagers."

True, but Storm's anger was a different beast. Their early relationship, despite being one of youthful affection, had only heightened his negative feelings. "We could spend from now until judgment day together, and he'd still hate me. All because of a stupid kiss in the fourth grade."

Grace raised her eyebrows and grinned. "You and Storm have kissed? Oh, do tell."

If Grace was excited about a kiss between two knobby-kneed kids, how would she react if Colleen told her she'd kissed a very grown-up Storm on an LA beach? She'd probably have to scoop Grace's jaw off the stable floor.

"When we were in fourth grade, Storm kissed me on the playground. When we got caught, everyone started making fun of me." She reached down to pet the orange tabby cat rubbing against her leg. The cat purred and wrapped around her leg, looking for more. "When I got home from school, my dad ordered me to stay away from that 'white trash.' You see, I'd been Storm's only friend, and after our kiss, I just wanted him to go away. You already know how we pranked each other throughout middle and high school. And then, I was a part of a really bad prank the night before graduation. Tyler and a bunch of his friends roughed him up pretty good."

Grace put up her hand to cover her mouth. "I heard a rumor about Storm being beaten up the night before graduation, but I hadn't heard you had anything to do with it. You should accept the fact that in his story, you are the wicked witch."

Would she ever be free of her past behavior? Frustration gave way to sorrow, and tears filled her eyes. "I'm scared we'll end up playing against each other for the prize money. I know he wants to start a farm and raise his daughter there. If I get in the way of his dream, I'll be so much worse than a wicked witch in his mind."

"Just wait and see if either of you gets picked." Grace looped an arm through Colleen's. "From what you said, a lot of people were at the audition. You both being chosen is a long shot."

As she exited the barn, Colleen squinted into the bright sunlight. She slipped on her sunglasses and saw Heath sitting on the farmhouse porch, rocking little John in his arms. "You're right. I shouldn't borrow trouble." Colleen walked toward the house, and then stepped into the cool shade of the porch. "Did I tell you I found the perfect property for the veterans' retreat?"

Heath lifted a finger to his lips in a *shhh* gesture. "Is the land close by?" he whispered.

Glancing down at the sweetly sleeping infant, she felt her sadness lift. "Mrs. Lyons is selling a fifty-acre plot from her late husband's farm about ten miles from here. The spot is perfect and has a flat section for the cabins and main buildings. Otherwise, the landscape is rolling hills dotted with a few ponds." A true smile pulled at her lips. "I finally picture the retreat as real and not just a dream."

"I never doubted your dream would become a reality." Heath stood and handed the little bundle of baby to Grace.

John let out a half-hearted cry then dozed again in his mother's arms.

Colleen couldn't help but wonder when she'd become a wife and mother. The right man had proven harder to find than an honest politician. She'd almost married once but luckily discovered he was an unfaithful lout before the wedding instead of after. He'd also been a raging alcoholic. In retrospect, she understood her fiancé was an image of her father, and she'd wanted nothing more than to finally earn her father's love.

Over the years since, she'd grown into a woman who was independent, honest, and strong. So, Storm Thompson could take his bad attitude and kissable lips and go jump off a tall cliff. She wouldn't let him get inside her head. Let him try kissing her again. Next time, he wouldn't be walking away so smug.

Next time? Where had that thought come from? Light tingles danced across her skin. She'd happily go to the grave without Storm's lips ever touching hers again.

Chapter Six

One month had passed since the live audition in LA, and in that time, Storm lost hope he'd compete for the one-million-dollar prize. Needing to earn some quick money, he got a temporary job with a local rancher. But with little money coming in and more going out, he'd run through his savings soon. Forget about buying land to start a farm, if he didn't find a full-time job soon, he and his mom would end up on the street.

To make matters more pressing, that morning Valerie informed him she accepted a one-year assignment in Brazil. She would leave in January, and Storm would have Harper permanently. But only if he proved he could provide a safe, stable home for their daughter.

Valerie would never sign-off on granting him full custody with his current lack of resources. In that case, his daughter would go live with her parents in New York—too far away from Liberty Ridge. Sure, he could take her to court, but a custody fight wasn't best for his daughter. He would move to New York, maybe leaving his mom in Texas—again.

His plan to start an organic farm was the key to keeping his family together. The reality show was his one and only lifeline in funding his dream.

Rose experienced several psychiatric episodes over

the past few weeks, but he handled them without much drama. Though, he still got freaked out when she talked to people who weren't there. She swore the voices she heard were real. As long as she kept the conversations confined to their apartment, everything was fine. But when she shouted in anger in the middle of a store, he received a phone call from a very concerned store manager.

Storm just disconnected from video chat, having tried to reach Valerie to talk with Harper, when his cell phone rang.

The female voice on the other end introduced herself as a casting producer for *The Great American Scavenger Hunt*. Without fanfare, she offered him a spot on the show.

His mind spun as she continued on with the details. He answered questions he barely comprehended. Yes, he'd love to compete on the show. No, he hadn't had a physical during the past year. Yes, he had an email address she could send all the details and forms. His heart pounded against his rib cage.

After he disconnected the call, he sat and collected his thoughts. He pictured winning the prize money, buying that land, and then driving a tractor over a field with Harper on his lap. His daughter could toddle around with the ducks and sheep, living the kind of life he'd always wanted for himself. More importantly, she'd grow up safe and loved.

This good news called for a celebration. Rose was at a pottery class at the community center so he was currently solo. He decided to walk downtown and treat himself to something yummy from A Bonnie Bakery. Normally, he avoided processed sugar, but right now his sweet tooth wanted to be satisfied.

Over the past month, he'd slowly grown comfortable in Liberty Ridge. Most everyone he interacted with was welcoming. Colleen was the only person he actively avoided. After what happened in California, he pretended she didn't exist.

After a walk, which took five minutes in ninety-degree heat, he opened the door to the bakery and stepped inside. Sugar and yeast scented the refreshingly cool air. Besides Bonnie working behind the counter, the bakery was empty. He ordered an apple turnover and a cup of tea, and then sat at a table by the window. The smell of warm apples and cinnamon wafted into his nose, and his mouth salivated in anticipation. The sweet scent reminded him of the taste of Colleen's lips. Memories of her appeared at the worst times—like when he was enjoying a little taste of victory.

As he savored the first bite of turnover, the bell over the door rang. A mixture of female voices filled the small bakery.

"I thought for sure I was out, so when they called me today, I couldn't believe it."

At the sound of Colleen's voice, Storm felt his stomach drop. Was it too much to ask that he get a peaceful moment to savor his own good news?

"Are you sure you're up for competing on a reality show?" Grace Carter stood beside Colleen and wrapped a tan arm around the petite blonde. "You really aren't the adventurous type. No offense."

Colleen laughed. "None taken. But who's to say this old house cat can't learn to enjoy exploring the backyard?"

The women headed to the counter and ordered.

With their backs to him, Storm let his gaze rest on Colleen. She was curvier now compared to the teenage girl who barely had enough hip width to hold up her cheerleading skirt. He liked the look of her woman's body. But, surely a lot of men did. She always had a long line of men at her beck and call. Was she in a relationship or single? Or was she playing the field?

Colleen turned toward Grace. "Part of the challenge is physical, but you're not going anywhere unless you have a brain to back up the challenges. I'll need to strategize. I can form alliances and get other contestants to trust me. I will play to win." Colleen took a cupcake from Bonnie and spun to face him. Her eyes widened.

She met Storm's hard stare. Was she talking about the *Scavenger Hunt* show? In his mouth, the sweet taste of apples turned bitter. He almost choked as he washed down the food with a sip of tea. Something in his life finally went right, and along came Colleen with a stick pin, smiling as she popped his balloon.

"Hey, Storm." Grace took a seat at another table. "Aren't the apple turnovers here fantastic?"

He didn't understand how Grace and Colleen could be friends. In high school, Colleen had teased Grace. Well, Colleen loved to tease everybody. Grace must be a bigger person. "Nothing tastes better than apples and pastry when you're celebrating." He lifted the china cup to his lips and took another drink of herbal tea.

Colleen sat across from Grace and set down her cupcake-topped plate, all while avoiding further eye contact with Storm.

"So, what are you celebrating?" Grace asked before sinking her fork into her pink frosted cupcake.

What would Colleen do when she learned he'd been cast for the show, too? Probably have her daddy call the show's producers and get him kicked off. Well, he wasn't going anywhere. He needed the prize money more. She had other means to get what she needed. He didn't. He stared at Colleen. "This morning, the producers of the *Scavenger Hunt* show called. They want to cast me, and I told them I can't wait to beat all the other contestants."

Colleen raised her gaze to meet his.

Her large, china blue eyes still had the ability to steal his breath. His heart fluttered inside his chest.

"Well, Liberty Ridge hasn't seen something this exciting since George Quinn was drafted by the St. Louis Cardinals," Grace said with a smile. "Colleen's been cast, too."

Like his life wasn't difficult enough. "You sure you want to even bother, Colleen?" He crossed his arms across his chest. "A pampered princess with nothing but a pretty face has no shot at winning. I've spent the last five years traveling and living off the land."

"So…you admit I'm pretty?" Colleen narrowed her eyes and glared back. "You underestimate me. Good."

How could he keep his composure while competing against her? A simple answer, really. He'd make sure she was the first one eliminated.

****

"I expressly forbid you to be on that show." Clive Gardner sat stiffly behind the desk in his office. "I won't stand by and watch my daughter made a fool of."

The little girl still inside Colleen shrank. Instead of giving in to her instinctual reaction to acquiesce, she stiffened her spine. She knew a fight with her father was inevitable over her involvement with the show. In a little over a week, she'd fly out to Washington DC and join the rest of the cast, regardless of whether she received her father's blessing or not. After spending the last two weeks thoughtfully packing her travel backpack, she was ready and raring to go. "If you haven't noticed, I'm a grown woman—capable of making my own decisions."

Her dad stood and closed the door to his office.

Wouldn't want all your employees to witness our argument. He cared so much about other's opinions but didn't bother putting on pretenses with his own child—which meant she saw the real Clive Gardner, warts and all. Once back in the safety of his own home, he'd pick up the bottle and become lost in a drunken haze.

"You may be grown, but you're still my responsibility. You could get hurt." He leaned back in his chair.

"For once in my life, would you please put some faith in me?" Despite her earlier calmness, she found her body tensing with each word. "Nothing you say will change my mind. I'm doing this, with or without your support."

Sighing, her dad reached into the mini fridge behind his desk and pulled out a bottle of water. He twisted off the cap and took a long drink.

Colleen saw the struggle behind his eyes and understood he wanted something stronger.

"When did you get so stubborn?" Clive set the water bottle onto a glass coaster on his desk. "The little girl I knew always wanted to make her dad happy."

Should she tell him that her attitude to always appease rated as one of her biggest regrets? Guilt hung around her neck like a heavy chain. She thought of her mom's death and her father's alcoholism, and the role she played in both. Followed by reviewing, her hurtful and mean behavior and how she'd heartlessly tossed aside Storm's friendship. Maybe she couldn't go back in time and change the past, but she still controlled the future.

"I'm just as stubborn as you." Colleen pointed at her dad before heading toward the door. "I leave next Friday. I hope to see you again before then."

"Still time for you to come to your senses." Clive leaned back in his large leather chair and turned his attention to the computer screen. "Come over for dinner on Sunday. I'll have Miriam cook something special."

As much of a blessing as he'd give. So, she'd accept his meager offerings with a grateful heart. As she walked out of the company office building, she let her mind wander to the starting line of *The Great American Scavenger Hunt*. With each passing day, her nervous excitement grew. Most people doubted she could really compete. Well, she'd show them and prove to Storm she was more than a pampered princess.

Her appointment at the salon wasn't for another thirty minutes. Hopefully, she wouldn't chicken out once in the stylist's chair. Fingering her long hair, she hardened her resolve. Ten inches of her beautiful hair would soon decorate the salon floor.

****

As he settled in for the night on his ex-girlfriend's couch, Storm tossed and turned in an attempt to get comfortable. But really, how could he ever be comfortable staying with Valerie? He'd only had enough money for a plane ticket and nowhere else to stay, so Val had grumbled but ultimately opened her home. In repayment, he was babysitter extraordinaire for Harper. He even sat quietly in the living room with Harper on his lap and watched the woman he used to love get dressed up for a date with another man.

He still found Val very beautiful. For the most part, they got along, even if their civility was mostly for Harper's sake. But any spark between them died well before Harper was born. They'd broken up a month before Val had stopped by his apartment with news of her pregnancy. At the time, the idea of fatherhood repelled him. Now, he couldn't imagine a life without his sweet daughter.

A door opened down the hall, and the shuffle of footsteps neared.

"You asleep yet?" Valerie whispered.

"Nah. What's up?" Storm cautiously adjusted to a sitting position, keeping the thin sheet covering his lower half.

She sat by his feet at the end of the sofa. "I'm glad you made the trip here for Harper's sake. She asks for you all the time."

His heart constricted with longing. He wanted his daughter with him every second. "I love Harper more than anything, Val. You know that. When I win the prize money, I'll make sure she has a good home. She'll be well taken care of while you're away."

"But what if you don't win? I've waited for years to get the opportunity for this study. I need to go, regardless of the outcome of your TV competition." She paused and twirled a piece of auburn hair around her index finger. "If Harper goes to live with my parents, they said you're welcome any time to visit."

Storm jerked forward, forgetting the sheet. Luckily, he wore a pair of boxers. "I get five thousand dollars just for being on the show. I can't buy the farm with just that amount, but it's enough to get by on until I find a good job in Liberty Ridge."

She threw up her hands. "Then what? You're already caring for your mentally ill mother. Do you plan on putting Harper in daycare, or will you let Grandma watch her?"

Arguing with Valerie always reminded him of why they were no longer together. Although, she was justified in being protective of their daughter. "I love Harper as much as you do. I'm not the one leaving to study plants."

She recoiled as if Storm slapped her. He didn't care he'd hit below the belt. Valerie was a well-respected botanist at California State University, Sacramento, and he understood her research of the anti-inflammatory properties of Amazonian plants could lead to huge medical breakthroughs. He just couldn't understand how she could leave her daughter for an entire year. Maybe longer if her research was successful.

"I'm not the one who moved to Texas." Valerie stood with her fists resting on her hips.

"You know why I had to go." He sighed in resignation.

"And you know why I took a job in Brazil. I honestly want Harper to live with you while I'm away. Go do the TV show and win the prize."

Once Valerie left for her bedroom, sleep still evaded him. He fell into a light sleep and was plagued by dreams of failure. He started the competition but fell violently ill. Harper was yanked out of his arms and handed over to Valerie's parents. At dawn, he awoke covered in sweat. Since he didn't want to go back to sleep and revisit those dreams, he put the kettle on the stove for tea. With a steamy cup in hand, he headed out to the patio for some fresh air. Maybe the cool morning breeze would help clear his mind.

Once Harper climbed out of bed and ran to him, he felt centered again. As long as he was with her, all was right with the world. He'd rented a car for the day, and Val installed her car seat. First stop was the store to pick up shovel and pails, and then he drove to Stinson Beach.

As soon as she saw the Pacific Ocean, Harper flapped her small arms and squealed. "Down," she commanded when Storm stepped onto the sand holding her. As soon as her feet touched down, she took off running.

He laughed at the determined hard line of her lips, which she'd inherited from him. As she wobbled across the sand with arms waving in the air, she reminded him of a newly hatched sea turtle on a quest to reach the ocean. Nothing would stop her, except for Daddy's protective arms.

"Oh no, you don't." Storm scooped her up just as her toes touched the water. "You need to hold my hand."

Harper crossed her arms and stuck out her lower lip. "Mean daddy."

Now, that label just wasn't fair. He wasn't mean daddy. He was cool dad—fun dad—but always safety-first dad.

A cool wind blew off the ocean, but the bright sun helped warm the air. Not a cloud in the sky.

He set down their beach towels and sand toys then took a firm hold of Harper's hand. They walked back to the water, and Storm played for almost an hour with her in the waves.

When she had enough, she ran back to their towels and plopped down. Harper lay still, with her tiny thumb stuck in her mouth and closed her eyes.

Storm sat beside her, gently rubbing her back. He remembered the soothing feeling of a soft hand rubbing his own small back—Colleen's hand. He could still hear her whispering, "Sleep, my Stormy. I'm right here." How had a five-year-old girl known the fears hidden deep in his heart? Colleen had been his comfort. She'd been his personal angel until she'd transformed into a taunting devil.

If he had never kissed her on the playground, would she have stayed his friend or eventually turned on him anyway? Guess he'd never know.

At the sound of barking, Harper's eyes popped open.

A group of seals had settled on a rock outcropping farther down the beach.

"Dolphin." Harper clapped her hands and squealed.

"Those are seals, honey." He lifted her into his arms and walked over for a closer look. He kissed one chubby cheek and inhaled. She smelled like sun block and ocean water. He ached with the thought of leaving her tomorrow.

"Love Daddy." She squeezed her arms around his neck and planted a wet kiss on his forehead.

Emotion lodged in his throat. Then and there, he committed to win the prize money, no matter what. He had no other option.

Chapter Seven

Tomorrow marked the start of the reality show competition. Each cast member already gave a preliminary interview. Now was Colleen's turn in the hot seat. She entered the Arlington, Virginia hotel room serving as a temporary production office. A camera and bright, hot lights took up one corner. Once a mic was clipped to her shirt, she sat on an upholstered stacking chair.

"Tell me the one thing you're most excited about as you embark on *The Great American Scavenger Hunt*?" The young show producer seated across the way glanced down at the notes on his lap. His long blond hair brushed his shoulders, with a few frizzy strands rising around his head.

"Since I usually use air travel, I'm looking forward to seeing the country from the ground." She purposefully relaxed her face for the camera and forced a smile on her lips.

"You met the other contestants at lunch today. Does anyone stick out as your biggest competition?"

She remembered the look Storm gave her when she'd walked into the hotel's conference room. He honestly appeared shocked. Did he think she lacked the moxie to show up? On a personal level, he was her biggest competition. He had the ability to see right through her. Even though they'd spent the last twelve years living apart, he knew her way too well. "Right now, no one stands out. I'll have a better idea after alliances form." Her lips stuck together as she talked. The room was so dry. She licked her lips and took a drink of water to relax her nerves.

"You and Storm Thompson grew up together. From what Storm told us during his audition, you two don't get along." His eyes widened. "Can our viewers expect fireworks?"

Why had Storm admitted their rocky relationship? She wouldn't play along. Colleen planned on being civil to Storm. Maybe offer to help once or twice and get him to lower his defenses. "Storm and I have an interesting history, but our relationship is in the past. I don't know him anymore, so don't expect any fireworks."

The young man leaned forward in his seat. "Storm also said you were the class bully. Is that true?"

Storm sure said a lot of things. Maybe he should learn to keep his big trap shut. What other secrets had he spilled in front of the camera? "I wasn't nice when I was younger. Now, I'm a Clinical Psychiatrist and work with veterans, which is more important than what I did as a teenager."

The young producer pushed his red-rimmed glasses up his nose and grinned. "We have talked to several people from Liberty Ridge to get a better picture of you. One was Heath Carter, who said your counseling saved his life. Other people mentioned you've done a lot of good since you opened your practice in town. Why do you think Storm is having such a hard time accepting the new you?"

Oh, for crying out loud. Colleen stood and

unclipped the microphone off her shirt then set it on the chair. "I'm finished. If you have any question not including Storm Thompson, let me know. Otherwise, I'm going back to my room."

The man watched slack-jawed as she marched out of the room. Why were these show producers so insistent on stirring up drama? With blood simmering, she turned the corner and slammed into a hard body. The impact sent her flying, and her backside landed hard on the carpeted hallway floor.

"I'm sorry." Storm reached down and, after a brief hesitation, took hold of her hand and pulled her up.

His touch sent waves of heat pulsing over her skin. *Please don't blush.* Of course, warmth rushed to her face anyway. "Thanks," she mumbled. "They need two-way mirrors up in the corners."

Storm didn't answer or didn't move. He just stood there, blocking her way.

She grew very uncomfortably hot in the cramped hallway.

"You cut your hair." He tipped his chin toward her and pointed to her head. "I'm surprised."

He actually noticed. Miracles do happen. She ran her hand through her pixie cut. The short length was something she was still getting used to every time she touched her hair or caught a glimpse of herself in the mirror. "I thought a short style would be easy to care for during the competition."

His lids shuttered slowly over his brown eyes. He inhaled and then reopened them. "I like your hair. The style suits you."

"So, what you're saying is this hairstyle is good for an evil witch?" Her voice held a hint of wry humor.

A smile formed on his lips. "It's all the rage for today's super villain."

"Thanks. So, are you ready for tomorrow?" She'd keep up the friendly banter and see if they could actually have a civil conversation.

"Can't wait. All this sitting around and answering stupid questions is getting on my nerves."

She loved the way his sandy-blond hair curled at the back of his neck. Storm had aged into a ruggedly handsome man. What a shame that years ago, she'd set fire to any chance of a relationship. "The show thinks they've struck gold with the two of us. I wish you hadn't shared our history."

He shrugged. "I regret sharing that myself. The producers are good at ferreting out information. Luckily, I'll be so far ahead that we won't have to worry about stepping on each other's toes."

"Ha, in your dreams, Thompson." Grinning, she swatted his arm. "I'm not losing to anyone and especially not you."

"I will win." His lips pressed in a firm line. "I made a promise to Harper."

Colleen fought a strong urge to go to him, curl up in his strong arms, and bury her head on his chest. He contained a whirl of contradictions—strong but vulnerable, filled with anger toward her but a loving son and father, a mouth that could slice her emotionally but still kissable. *Storm might be the death of me.*

She didn't have the energy to fight right now, so she stuck with a subject she knew would soften him. "How is Harper? She really is the sweetest little girl."

His smile deepened the creases around his eyes. "I saw her last week up in Sacramento. She's a handful."

"She must take after her dad." Another smile lit up his face—a metamorphosis from good looking to breathtakingly gorgeous. Her pulse quickened. Guess talking about his child made him happy, regardless of who he was with.

"Harper is stubborn like me, but she's kind, like her mom. Valerie says when she sees the firm set in Harper's lips, she knows she won't win."

At the sound of the other woman's name, Colleen suffered a cold bite of jealousy. "Is Valerie Harper's mother?"

"Yes." He crossed his arms across his chest. "She's a botanist at the university in Sacramento. In January, she'll head to Brazil for at least a year. I'll be awarded full custody if I can prove I have a stable home for Harper." His lips pressed together and his brow furrowed. "I need the prize money so I can buy land and start a farm."

"Oh." Concern replaced her earlier excitement. Her determination to win this competition put her in between Storm's goal to raise his daughter. She shook off the guilt. Every person here competed for their own valid reasons. The retreat she wanted to build was just as important, probably even more so, as anyone else's dream. She wanted to help others—veterans who desperately needed the services she could offer.

"Well, I'm calling it a night," Storm moved passed her. "See you bright and early."

As his hand lightly brushed against hers, electric charges sparked on her skin. "Sleep well, Stormy." Her old nickname slipped past her lips. She hadn't called him Stormy in years. Despite sensing his gaze on her, she continued walking. Once inside her room, she leaned against the door. Tears welled in the corners of her eyes. Years ago, she'd called him 'my Stormy.' Did he remember those days with fondness like she did?

If she could find a way to crawl back in time, she would change so many things. Unless she stumbled across a time machine, changing the past was impossible. Colleen steeled her emotions and set her feet firmly in the present. She had a competition to win.

Chapter Eight
The Great American Scavenger Hunt: Day 1

Storm stood on the stairs of the US Capitol Building, and the weight of his travel pack dug into his shoulders. Before sunrise, all the contestants were bussed seven miles over from their hotel in Arlington. A few other contestants started conversations, and his minimal replies made clear he wasn't here to make friends. Colleen ignored him, which was good. Her mere presence provided enough distraction.

He had a good view of her down at the other end of the line. How could she stand upright underneath the weight of her pack? The thing looked as heavy as her. He'd bought his at the secondhand shop in Liberty Ridge. Colleen probably shopped at a high-end outdoor store that carried the latest gizmos and gadgets. Her pack and its contents might cost the equivalent of a small country's GDP.

When he'd seen her yesterday at lunch, he almost didn't recognize her. Her short hair looked amazingly sexy. This morning, she wore a tousled look, like she'd just rolled out of bed, which she likely had being that the clock just struck seven-thirty am.

The host of the show, Burt Blackstone, walked before the assembled group. He stood medium height, with a trim build, and a head of closely cropped, salt-and-pepper hair. Today, Burt wore khaki shorts and an orange button-up top. "I want to wish every one of you good luck. We'll start filming shortly. I'll go over the rules once more, mostly for the audience's sake. Then, I'll give the signal, and you'll be off."

A low murmur drifted over the group.

Storm shifted the weight of his travel pack and mentally walked through his plan. He held a red envelope, which was identical to the ones given to the other contestants. *Let's rock and roll.*

A producer gave a shout, and the camera lights blazed.

Burt adjusted the small microphone clipped to the front of his shirt and plastered on a wide smile. "Welcome to *The Great American Scavenger Hunt*. My name is Burt Blackstone, and I am your host for this race across the country. Standing before me are twenty contestants, all playing for a chance to win the grand prize of one million dollars!" One arm swooped upward in dramatic flair.

The cameramen turned toward the assembly on the stairs, panned across, and then re-focused on the show host.

Burt stepped closer to one of the cameras. "The first one to reach the final destination will be declared the winner. Each clue will lead them to the next, zig-zagging our contestants across wilderness and deserts, as well as through city and country roads. Our rules are simple but will be enforced, so pay attention." He turned his attention from the camera to the contestants. "Our group assembled here already has the first clue, one thousand dollars cash, a map, a credit card only for gas, and keys to a car. They may only travel from six am until eight pm. Anyone on the road after eight pm will receive a two-hour start time penalty the next morning plus the number of minutes past curfew. Safe Houses are marked along the route, and each contestant has a list of their locations. Sleeping and eating at a Safe House are free to contestants, but they are scattered, so plan accordingly. Otherwise, use your cash allowance to stay at a motel."

Burt paused and moved toward another camera. "Every few days, the contestants will receive a Time-Out stop—a meeting spot where all contestants enjoy a twenty-four hour break. Time-Out stops are also elimination checkpoints. The number of contestants eliminated will be stated on the previous clue."

Come on, let's go. Storm's new boots pinched his feet, and the rising sun burned his eyes. His fingers itched to open the first clue and get moving.

As they filmed, every so often a black luxury car pulled up to the side entrance of the Capitol. He assumed the backseat occupant was a power suit coming in for a day to make deals and accept bribes.

Burt Blackstone droned on. "By the final clue, only two contestants will remain. Play smart, be safe, and don't forget to have fun. Are you ready?"

A cheer rose from the contestants lined up on the Capitol stairs.

Colleen leaned forward and peered around the crowd, smiling at Storm.

The expression wasn't a wish of good luck. He recognized the glint in her eyes as a challenge. She resembled a little black bear, so cute and cuddly, until the animal decided to rip out your throat. He sent her an easy smile in return, attempting to convey his disregard.

"The hunt has begun. Open your first clue!" Burt

yelled.

The sound of ripping paper drowned all other noise.

Storm pulled out a yellow piece of paper and read.

Gym, Tan, Laundry might have placed it in the national spotlight, but this shore has been a destination for close to two hundred years. Find Lucy the Elephant. Your car is waiting outside the Crystal City Metro Station.

Storm had already studied a map of DC and knew a Metro Station stood to the southeast. Along with the other nineteen contestants, he ran past the Library of Congress and down First Street until the small sign for the Capitol South station appeared. After a brief escalator trip underground, he found himself in a room full of ticket vending machines. He did a lap around, reading the color-coded list of stations and costs, and panic built in his chest. The signs could be in another language for all the good the names and prices did him.

He needed help navigating the confusing system. Where was a transit employee? Other contestants had arrived and bought their tickets, while he stayed stuck here like an idiot. A familiar voice sounded at his side. He turned toward Colleen.

"Buying Metro tickets is so confusing." She pointed to the sign about the ticket vending machine. "You need a Metro Pass."

She walked him through purchasing the pass, and then bought one for herself. "Follow me. We need to catch the next train."

Like a pro, she navigated the station. Before he could complain, he stood beside her on the waiting platform.

"We're taking the Blue Line to Franconia-Springfield. From what the sign says, the train looks to be three minutes out. Hold on to your card, because you'll need it to get out of the Crystal City Station." Colleen shrugged off her pack and set it at her feet.

If Colleen hadn't helped him, he'd still be stuck upstairs. What kind of game was she playing? Was she pretending to be his friend then stab him in the back? Whatever her motives, he could at least thank her. "Thanks. You must have done this before." With her dad's money, she'd probably traveled a lot, both domestically and internationally.

Nodding, she smiled. "I visited DC every so often during college. The Metro is the easiest and cheapest way to get around."

A rush of stale wind heralded the arrival of their train. The train doors swooshed open, and they stepped inside. He took a seat across the aisle from Colleen and gazed out the dark window. Every so often, he'd peer over at her, and then berate himself for his lack of willpower. As the train moved, he worked on deciphering the first clue. By the time the train arrived at the Crystal City stop, he hadn't come any closer to an answer. He stood and grabbed his backpack then waited at the door, ready to go. "Try not to trip on your way out." He looked over his shoulder at Colleen. "Doubt I'll see you at the next stop."

She gave him an easy shove on the back. "Don't lose that overconfidence. See ya on the road, Stormy."

The doors opened, and he darted toward the marked exit. Storm bounded up the escalators until finally reaching fresh air and sunshine. To his right sat a lineup of green cars parked on the street. Storm found the one with his name on the windshield. He tossed his backpack on the passenger seat and hopped inside.

Again, he read the first clue. What the heck was Gym, Tan, Laundry? Some contestants drove away. *Don't panic. Sit here until you figure out the clue.*

With no cell phone and no internet, he'd work out the problem on his own. How would he win if he couldn't even solve the first clue? He pounded the steering wheel. Storm focused on the word "shore." His destination was somewhere along the Atlantic Ocean. He relaxed his mind and took deep breaths. A new calm evicted all earlier stress.

The image of tan and beefy teenage boys with greased spiky hair materialized in his mind. He remembered a reality show where the cast was known for their bad behavior. *Bingo.*

After starting the ignition, he opened his map. What was the fastest route to the New Jersey shore?

****

Colleen sat in her car, studying her map. She knew where to go, just not how to get there. First challenge— getting out of the metro DC urban knot. Next, she'd need the quickest route to New Jersey. Map reading proved a challenge. She'd been spoiled by the GPS on her cell phone.

Cars around her left, but she refused to panic. She'd stay put until she became confident in her directions. How many of those schmucks would end up lost because of their rush?

Storm, who was parked in front of her, pulled out onto the street and drove away. Would helping him navigate the Metro bite her in the rear? In the end, Storm was a good man and had once been her friend.

She'd help him again, as long as helping didn't hurt her chances of winning. Finally, she set a route. Colleen started her car and put it into Drive. A flood of nervous excitement filled her body. This moment marked the beginning of the biggest adventure of her life.

Her dad was back home, powerless to interfere. All her friends had written notes of encouragement. She decided to read one each night before bed. Storm Thompson, for better or worse, would be a partner in her journey. The road lay ahead like a silver ribbon, inviting her to explore the country's wonders. And one million dollars waited at the finish line—a pot of gold at the end of the rainbow.

She still hadn't figured out the exact location of Lucy the Elephant, so she'd ask someone once she got closer to the shore. Hopefully, the landmark was well-known. Personally, the only time she'd ever spent in New Jersey was inside the Newark International Airport.

As she entered Atlantic City, her first goal was to figure out where Lucy the Elephant called home. She stopped at a little, yellow shack whose weather-beaten sign listed it as a souvenir shop. Before going inside, she asked a few people mulling about on the sidewalk. A kind woman in a hibiscus floral top pointed to Margate City on the map. Then, she launched into the long history of the elephant statue. Not wanting to appear rude, Colleen listened for several minutes. Once the woman's story reached the 1950s, Colleen politely excused herself.

The little beach town of Margate City was not far. Driving down Atlantic Avenue, she searched for the clue stop. Lucy the Elephant, standing six stories tall, was impossible to miss. She parked on the side and ran up to a red flag by the open gate.

Several other contestants were there, including Storm.

Darn! She reached in the basket to grab her next clue.

Side Trip—*Let's go fishing! A charter boat waits for you in the Cape May Harbor. Look for the marina with the red flags. Hire a boat to take you fishing. You must catch two ten-pound fish (or heavier) in order to receive the next clue. Make sure you get a picture with your fish.*

Nothing she hated worse than fishing. Long stretches of staring into the water, praying for a bite. Maybe a professional charter boat would help?

Happy fishing. Yeah, right.

****

During the ride to New Jersey, Storm had done some serious strategizing. He'd sized up the rest of the contestants during their brief time together at the hotel in Washington DC—ten men and ten women. A few looked like Hollywood types, whom he dismissed on sight. A few groups had formed, and he assumed they'd stick together, at least in the beginning. He wasn't interested in making friends or alliances.

He hadn't figured out Colleen's angle. Would he accept her help? Sure, he'd take any advantage. He refused to help anyone, especially Colleen.

Now, he grabbed the second clue from under the large frame of Lucy the Elephant and drove to the blue water of the Cape May Harbor. Getting out of his car, he breathed in the salty air. The scent of fish permeated the breeze, and white boats bobbed on the surface of the water, lined up like a flock of birds resting on a wire. Storm placed his baseball cap on his head and set off toward the dock. A red flag blew in the stiff breeze over the entrance to one of the piers.

Another contestant, a middle-aged man with a receding hairline, arrived a minute before Storm. The man made arrangements with a charter captain while Storm looked around for another boat.

A salty-looking man wearing faded jeans and a tan canvas coat sat on an overturned bucket. The man waved him over.

Storm approached and after a quick exchange, the seadog motioned to board his boat.

Captain Hook—Storm had a hard time believing that was the man's real name—gave a quick lesson on deep sea fishing, and then they were off. As the boat pulled away from the dock, he saw Colleen exit her car. She was right on his heels. With any luck, he'd catch his fish and be back before she left shore.

Two hours later, he was ready to throw his pole into the ocean. His line snagged a few bites but no real takers. The wind picked up, making the small fishing boat sway in a nausea-inducing dance. While he was stuck out in the water, four other competitors' boats headed back to the harbor. Annoyance churned in his gut. Had Colleen caught her fish yet, or was she still drowning worms like him? Actually, he was drowning shrimp, not worms. Storm looked at his watch—three-ten pm. If he didn't get a fish soon, he'd be stuck in Cape May all night.

Just as he was ready to fall down on his knees and beg Poseidon for a gift from the sea, his pole jerked once then twice.

Captain Hook yelled, using a unique blend of curse words.

Storm grabbed hold of the pole and pulled with every ounce of his strength. His muscles burned as he reeled in the line. Before long, a beautiful scaly fish was flopping away on the deck.

"Is it over ten pounds?" Storm crossed his fingers. If so, all he needed was one more good catch, and he could head to shore.

"Well." Captain Hook held up the fish by the tail. "You caught a pretty Striped Bass. Let's weigh the fish but if I had to guess, I'd say it's at least fifteen."

"Yeah!" He pumped his fist. Half-way there.

His luck improved. Within thirty minutes, he'd caught his second fish, and the boat headed back to the harbor. Storm posed for a Polaroid picture—proof he needed to submit at the Time-Out stop. Captain Hook wrote the fish species and weight on the bottom of the picture, shook Storm's hand, and gave him the next clue.

The time was now five pm. Three more hours until he had to stop for the night. Not wanting to waste any more time, he ripped open the envelope.

This quiet farm field witnessed one of the bloodiest battles in Civil War history. There, a 'little' hill served as a Union Army stronghold and the location where Colonel Chamberlain called for a final charge on the advancing Southern troops. The Statue of Union chief engineer Governor K. Warren holds your next clue.

No time lost solving this riddle. He got back into his car and took out his map. What was the quickest route to Gettysburg?

****

For Colleen, fishing had gone better than expected. She hadn't been out on the water for more than fifteen minutes before catching her first fish. The boat captain classified the type of fish she'd caught, but as long as the weight was over ten pounds, she was good. Fish number two was reeled in about thirty minutes later. Her goal was to get to Gettysburg by eight pm—their daily deadline. With any luck, she'd be one of the first at the park's entrance tomorrow morning.

As she drove, she pressed her hand over her rumbling stomach, which reminded her she'd only eaten a protein bar for lunch. After a quick stop for a burger and fries, she was back on the road. The closest Safe House to Gettysburg was in Lancaster. Too far away from her destination. She'd spend the money for a cheap motel room in close proximity to the park. *A wise investment.*

After almost four hours on the road, she found a small, roadside motel and checked in. With her first day coming to a close, she let her road-weary body fall on the squeaky motel bed. She bounced up and down a few times, laughing at the possible reaction of the people in the next room. *Sorry to disappoint, but no one's getting lucky in this room tonight.*

Colleen set the old-style alarm clock for five am and burrowed under the comforter. As her eyes drifted closed, the memory of Storm's kiss on the California beach drifted through her mind. Could she fight her attraction while keeping focused on the competition? She had to or run the risk of failure. After tossing and turning for several minutes, she banished all thoughts of Storm and finally fell into a deep sleep.

Chapter Nine
Day 2

At the sound of a rooster crowing, Storm awoke with a start. He grumbled and rolled out of bed. The farmhouse was otherwise quiet, which meant nobody else was up, and he could get first dibs on the shower. Four other contestants stayed at the Lancaster Safe House. An elderly couple served as hosts. Last night, Mrs. Gifford cooked the most magnificent dinner. The meal alone was worth the small delay in not reaching Gettysburg.

After a quick shower, he dressed and went down for breakfast. Cereal, milk, and a variety of muffins were set out on the dining room table. Beggars couldn't be choosers. He'd eat the basic breakfast and be happy, not knowing when the next time he'd eat today.

Last night, he'd researched his next stop with Mr. Gifford in his study and learned the clue waited at Little Round Top hill in Gettysburg National Park. He had about a ninety-minute drive to Gettysburg. With the park opening at six am, the contestants who arrived in Gettysburg last night would have the advantage. He needed to hustle and make up lost time.

At six on the dot, Storm turned the key and drove away from the Lancaster farm house. Little Mrs. Gifford, wearing a calf-length floral dress and pink apron, stood on the front porch and waved. Once he arrived in the town of Gettysburg, he picked up a park map from a gas station and took a minute to study the route to Little Round Top hill. A series of one-way roads wound around the park, taking visitors past different attractions.

The drive through the park was slow going, with early-morning bikers taking up much of the road. When he finally crested the hill, a jolt of exhilaration hit him. The breathtaking scene overlooked acres of farm fields, which had witnessed thousands of men die at the end of a bayonet or cannon ball. A tall, bronze statue stood watch over the gathering crowd. Storm counted seven contestants either arriving or leaving with their clue. He pushed aside panic. Plenty of time to get ahead.

A red flag marked the basket of clues. Storm reached inside and noticed only six were left. He was in the back of the pack. A new sense of urgency increased his pulse. Opening the envelope, he read the directions.

Gettysburg National Park is a living memorial to the lives lost during the three-day battle. If you listen carefully, you can hear the whispers of the ghosts still walking the fields. Task: *Ride the provided bike around the park. Five stops are marked along the route. At each, collect one musket ball from the container. Finish back on Little Round Top and present your five musket balls to the Park Ranger. Then, you will receive the next clue.*

Storm ran back to his car, grabbed his water bottle, and hopped on one of the few bikes left. He stuffed the park map into the back pocket of his shorts. Attached to the bike helmet was a video camera, but several cameramen sat on bikes at the foot of the hill, ready to follow the contestants as they departed.

Coasting downward, he focused on locating the red flags. But his attention was drawn to the peaceful beauty surrounding him, as well, and he imagined the destruction that took place here two-hundred-and-fifty years ago.

He approached a small, white house, and a red flag greeted him, waving in the breeze. A small monument marked the house as General Meade's Headquarters. Storm stopped and reached into the ceramic jar, pulling out his first musket ball. He slipped the round piece of lead into a pouch strapped across his body. *Only four more to go.*

At the Gettysburg Address Memorial, he found musket ball number two. The third rested beside a cannon at McPherson's Ridge. He'd just finished picking up the fourth at the Virginia Monument when he saw ahead the backside of someone familiar— Colleen. He increased his speed to catch her. "Hey, turtle." He pedaled alongside her.

Her cheeks were red, and sweat dripped down her face. "You," she huffed. "Go away."

"How many musket balls do you have?" He struggled not to smile. She really looked cute.

"How many do you have?" Laughter punctuated her reply. "I was crazy to sign up for this torture side-show."

Yesterday on the fishing boat, he'd had the same thought. "I'm having the time of my life. Did you get to Gettysburg last night?"

"Stop pumping me for information. I won't tell you a thing." She focused her gaze on the road ahead.

"Fine. Enjoy the view as I ride away." Storm pedaled faster. When he heard Colleen call out his name, he slowed.

"I will tell you one thing," she shouted. "A pack of other contestants is up ahead…an alliance. Five total, three men and two women. They're blocking the road so no one else can pass."

His mind raced with the information. Storm circled around and drew up alongside her. "Have you tried getting by them?"

"No, I don't have the energy." Her chest rose and lowered with each deep breath.

After a moment's thought, a strategy emerged. What if they teamed up to pass the group? Just like car racing. Could he stomach forming an alliance with this woman? He weighed the options, alternating pros and cons like a seesaw. Sure, if doing so helped him get ahead.

They biked for about ten minutes until they approached the group. Tall oak trees and leafy shrubs lined both sides of the shaded road.

The cluster of riders cut a wide path, blocking the entire width.

On his signal, Colleen rode forward on their left.

The group acted like a flock of birds, all shifting to the left to block her.

Their mob mentality and predictability amused him. With an opening now on the right, Storm zipped past. With a few shouts and gasps, the group flocked to the right.

Head down and pumping hard, Colleen then passed on the left.

He ignored the outraged yelling behind him. Laughter bubbled in his chest. "We played them perfectly."

"Yahoo!" With her feet pumping fast on the pedals, Colleen reached across to give him a high-five.

"You did good, babe." The words left his lips before the filter in his brain activated. A little encouragement didn't mean he wanted to be best friends again. Some of the ice he'd built around his heart melted with her smile.

Storm spotted the last flag marker along a line of split-rail fence that bordered the road. He grabbed his last musket ball and pedaled like someone chased by the devil, resulting in almost losing Colleen on the trip up Little Round Top hill. He slowed to look behind him.

She gritted her teeth and kept moving until she met him at the top.

After parking his bike, he hopped off and sprinted over to the Park Ranger for his next clue. Colleen followed, breathing like someone who'd just finished a marathon. Even sweaty and flustered, she still looked gorgeous.

She removed her bike helmet, and her short, damp hair stuck out in all directions.

"You remind me of a porcupine after enthusiastic mating," Storm shouted as she walked past.

"Gross." She reached her car then glanced back. Her nose scrunched, and her eyes narrowed. "How do you know what a porcupine looks like after mating?"

"A kid learns a lot growing up on a commune." He couldn't stop laughing at her skeptical expression.

"You're so weird." Colleen climbed in her car and closed the door.

He hated to admit sometimes two were more effective than one. For better or worse, he and Colleen were in this competition together. And shockingly, he might be okay with that. He ripped open the envelope flap.

An NFL regulation football is the next item you need to collect. The stadium that holds your next clue is a temple to the great condiment of ketchup. Steel yourself for another physical challenge.

****

Colleen read the clue five times and still had no idea where to go. Storm was long gone. Guess teaming up once was enough for today. Although, he'd surprised her earlier by asking to work together. Would wonders ever cease?

Okay—enough thinking about Storm and how attractive he looked riding on a bicycle. Drooling over him would not get her any closer to solving this clue.

Before Colleen left Liberty Ridge, Grace gave her a book of tourist spots all over the country, sorted by state. Colleen grabbed the book from her pack and thumbed through the closest states. She needed an NFL football stadium, which should help narrow her options. When she saw the bold lettering of Pittsburgh Steelers and Heinz Stadium, she wanted to scream in relief and frustration. *Finally*! After consulting her map, she drove west toward the Steel City.

The long drive was welcome, since her legs still trembled from the biking excursion. She was a regular at spin class but riding a real bike over lofty hills was definitely more of a challenge. On the trip, she found a classic music station, and her mind became lost in the melodies. By the time she pulled into the parking lot of Heinz Field at noon, her body and soul were rejuvenated.

As she entered, Storm ran out, waving a sheet of paper. "Move fast and keep your head down," he yelled in passing. He sported a red welt on his forehead. "See you at the Time-Out."

Her heart leaped. The next clue would lead to a Time-Out stop, which meant if she was one of the last there, she'd be eliminated. With adrenaline rushing through her veins, she sprinted into the stadium.

Colleen followed the show's signage, through a switchback series of halls, until she was in the locker room. Without fanfare, she ran through the tunnel and onto the football field. The words of her next clue glowed on the massive TV screen set at the end of the field.

This field is 100 yards long. Get ready to run. Remember gophers from high school gym? Get ready for gophers on steroids.

Start at the end zone and run to the 20-yard line. Touch back at the end zone and run to the 50-yard line. Touch back at the end zone and run to the 80-yard line. Touch back at the end zone and run to the opposite end zone. Sprint back across the field and end at the goalpost.

All while avoiding footballs thrown by the Steelers' quarterback.

She stomped her foot in protest, and then watched the quarterback sling footballs. The man had an arm like a rocket. Instead of worrying about the quarterback, she ducked her head and ran for her life.

After several minutes of burning exercise, she dropped onto the turf in the end zone next to the goal post and clutched her stomach. *I think I'm sick.* Thankfully, she'd avoided getting hit by footballs thrown by the lumberjack-size quarterback. She allowed several seconds to catch her breath before stiffly rising to stand. As she limped to the tunnel, the quarterback winked. She scoffed. Did he honestly think she'd flirt after he'd used her as a moving practice target? Maybe he figured going easy on her would increase his luck. Not likely. Disappearing back into the stadium, Colleen opened the envelope.

Next up is a Time-Out stop. Last three *contestants to arrive will be eliminated. From 1876 to 1995, this Gothic stone structure was home to many of West Virginia's most violent prisoners. Find Old Sparky to check in.*

She would have jumped for joy, if her legs weren't ready to give out. Not long ago, she'd seen a *Ghost Hunters* episode filmed at the West Virginia Penitentiary. Checking with her map, she found the prison in Moundsville, WV. A short drive—only an hour away.

As she drove, the *Ghost Hunters* episode replayed in her mind. The West Virginia Penitentiary was creepy, to say the least. She hoped they wouldn't stay overnight. But she was on a reality show—so, of course, the show's producers would house them in the haunted prison. Would Storm protect her from the ghosts of the prisoners who wandered the halls? Not likely. To be honest, the feelings he stirred inside her were scarier than any ghost.

****

As Storm entered the massive stone main building of the West Virginia Penitentiary, he felt his skin prickle. The place looked more like a haunted medieval castle than a prison. He stopped at the office for a map to find Old Sparky, and then he headed into the dank bowels of the empty prison. As he traveled, a row of abandoned cells flanked him on one side. On the other was a line of chain link fence. What had a man felt to be caged in one of these small cells, waiting to be led down for his date with death? Some weird electricity charged the air around him. Probably just his imagination.

After about twenty minutes of walking and a few wrong turns, he found his destination. Entering the execution room sent chills down his spine.

Inside a sterile white room, the host of the show, Burt Blackstone, waited. He stood before Old Sparky, the famous electric chair. "Welcome to the West Virginia Penitentiary in Moundsville. You are number eight to check in," Burt Blackstone announced.

Storm's body relaxed with instant relief. He was still in the game.

"You'll stay on the prison grounds for the next twenty-four hours. Each contestant will leave in the order in which they've arrived."

Storm turned toward the next contestant, who'd come in behind him and unfortunately was not Colleen. He wondered if she was on site already or still on the road—and hoped she arrived soon enough to stay in the competition. *Be a shame to say good-bye already*. He left the room and found a tour guide waiting, who escorted him to his lodgings. Or should he say his prison cell.

When he got to his cell, he halted outside the bars. His feet refused to move. After a few deep breaths, he passed into a cramped space that made his skin crawl. *Well, staying here will make for a memorable night.*

The walls of the cell were made of cold metal and plaster and had served as a medium for its former inhabitant's artwork and written compositions. Some were more colorful than others. A bio-hazard-looking toilet and sink were attached to the back wall.

Might as well get comfortable. He unpacked a blanket, which he laid over the plastic-covered mattress on a rusty metal frame bed to take a little nap. With his eyes closed, the rotting smell of his surroundings intensified. A cold breath passed over the bare skin of his arms—seriously creepy.

Sleep might be impossible after dark, when his mind would play even more tricks. He dozed off for about an hour, and then woke to go exploring. He passed several occupied cells filled with other contestants. So far, no ghosts.

In the last cell on his level, he found Colleen and immediately suppressed a smile. She read, curled up on her bed like a child. "You made it." He stepped inside and relaxed for the first time since entering the prison. "How did you place?"

"I came in tenth. Dead middle of the pack. I'd hoped to do better." She took off her glasses and set them on the bed.

"You must have arrived soon after me. I was number eight."

Colleen peered up with bright blue eyes. For some reason, instead of appearing cold, they reminded him of deep pools of tropical water—ones he wanted to dive into and become lost. If he didn't keep up his guard around her, he'd witness his own undoing.

She swung her legs off the side of the bed. "How did you figure out the Pittsburgh clue so fast? I must have lost twenty minutes on that one."

Pride straightened his posture. "I might have been raised on a hippy commune, but I know football. Heinz Field, Pittsburgh Steelers—that one was easy."

She reached into her pack and pulled out a plastic bag. "I brought along some nuts and dried fruit. You want some?"

"Sure." On cue, his stomach growled. He held out his hand, and she poured a portion onto his palm. "Thanks."

Watching him, she grinned. "You still eat all the cashews first."

He couldn't believe she remembered. "They're my favorite." When the cashews were gone, he popped the rest of the mix into his mouth and chewed.

"Do you want to go for a walk?" She marked her place in her book then snapped it shut. "Being here alone gives me the creeps."

"I still have to do my interview and the confessional booth thing." The traveling and challenges were fine, but he hated sitting in front of a camera and answering stupid questions.

"I have to do that, too. We can go together." Colleen stood and followed him out into the corridor.

Even after all these years, he continued to be drawn to Colleen. Maybe because she was the only familiar person in this crazy adventure. He didn't like her and didn't trust her, but they shared a history. Her presence gave him comfort, just as when he was a small boy. Remembering that time in his life filled him with unease. He'd been vulnerable then, and he despised the dependency he'd experienced throughout his childhood.

As they walked in silence, the sound of their

footsteps echoed through the chilly air.

When they arrived at the show's headquarters, housed in the old warden's office, Colleen halted. "You can go first. I'll wait outside. Come get me when you're done."

With as much enthusiasm as a condemned man being led to Old Sparky, he entered and sat across from one of the show's producers. The crew miked him up, and the camera's light glowed.

"Storm, you had a setback during the fishing challenge. Tell us what happened on the boat." The redhead female producer leaned forward in her chair.

He suppressed his instinctual growl and kept the expression on his face passive. "I caught my fish. Just took a little longer than I would have liked."

"You and Colleen appear to have teamed up." She crossed her legs and drummed her fingers on her thigh. "From what we learned during the preliminary interviews, you two were more enemies than lovers. So, what's changed?"

The producer's eyes sparkled with predatory excitement. He'd throw cold water on any implication he and Colleen had hooked up. "The bike incident was out of necessity. An alliance had blocked the road. Neither of us could pass them on our own. You'll have to ask Colleen why she helped me navigate the Metro back in DC."

"She's a very pretty woman and a doctor to boot. Can we expect any sparks to fly?" Her eyebrows waggled.

Storm frowned. "Don't hold your breath."

Her smile transformed into a grimace. "Okay, Storm. We're done. Can you ask Colleen to come in?

Then, step into the confessional booth and talk for about five minutes on your experiences so far."

He walked outside and found Colleen sitting on the ground in the enclosed former exercise yard. Her face lifted toward the sun. The image stirred feelings he'd forgotten. For the first time since moving home, he wished he and Colleen didn't share such a toxic history. If only he was just a guy and she was just a girl, and they met as adults and slowly got to know each other.

Had she really changed so drastically? According to the word around town, she was a reformed person. Even his mom thought she walked on water. He couldn't get drawn back into Colleen's aura. He'd win the prize money, which meant she'd go home disappointed. He was sure situations would arise, and he'd step on her toes more than a few times in order to win. Harper and their future together were more important than anything else.

Chapter Ten
Day 3

Colleen's night was anything but restful. During the dark hours, she sensed the ghosts of former prisoners wandering past her cell. Now, in the light of morning, she sat hunched over a table in the common room, nursing a cold cup of coffee. After breakfast, she wanted to do a little exploring. She had time to kill, and the wait would go faster if she kept her mind occupied.

Her check-in time was one forty-five the previous afternoon, which meant she'd leave at the same time today. Her feet hurt, her back ached, and she noticed two newly formed pimples on her face.

Wonder how Storm is holding up? She glanced at him sitting across the room. He was alone, so she stood and walked over to join him. "So, how did you sleep last night in the jail cell?"

He grunted. "Terrible. I dreamt someone shut all the cell doors. I tried opening mine and couldn't escape. Can't wait to get out of here."

"I was thinking about taking a stroll around the prison. Would you like to join me?" The new goodwill between them was as fragile as a bird's nest, wound together with scavenged bits from their past. One strong wind, one wrong word, or misconstrued action, and their truce would scatter onto the ground.

He shook his head. "I want to study my maps and

get familiar with the roads around here. See if I can't figure out where they'll send us next."

"Okay." Her overly optimistic heart stuttered with disappointment. *Of course, he doesn't want to spend the morning with you.*

He dropped his gaze and went back to shoveling watery scrambled eggs into his mouth.

"Well, good luck today." Colleen stood and turned to leave. Storm remained silent, so she left him to his breakfast. He obviously wanted to be alone. *Stop extending an olive branch.* How many times did she have her hand bit before she'd learn? What was the saying? *Apparently, one more time.*

Five-and-a-half hours later, she stood before the show's host and reached out to receive her next clue. She tore open the envelope, and the camera crew hovered, recording her action.

A Grand, Gloomy, and Peculiar Place. Your next stop is the world's largest known cave system. So, don't get lost! Look for the red flag at the Visitors' Center. Hours of operation: eight thirty am to five-fifteen pm Central Time. Tents provided at the park's campground.

Earlier, Colleen copied Storm's idea and studied her maps and travel book. This clue must be Mammoth Cave. The four-hundred-twenty-five miles was too long to make the drive by the time the cave closed today. She'd have to camp overnight then get in line at the entrance at sunrise. Storm left only fifteen minutes prior, so he'd be camping as well.

Colleen tossed her pack in the back of her car and slid into the driver's seat. After leaving West Virginia and the eastern part of Ohio, the trip presented long stretches of flat interstate peppered with truck-stops and all-you-can-eat diners. She approached Cincinnati, and the landscape evolved into rolling hills and valleys. Once she crossed the Ohio River and traveled south of Louisville, the scenery turned more robust, with dramatic rises and falls in elevation covered in autumn foliage. After a six-and-a half hour drive, she pulled into the Mammoth Cave campgrounds, just barely beating the evening curfew.

The sun had set, so besides the few campfires burning, the grounds were dark. The crisp autumn air rejuvenated her after the long car ride. As she carried her travel pack to the circle of tents, she shivered. With only six tents for the twelve contestants who'd arrived, she quickly came to the conclusion they'd have to share.

Not ready to turn in yet, Colleen sat on a split log bench beside the fire pit and talked with a few other contestants. She devoured a cold hamburger and chips while the camera crew kept to the edges of their gathering. She hadn't seen Storm but heard from someone else he was there. She was so nice and warm, the thought of leaving the fire to sleep in a cold tent delayed her choosing a tent mate. Before she knew what happened, the other contestants paired up, leaving her sitting alone by the fire.

One spot had to be open, preferably with one of the few females who'd made it here, but in which tent? Should she go around knocking on each tent? *How exactly does one knock on a tent?* Approaching the closest one, she cleared her throat. "Knock, knock. Anyone home?" The rip of a zipper opening gave her hope.

Storm poked out his head from between the tent flaps. "What?"

Her heart fluttered. "Nice to see you, too. Are you all alone in there?" She peered inside, past Storm's body and through the zippered opening. Two sleeping bags were laid out, but only one occupant. Of course, no one wanted to be his bunkmate. He probably scared them all off.

"I am, and I'm keeping it that way." His gaze scanned the camping area and then rested back on her. A smirk pulled at the corner of his mouth.

"Come on, let me in. It's freezing out here." She wrapped her arms around her body and shivered for added effect.

"Go find somewhere else. You're not sleeping next to me." He reached up for the pull to slide the zipper closed.

"Look." She pushed past him. "I'm tired, and so are you." Sighing, she tossed her bag on the floor of the tent. "Sleeping arrangements aren't worth fighting over."

The scowl on his face deepened. "Fine." He grabbed the extra blanket off his sleeping bag and tossed it over the center pole of the tent, making a boundary. "You stay on your side, and I'll stay on mine—like we each have our own tent."

Might work. She'd just pretend he was somewhere far, far away. Not within arm's reach. "Deal. But I'm warning you, don't try any funny business."

He snorted. "Your honor is safe with me."

After a trip to the bathhouse, Colleen cocooned herself inside the warmth of her sleeping bag. The evening song of hooting owls had her drifting off to sleep within minutes.

Sometime during the night, she felt warm breath on her face. Then, she became aware of the weight of an arm resting on her body. Fighting panic, Colleen slowly opened her eyes. In the dim moonlight, she could make out Storm's sleepy face only inches away. His wavy hair hung over his eyes like overgrown sheep's wool.

He was definitely on her side of the tent. Did he have any idea? Most likely, not. But right now, his dislike of her didn't matter. She'd take full advantage of his lack of cognizance and make use of his body heat. Curling up, she closed the small gap between their separate sleeping bags. The pure male scent of him mixed with the freshness of mint from his toothpaste was heaven.

Tomorrow, they'd go back to being enemies. Tonight, she'd ignore the hard, lumpy ground and enjoy the comforting feeling of Storm's warm body.

Chapter Eleven
Day 4

Storm was having the best dream. He was in bed with a woman, who smelled like campfire smoke and floral shampoo. A bulky blanket lay wedged between them, and he needed to remove it to get closer.

Filtered sunlight permeated the lids of his eyes. When the woman at his side moved, he pulled her in tighter. She was soft and warm, a stark difference to the cold air. Storm's sleepy brain drifted until with some effort, he came to consciousness.

He rested in a tent. Yesterday, he'd traveled to Mammoth Cave in Kentucky. He was competing in *The Great American Scavenger Hunt*. The woman who he slept next to was—Colleen. He tensed, his eyes popped open, and he focused on the face inches from his own.

"Good morning." Colleen smiled. The whiteness of her teeth glowed in the dim light. "I enjoy cuddling as much as the next person, but we really should get moving."

Storm jerked away his arm like he'd been shocked. "What do you think you're doing?" He looked up at the dividing blanket. "You're on my side."

Wiggling out of her sleeping bag, she sat upright. "Your side is over there." She pointed to the empty portion of the tent. "This side is mine. Until you rolled over here."

Looking at the zippered door, he ran a hand down his face. Which side had he started on? He'd taken the right side, and Colleen the left. Somehow during the night, he'd moved. Nerves pinged in his gut. "Why didn't you wake me?" He rose to rest on his elbow. "A swift kick would have sent me back."

"I was cold and enjoyed your body heat." She stood, hunched to avoid hitting her head on the roof of the tent, and unzipped her pack. "It's seven now. We have about an hour and a half to get ready before the Visitors' Center opens. We should go to the bathhouse and shower."

She used the pronoun "we" a lot lately. There was Storm, and then there was Colleen. Definitely no "we." He might be forced to work with her in order to get ahead, but they'd never be a team. "Just because *we* shared a tent doesn't mean *I* need *you* to tell me what to do." He kicked out of his own sleeping bag. "Don't forget, you need to beat *me* in order to win the prize money."

With her arms full of clean clothes, plus soap and shampoo, she stared back, blinking. Her short hair stuck up on one side. "In order for either of us to win, we'll eventually team up with someone. A simple strategy. If you don't want my help, that's fine. I'll see if I can work my way into another group. But I think, despite our history *and* your bad feelings toward me, we make a good team."

The knot in his chest tightened. "What I feel toward you is more than a few bad feelings."

She exhaled a long sigh. "What do you want me to say, Storm? Yes, I was a mean, horrible person when I was younger. But you were no angel either. Remember the time you put glue in my face moisturizer at school?"

One side on his mouth twitched in a grin. "That prank was great."

"I spent a week scrubbing that junk from my face to feel normal again." Her mouth twitched with a smile. "Stop laughing."

He shrugged. Time to admit he could use a partner, especially a smart one. "We can team up temporarily. But if you start dragging me behind, I'm out."

"Same." Colleen shuffled the items in her arm, bent down, and then used a free hand to unzip the tent. "And in the end, if we both are still in this thing, all bets are off. We play to win."

Fresh, cool air rushed inside. The playful curve of her lips had him smiling back. "Winner takes all."

"Winner takes all." She nodded before stepping outside the tent.

Last night, cuddled next to Colleen, he'd had the best night's sleep in a long time. Maybe only a result of his growing exhaustion. Right, he'd been overtired and sought out a warm body. The stress of competition must be getting to his head. He couldn't let Colleen get to his heart.

****

When she returned from her shower, Storm waited by the tent. He tossed her a protein bar and yelled to hurry up. Somehow, he'd showered while she'd been gone. He looked rugged in hiking boots, shorts, and a flannel shirt—every bit the true naturalist he was at heart.

Colleen grabbed her pack and followed Storm over to the Visitors' Center. Four other contestants were already there. They formed a semi-organized line.

At eight-thirty, the doors of the building opened. Storm and Colleen rushed inside, and she picked up their next clue.

Take the Violet City tour of Mammoth Cave. Pick up lanterns at the Historical Entrance and follow the flags through the cave system. Stay on the marked path and don't stray, or you might never find your way out! In Wright's Rotunda, find the basket filled with reed torches and take one. Reed torches were used by Native Americans to explore the dark cave.

Grabbing a park map, Colleen unfolded it and located the red dot marking the Violet City tour. The Historical Entrance was nearby, but their hike would end some distance from the Visitor's Center. Once she completed the task, she'd hitch a return ride.

"Come on." Storm stood by the open door.

"Leave your pack here." She dropped hers behind the reception counter. "The extra weight will slow us down."

Once outside, Colleen ran beside Storm toward the cave opening. She grabbed one of the lanterns set out on a table, and she counted three contestants ahead of her.

A long staircase descended into the dim cave. The scents of rock, minerals, and age ladened the dry air. Only a few upward-pointing lights marked the path. She relied mostly on their lanterns to illuminate the twists and turns of the cave.

After an hour of strenuous hiking, her legs shook in exhaustion. "I need to sit and catch my breath." Thankfully, a wooden bench occupied a niche just up ahead. She lowered onto the seat, and her leg muscles rejoiced. The physical challenges of the last two days were extracting payment from her body.

Storm peered over his shoulder. "I don't hear anyone behind us. Let's take a two-minute rest. Drink some water. Then we'll get back to work." He sat and took a long drink out of the water bottle in his hand.

"You're actually sticking with me?" After his speech that morning about not letting anything slow him down, she was surprised he'd wait.

"I'd be stupid to try navigating this cave alone," Storm said.

The bite of disappointment stung. What did she expect? He wanted to stay because he cared? She was delusional if she thought he'd ever see her as anything but the enemy. The only reason he'd teamed up was for his own advantage. To be honest, she was using him, too. But deep down, she did care. At the end of the contest, she'd beat him and when the time came, the action would break her heart. "Okay, let's go." She pushed off the bench. Blisters burned the underside of her feet and backs of her heels.

Storm lifted his lantern and moved along the dark path. "Do you remember seeing Wright's Rotunda on the map? Are we almost there?"

"We passed the Tuberculosis Hospital Ruins, so it should be up ahead. Hard to judge distance down here." She squinted to read her map. After she rounded a corner, the warm glow of lights greeted her. As she entered the Rotunda, she raced Storm to the basket.

Of course, he got there first and pulled out a reed. "Let's go." He waited while she collected hers, and then pushed on toward the cave exit.

In the low light, Colleen moved as quickly as she could manage without twisting an ankle or tripping.

The formations of the cave were amazing, but in her rush, she moved past them like a ghost in the darkness, barely noticing the grandeur. Some of the narrow paths made Colleen fear the dark walls were moving in to surround them. She'd never escape. At the idea of getting lost underground, panic built inside her chest. She struggled to breathe. Her lungs were heavy and thick with anxiety.

Storm moved ahead and disappeared around the corner. "I see stairs," his voice echoed.

Thank goodness. I need fresh air and sunlight, or I'll go mad. She rushed up the stairs to freedom. As she pushed open the metal door, she became blinded by the light. She blinked, letting her eyes adjust. Cool, damp air filled her lungs and blew across her face, causing her skin to tingle with joy.

A man stood about twenty feet away with a video camera, waiting to capture the contestants exit the cave.

By now, Colleen barely noticed the cameras, which were as pesky and unwelcome as mosquitoes. Out of the corner of her eye, she saw a red flag, and a stack of white envelopes waited.

Hurry to the Birthplace of the Blues. The lion might be the king of the jungle, but this King created his own Jungle Room. Your next clue is there.

"Graceland." He swayed his hips. "I didn't pack my blue suede shoes."

"You can sing and dance later." She stifled a laugh. "We need to get back to the Visitors' Center." For a normal cave tour, a bus would transport the pedestrians, but the show's contestants weren't so lucky. Her two-and-a-half-hour hike through the cave had wiped her out. The thought of more walking brought tears to her eyes.

As another two contestants exited the metal door, Colleen grabbed Storm's hand and pulled him to sit on a small bench. "They'll take the hiking path. We need to take the road so we can flag down a ride." She waited another minute, until the others were well out of sight, and then led Storm toward the paved road. By this point, her legs were so tired, her muscles quivered. Driving to Graceland would give her a chance to sit and let her poor body recover.

The sun climbed higher in the sky, heating the crisp October air. Dry leaves crunched under their feet. Besides the bird's songs coming from the surrounding forest, the world around her was quiet. Storm moved closer and pulled her arm up to rest over his shoulder, helping to support her weight.

Her heart skipped when she heard the distant rumble of a car engine. If they could get a ride, she and Storm would most likely be the first to leave for Graceland.

On the road, a dark green truck approached. She stepped out to wave it down. Thank goodness—a Park Ranger. "Let me handle this," she whispered as the truck's passenger window rolled down. "Excuse me, sir," Colleen said in a sweet-as-sugar southern drawl. "I am so tired. Is there any way you could give my friend and me a ride back to the Visitors' Center?"

The man's wide-eyed gaze did not leave Colleen. He gave her a toothy smile and adjusted his beaten, olive-colored baseball cap. "Are you a contestant in that reality show they're filming here?"

She batted her eyelashes. "Yes, we are. A ride would really help. After the long hike through the cave, my legs are so tired, they're ready to give out."

"Well, ma'am, we wouldn't want that. You and your friend hop on in. I'll get you back to the Center lickety-split."

Behind her, Storm snorted.

Ignoring him, she climbed into the cab of the truck and scooted over to the middle, placing her next to the driver. In less than a five-minute drive, she was back at the Center. "Thank you for your help," Colleen said to the Park Ranger as she hopped out of the truck.

"*No problemo*." He leaned toward the open passenger door. "I'm always happy to help a damsel in distress."

Colleen opened her mouth to reply, but Storm grabbed her arm and yanked her toward the Visitors' Center and their waiting packs. All she could do was wave good-bye.

"Come on...stop flirting with Yogi Bear," Storm growled. "We need to get back to the campground and our vehicles."

She yanked her arm out of his grasp. "You shouldn't act so rude. He saved us time."

Storm's long-legged stride carried him to the covered entrance of the limestone building. "You shouldn't feel the need to flirt with every man you come across."

"I'm being nice. You should try it sometime, and I'm not a flirt." She huffed with the effort of keeping pace.

"You are not nice, and you use people to get what you want."

"Oh really?" Colleen picked up her pack and slung it over her shoulders. Her temper flared. "Here you go again…hurling accusations in my face. What did I want from you back in DC when I helped you with the Metro?"

Storm marched silently until they reached their cars, and then stopped. "I haven't figured out your game, but I know you have one."

"You're impossible. My only game is to win." Opening the rear door of her car, she tossed in her pack. "I've never met someone so thick headed. What game were you playing last night when you put the moves on me?" His face turned as red as the autumn leaves surrounding them.

"I was cold," he sputtered. "Don't think too highly of yourself, princess. I wanted nothing more from you than extra body heat."

She didn't stop the spreading grin. "And our kiss? Was that about capturing my body heat?"

"I didn't kiss you." He swung open the door to his car. "Except in your dreams."

Laughing at his flustered expression, she hopped into the driver's seat and started the ignition.

He'd been right to accuse her of playing games. But her goal was not mean spirited. Exactly the opposite. She wished he'd loosen up.

As a child, Storm had been tightly wound. He suffered stomachaches due to anxiety, and his surly personality might be his way of coping with those same issues as an adult. During his time away, Storm had grown into a man and became a father. He was good-looking, strong, and smart. So, why was he still holding on to the baggage of his youth?

As she drove out of Mammoth Cave National Park, she caught a glimpse of her reflection in the rearview mirror. Her eyes stared back accusingly. How dare she judge Storm for holding on to the past when she was just as much a prisoner to it herself. Every day, she lived with the insecurity and fear her dad created inside her. After moving back home as an adult, she still felt compelled to win his approval. Why did she try so hard to impress an alcoholic?

Because a lifetime of learned behavior didn't go away in the blink of an eye.

She had a four-hour drive through the scenic mountains and foothills of Tennessee and didn't want to spend the entire trip psychoanalyzing her and Storm's childhood traumas. She focused on winning the prize money. The veterans she'd help were deserving. What they had endured made her family's problems seem small.

A deep longing for her mom hit her heart, and her chest tightened. To Colleen, her mom was an enigma, like a patron saint, always with her in spirit but not a real part of her life. Since losing her mom at a young age, she didn't have many solid memories of their short time together. Now as an adult, she wished she had a mother to go to for advice. If she hadn't acted like a spoiled child the day of the car accident, her mom would still be alive.

Long enough for a pity party.

She turned on the radio, and the upbeat melody of "All Shook Up" caused her left foot to tap along to the beat. A fitting send-off for a trip to Graceland.

****

At three pm, Storm boarded a small bus and took the short ride across the street to Graceland. His first stop once inside the mansion—the Jungle Room.

Standing in the viewing hall, he glanced around the legendary space. Green shag carpeted the floor, and wood paneling covered three of the four walls. The fourth wall was wrapped in faux greenery and brick. The room looked like a trip to Hawaii on LSD—wild with a hint of crazy.

Under a hanging red flag sat a basket of clues.

Time to sing the Blues—at The Blues Hall. Your Choice: either sing on stage with the band or dance with a partner for one song. Doors open at five pm.

Colleen stepped beside him and glanced around the room. "I should hire Elvis's decorator for my next house."

Whether he wanted her presence or not, she always seemed to be nearby. Almost like they'd established some strange gravitational pull. "A carpeted ceiling looks great in any living room." With his success at each stop, Storm's mood lifted. The farther he traveled, the closer he got to the million dollars.

"We're supposed to go to the Blues Hall. Do you know where that is?" Colleen pointed at the paper in her hands.

He shrugged. "No idea."

They exited the home through a side door.

Colleen sprinted ahead and flagged a couple of tourists strolling by. After a brief conversation, she darted toward the bus that took them back to the parking lot.

He fumed and ran after her. Did she really think she'd leave without sharing the location of the Blues Hall? "What happened to working as a team?"

"Calm down." She rolled her eyes. "The bus wouldn't leave without you. Follow me to Beale Street.

The Blues Hall is down by Handy Park."

Back at his car, he scanned the parking lot for other competitors' cars. Not a one. He and Colleen must be in the lead. On the drive to Beale Street, he maneuvered like a racing pro to keep up. Her turns were performed last second with no blinker. On the ramp to the freeway, she gunned it, and for several minutes, he'd lost sight of her. Since he hadn't looked at the map before they'd left, he was totally reliant on Colleen. A stupid move on his part.

Just as he pulled up behind her, she rocketed from the far left lane over to the exit ramp on the right. Horns blasted as he jerked the steering wheel to follow across the lanes of traffic.

Once parked, he marched over to meet her by her car, temper burning. "Don't tell me to follow you then go drive like a maniac."

She grabbed her pack out of the back seat and turned to face him. "You drive like an old lady."

"You tried to lose me." He moved to within inches, and his gaze swept her face and down her body. "What's the matter, Colleen? You threatened by me?"

A red flush crept up Colleen's neck to color her cheeks. "Threatened by you? Not likely."

He wrapped an arm around her waist and pulled her close. Heated blood pulsed through his veins. "Admit the truth. I'm tougher, smarter, and always got the best of you."

"You're so full of it." She pushed off his chest. "The last time you got the best of me was junior year, when you put the ad in the newspaper for lice treatment using my school picture."

Storm grinned. "I forgot about the lice ad. I really

got you good." He nudged her with his elbow. "Come on…admit it."

"*Humph.*" She walked away. "I wouldn't admit anything. People called me lice-head for the rest of the school year." Jerking to a halt, she rounded on him. "I don't need underhanded tactics to win."

"All right." Storm took a step back, hands raised. "Sorry about the nickname. Kids can be cruel."

"I know." Her gaze dropped to her feet.

"Come on." Taking her hand, he pulled her forward. "Enough fighting. Let's go."

With Colleen at his side, he followed the sound of music to Beale Street. People lazily strode along the sidewalk, seemingly with nowhere to go. Jazz and Blues drifted out of the establishments he passed. A few bars of melody hung in the air, and then he'd move along and another song took its place.

Above a teal awning hung a blue sign with white letters reading *Blues Hall*. No other contestants were in sight. Right now, he and Colleen were in first place. The thrill of success sparked in his chest. But he'd have to wait for almost an hour before the hall opened. By then, who knew how many others would have caught up?

Colleen sat on the sidewalk with her back resting on the building and closed her eyes.

How could she even think of sleeping? He was too keyed up to rest. Still standing, he observed the crowds moving by and watched for the now-familiar faces of his opponents.

"You know…if we're working together, you should trust me." Colleen glanced up and shielded her eyes with her hand.

"No way. And if you're smart, you won't trust me, either." He turned away and put an end to the conversation. Trust had to be earned, and right now, it came with too high a cost.

When the doors to the Blues Hall finally swung open, Storm and Colleen were still the only ones waiting outside. Finally, luck was on his side.

The building was fairly empty, beside the bartender, several waitresses, and the band on the small stage. The place smelled like stale cigarette smoke and beer—a fragrance produced from the classic mixture of music and booze.

"Sing or dance?" Colleen asked while they waited for the band to warm up.

"I can't sing to save my life. I'm finding someone to dance with." Storm stepped away toward a group of waitresses by the bar.

She reached out and jerked his arm. "If you're dancing with anyone, you're dancing with me." Stepping out onto the dance floor, she curved a finger for him to follow.

Torn between humor and irritation, he joined the bossy woman. Of all the people in the world, he'd joined forces with her.

Tables and chairs had been pushed against the wall, leaving a small space of well-worn wooden planks. A few chords sounded from a bass guitar, followed by the rhythmic beating of a drum. The band's singer, a black man wearing a stylish cobalt suit and a gray fedora, stepped to the microphone. His deep baritone voice crackled through the speakers on stage.

Storm placed an arm around Colleen's waist and pulled her close. His other hand smoothed back the strands of hair on her face. She was soft and warm, and smelled as good as he remembered.

Their bodies swayed with the strong beat of the music.

"*Just can't shake loose these chains and things.*" The singer's soulful voice echoed off the walls.

Colleen swung her hips and dipped low. Her face lifted with the seductive curve of her lips.

She played with him, and at that moment, he didn't care. He didn't give thought to the camera man standing in the corner, recording their dance. The music had cast a spell, like a snake charmer's flute for a cobra. He couldn't take his gaze off Colleen and the way her body moved with his.

Her hand moved to the back of his neck and fingered the curls of his hair. "Why didn't I see it sooner?" she whispered. Her other hand rose until it rested on his shoulder and caressed the muscles lying just beneath the thin fabric of his shirt.

"See what?" He swallowed hard.

"You...the man you'd become."

Storm shivered under her light touch. "I may have grown up, but I can't forget what you did the night before graduation."

"I know." She closed her eyes and rested her head on his chest. "I'll never forgive myself for what happened at the party. I didn't know they'd be so cruel. I'm sorry, Storm."

Memories of the worst night of his life washed over him. Colleen had taken part, exploiting his teenage hormones to lure him to a private spot. Once she'd left, members of the varsity football team took care of the rest. They tied him to a tree and took turns pounding his gangly, teenage body until he passed out.

Was she aware of the true extent of what happened? That he spent all night in the cold and bleeding? The rope cut so tight into his wrists, he'd spent painful hours working to get free. Remembering the pain, he shivered. No use thinking about high school. Now, he was a grown man and a father of a wonderful girl. And he had a competition to win.

The song ended, and so did Storm's chain of thought.

Colleen hurried toward the bar to take the envelope from the bartender's hand.

Once he regained his focus, Storm followed.

Another contestant darted inside.

Darn. His pulse and pace quickened with renewed urgency. As he exited the bar, Storm ripped open the envelope.

You might be familiar with the never-ending party that is New Orleans, but this state offers another kind of wildlife. Outside the city of Lake Charles, the Gator Bayou Tour Company awaits your arrival. Hours of operation: nine am to five pm. Rent a kayak and paddle through the bayou in search of alligators. Use your digital camera to take pictures of three different alligators. Then head back to the docks to find Cajun Jim. He will provide your next clue.

He sprinted back to his vehicle and drove away, not waiting for Colleen, who couldn't run at his speed. Putting distance between them was imperative. She'd gotten under his skin—like a tick. A pesky, annoying, dangerous, but breathtakingly beautiful tick.

****

Colleen drove until seven-thirty then found a small

town in Mississippi to stop for the night and sleep. The Safe House along this route was too far away to arrive before curfew. As she drove into town, she searched the main road for a decent motel. The first one she saw looked like the Bates Motel from *Psycho*. *Nope*. Rather not get stabbed to death while in the shower.

The next one she found was only marginally better, but she was running out of time. She put away her pride and parked under a rotating neon sign that flashed *Vacancy*. When the elderly man working the front desk handed her a room key, she nearly doubled over with exhaustion. Her arms hung heavy and weak. The simple walk to the motel room became as draining as if she was moving underwater. An intense throbbing pulsed behind her eyes. She needed sleep but hunger won.

After dropping off her pack inside her room, she shuffled over to the family restaurant across the parking lot. With her tummy content from the club sandwich and fries she'd downed, she savored a hot shower and collapsed into bed. Something was missing tonight— more like someone. Last night, inside the tent, she enjoyed the comfort of Storm's presence. Now, with worry weighing heavy on her heart, she drifted off to sleep under a blanket of renewed loneliness.

Chapter Twelve
Day 5

The next morning, as the sun rose over the eastern horizon, Colleen drove south. The landscape passing by her car window turned lush and green. Spanish moss hung from tree branches like velvet draperies. At a freeway truck stop, she bought a protein bar and a bottle of water. The welcoming, thick Southern accent of the cashier was delightful.

Once back on the road, she thought ahead to the kayak trip through the bayou and the waiting alligators. Despite the warmth, she quivered. She imagined gleaming white rows of teeth in the open mouth of the leathery beast. Heaven help her get through this next task.

She made good time and didn't hit much traffic going through Baton Rouge, arriving in Lake Charles by ten-thirty. A friendly woman at the visitor center off Interstate 10 gave her directions to Gator Bayou Tour Company. After a fifteen-minute drive past hulking oil refineries and down a dead-end road, she saw the sign in the shape of an alligator, which marked her destination.

She parked next to Storm's car, grabbed her camera, and ran to the little shack serving as the ticket booth. Her stomach threatened to toss up her protein bar at the sight of the small kayak she'd entrust with her life. The smell of stagnant water didn't help, either.

After receiving a few brief instructions, she descended into a kayak and paddled out into the murky water. Algae floated on the still water surface like Elvis's shag carpet. Tall trees loomed above, their roots somehow set firm in the earth of the muddy swamp.

She paddled for twenty minutes, while her gaze darted back and forth, searching for telltale ripples on the water's surface. She wanted to find an alligator, but then again, she didn't. Her heart beat a staccato rhythm, fast and hard. Starbursts flashed in her vision. Her brain screamed to turn around and go back. A panic attack loomed.

A long time had passed since her last one during the final days of writing her doctorate dissertation. She remembered vividly the warning signals her body sent off before her anxiety fully crested. Colleen forced her breathing to slow. She closed her eyes in order to refocus. Holding the kayak paddle out of the water with shaking hands, she sat still and allowed her body to fall into relaxation. *Forget about the competition, forget about the alligators, and forget about Storm. Focus on the here and now.*

Slowly, she opened her eyes. Fighting her body's natural reflex to tense, she stayed calm. Directly ahead, above the water line, floated a bumpy log with two black eyes. Making slow movements, she lifted her camera and snapped a picture.

The alligator disappeared under the water, sliding away without any surface movement.

Yuck. One down—only two more to go. Then she could get the heck out of here. Luck played nicely today, and she found two more alligators fairly easily.

She paddled back to the dock and approached a narrow passage, when two other contestants came from the opposite direction.

She wasn't willing to concede the right of way, and the two other women stared back, unmoving—which meant she was at an impasse in the narrow section of the waterway.

The other two kayakers moved forward.

As she found herself pushed backward, she cursed under her breath.

"Your boyfriend's leaving you behind," Jody, the kayaker on the right, taunted.

Every time she saw Jody, the woman wore a smirk. With dark hair and a tall, lean body, Jody might be pretty if she ever lost the condescending attitude. "You mean Storm?" Why would anyone think he was her boyfriend? Didn't they notice his look of aggravation every time they were together?

"Yeah. The really hot guy who's always wearing tight T-shirts." The other female kayaker, Betty, brushed off a bug from her bare shoulder. Her olive complexion showed only a hint of pink from the sun.

"Storm and I have teamed up on occasion, but we aren't in a relationship." Colleen was finally back far enough so the two kayakers could pass. They moved around her, one on each side, like a pair of wolves preparing for an attack.

"Well," said Jody. "Good to know he's available. He'd make a great addition to our alliance. If nothing else, I'll enjoy looking at him."

Before you eat him alive. "Don't get your hopes up," Colleen shot back. "He's not in the market for partners, in the competition or otherwise. Good luck with the gators. They're hungry today. One almost bit a chunk out of my kayak."

As she heard the women gasp, she laughed. A small alligator approached her kayak and glided alongside for a while. Then, in an instant, it quickly submerged. Guess the little guy preferred fresh fish over eating plastic kayaks.

Saying a prayer of thanksgiving, she pulled her kayak alongside the dock and carefully climbed out.

Big Cajun Jim, wearing overalls with no shirt underneath, handed her a clue.

****

Next stop—the mighty Mississippi River. The White Oak Inn in Natchez, Mississippi, is a Time-Out stop. The last three *contestants to arrive will be eliminated.*

After Storm returned to Cajun Jim with his gator pictures, he didn't waste any time. The Time-Out stop was a three-hour drive. More time in the car. With about thirty miles to go, his check-engine light flashed. He pounded the steering wheel in frustration. Then, he watched the temperature gauge slowly creep over to red. If his car broke down on the side of the road, he'd be stuck. He should have never left Colleen to strike off on his own.

Should he stop at a gas station or just keep pushing forward? He decreased his speed but didn't stop, praying the hunk of American-made steel would keep chugging along. He refused to be one of the last three contestants and be eliminated.

Another contestant blew past, honking repeatedly.

By the time he had one mile remaining to his destination, his shirt was soaked with sweat. When he pulled into the parking lot of the White Oak Inn, he counted only three other cars already there. Driving with car trouble reinforced that playing with a partner, at least in the beginning, was smarter. All the other contestants had formed into loose teams. They traveled together and watched one another's backs.

At this stop, he'd have a chance to speak with Colleen and maybe put together a plan. Colleen was a smart player. *Keep your enemy close.* If they worked together, they could pull ahead of the competition. Then, when they reached the end of the race, he'd figure out a way to leave her behind.

His strategy was smart, and maybe a bit underhanded, but he had to ensure he crossed that line first. He ignored the scratching at the door of his conscience, which sounded a lot like his mother's chiding voice. He refused to feel guilty about playing the game in order to win.

Because he had to win. Harper's future counted on his success.

****

Colleen dipped her toes into the refreshing blue water of the hotel's pool. The air temperature was pleasant, and the heated pool water pampered her body after a rough few days. She sat on the edge then slid in. Her weightless body floated on the water's surface as she stared upward at the cornflower blue sky. The white clouds above resembled the cotton she'd seen growing in roadside fields—soft and wispy.

Earlier, when she'd arrived at the check-in, she was surprised to learn she ranked first. Jody and Betty, the two women she'd passed during the kayak challenge, were second and third. Storm arrived fourth.

After a mental debate, she'd decided to stop

attempting a friendship with Storm. She was through being a doormat—only useful for his needs. A team meant working together toward a common goal.

Pushing Storm's self-centered attitude out of her mind, she enjoyed the peace and relaxation of the pool. Deep voices sounded, and she turned her head to see two men, fellow contestants, exiting the inn.

"Hey." Rob pulled off his shirt. He was tall, with short dark hair and a wide chest. "Mind if we join you?"

"Of course not." Colleen let her feet sink to the bottom of the pool. She could use a pleasant conversation.

"That's cool you came in first today. I'm Rob, by the way. This is Brad." He pointed to the quiet guy standing beside him.

Brad waved.

He was cute, in a grown-up, frat boy kind of way. And his wide smile made her insides glow. "I remember your names. I'm Colleen. Nice to get a break, huh? How did you guys do today?"

"I came in fifth, and Brad is in sixth." Rob stepped down the pool stairs and swam toward her.

Brad did an elegant dive and joined them in the center.

"Are you guys working together?" As she stood between two handsome men, Colleen enjoyed a body sparkling reaction.

Fat water droplets dripped off Brad's hair then trickled in random paths down his body. "Yeah," Brad said. "Since the last Time-Out stop at the prison. We plan on sticking together for as long as possible. Better chance working with another person."

She agreed, which was one of the reasons she'd wanted to form an alliance with Storm. The other reason was more personal.

The three spent the next half-hour engaging in small talk. When Colleen exited the pool, the two guys followed her to the lounge chairs. One sat on either side. Wow—two good-looking guys giving her their rapt attention. Not once had she apologized for something she did in the past. She hadn't tip-toed around subjects like she did with Storm. *So nice to just be myself.*

"Why don't you join us for dinner?" Rob asked. "I don't know about you, but I'm starving. The show set up a buffet in one of the conference rooms."

She glanced over at Brad, whose warm smile had her agreeing to practically anything. "Sure. Let me put on regular clothes, and I'll meet you in the lobby."

"I hate to see you change out of that bikini." Rob offered her a hand and pulled her onto her feet.

Colleen laughed and grabbed her pool towel. Back in her room, she took a quick shower, put on a touch of make-up, and styled her short hair. After dressing in a clean shirt and shorts, she went down to the lobby.

Storm stood at the bottom of the stairs, like an overprotective father of a daughter heading out on a date. As she approached, she cringed at the always present scowl marking his face. "You keep frowning and your face will stay like that forever." What she wouldn't give for him to smile like when he was younger. He'd always had the sweetest smile.

"Let's eat. We can talk strategy." Storm came to stand alongside her and cupped her elbow.

What nerve? He took off without her back in

Memphis after their slow dance. Now that she was in first, he figured she'd be useful again. "I've already made plans to eat with Rob and Brad."

Storm stiffened. "What?"

Raising her chin, she looked him directly in the eyes. The brown pools churned with something resembling anger. *Don't be intimidated, and don't let your feelings cloud your better judgment.* "I assumed you weren't interested in working with me anymore, so I looked elsewhere for a partner. I don't need you, Storm." Turning on her heel, she walked away. She joined Rob and Brad, who stood at the entrance of the conference room.

Over dinner, she firmed her decision to team up with Rob and Brad—temporarily. They seemed nice, although in this situation, she could never be sure of anyone's true character. Although she'd leave one hour before them tomorrow, they'd assist each other whenever their paths crossed. If things went according to plan, the three would gain the lead on the other contestants.

As she ate, she peered over at Storm, who sat at a table alone. He wore his normal look of displeasure, of course, but she sensed something deeper. Disappointment, maybe? Hurt? After all his huffing and puffing about how much he didn't like her, deep down did he still care? They had a connection, a dysfunctional one, but the bond was still there.

Reluctantly, she met a producer for a short contestant interview before taking her turn in the confessional booth. In an attempt to keep the topics light, she focused her conversations on recounting her experience kayaking through the bayou and how a task she'd feared turned out kind of fun. She purposely avoided any talk of Storm.

Finally, around eleven, after a couple of drinks at the bar, Colleen said goodnight. She left Rob and Brad and strolled to the elevator. When the door slid open, she stepped inside and leaned against the back wall for support. Was the elevator spinning? Before the doors closed, a hand reached in to force them open.

Storm came striding inside, looked her up and down, and pressed the button for the fourth floor. "You look terrible," he said.

She stared at his broad back. "Thanks. No wonder you're so smooth with the ladies."

"Drinking too much alcohol is not good for you."

A reply surfaced in Colleen's fuzzy brain. "Are you too pure and organic to have a little fun?"

Slowly, he turned to face her. The door pinged open to their floor.

"For me, alcohol was never about fun." He halted in the hallway outside the elevator.

He took hold of her arm, leading her out like a child. "I remember you having fun the night I caught you drinking at the grain elevator with Marsha Underwood." She giggled.

Deep creases formed on his tan forehead. "I started drinking heavily my junior year. After high school, I turned into a full-blown alcoholic."

"I…" Her voice trailed off. What could she say? Tears filled her eyes, blurring her vision.

"My home life sucked, and school was hell. The only way I could get away from the pain was to drink." He moved toward her.

In the cramped hotel hallway, Storm stood within

inches. His breath smelled like the peppermint candies restaurants supplied after dinner. She wanted to run and get away. She knew the wickedness of alcohol abuse firsthand. Her dad used scotch as an escape after he'd lost his wife.

"Do you still drink?" she asked.

"I haven't touched booze in five years." Tension released from his face and body. "I stopped drinking when I became interested in organic farming. Spending time in nature forced me to reexamine what I was doing to my body. I started eating clean and exercising."

Her earlier buzz evaporated. Storm lowered his defenses and made himself vulnerable—he wanted her approval of the man he'd become. "I'm proud of you. Removing alcohol from your life is not an easy accomplishment."

"Is that a line from one of your shrink textbooks?" One eyebrow twitched.

She couldn't tell the connotation behind his words. A joke or a jab? No matter. He lived under the assumption her life had been perfect, and she wouldn't spoil the illusion by confessing her own father was a drunk. Storm was as thick-headed and stubborn as they came. Nothing she'd say would change his mind.

"Sure, that's right…a textbook." Colleen stepped around him and headed down the hall. Her hand trembled as she slid the keycard and turned the handle. She couldn't wait for Storm to be eliminated. Her focus should stay on winning, and he was a distraction. A very big distraction.

Chapter Thirteen
Day 6

Storm watched as Colleen sauntered into the hotel conference room where breakfast was served. She piled bacon and eggs onto her plate, and then joined her new boyfriends, all the while not looking his way. But his gaze hadn't left her since the moment she walked into view.

She had a new spring in her step. Could be the extra sleep she'd gotten last night. He'd enjoyed not waking early to hit the road. Colleen would leave at three today. He'd follow a half an hour later.

The size of the crowd of contestants had shrunk. After the three eliminated yesterday, he had thirteen people to beat, including Colleen. Especially Colleen.

Tipping back her head, she laughed. The delicate arch of her neck caused his heart to thud against his ribcage. He imagined leaving a trail of kisses up her ivory neck, until he reached the tender spot behind her ear.

Not giving his mind more latitude, he tossed his fork onto the linen tablecloth next to his empty plate and strode away. He walked through the hotel lobby and out the sliding glass doors.

Outside, the cameramen and show's producers huddled in a morning meeting.

Not wanting to eavesdrop, Storm followed the path

overlooking the Mississippi River. The river ran wide and powerful. Coffee-colored water churned toward the end of its long journey.

Last night, why had he admitted to Colleen he was a recovering alcoholic? He never discussed that portion of his life. One of the things he'd learned in recovery was to take responsibility for his decisions, yet he threw accusations at Colleen like Mardi Gras beads.

When he'd started drinking heavily in high school, Colleen had acted like he didn't exist. Her time was spent chasing her boyfriend, who was, of course, the star of the football team.

He remembered walking past her in the school hall—Colleen standing in front of her open locker. She always checked her reflection in a little, heart-shaped mirror. She smelled like vanilla and citrus, and he wanted to reach out and touch her—to feel the smoothness of her skin against his fingertips. Better judgment always held and he kept walking, knowing she wasn't aware of his presence. He wanted her so badly, he ached. Colleen was like a diamond necklace locked underneath glass—look but don't touch.

Alcohol numbed the pain and helped him forget things he couldn't have. The night of the graduation party, he thought he finally had a chance. When he arrived, she showered him with attention. They hung out around the fire pit and talked like they had when they were kids. Then, she asked if he wanted to go somewhere alone. He should have known better. If he hadn't been drinking, he would have shown sounder judgment.

Drinking turned his pain into anger—love into hate. Looking back, Storm understood his feelings were of a boy who didn't like himself, let alone anyone else. Once he'd reached sobriety and cleaned up his life, he'd let go of most of his emotional baggage—with the glaringly obvious exception of his feelings for Colleen. Somehow, she still brought out the worst in him. He should forgive her and move on. Harper's wellbeing was his main concern now. His daughter would never doubt his love.

He strolled along the path back to the hotel. Could Colleen forgive him for how he'd treated her? Would she agree to team up again? Maybe, if he turned on the charm.

Not sure if he'd ever consider himself charming, he laughed. Committed, hardworking, eco-conscious, but not someone who had an easy time with women. Valerie had been different because they shared interests. He could talk about organic bug spray and crop rotation with her. Other women, not so much. He passed through the inn's lobby and noticed all the contestants standing in a line.

"There you are." A show producer approached and handed him a slip of paper written with the numeral two.

"What's going on?" Storm asked the tall woman named Monica who stood beside him.

"Team challenge," Monica whispered. "We've divided into two teams. Winning team gets to leave early today."

Burt Blackstone appeared in front of the camera. "This morning, the remaining contestants will compete in a team challenge. Team One, gather to my left. Team Two, go to my right."

All fourteen contestants moved as instructed to

form teams.

Just his luck, he was placed on the team with Colleen, who completely ignored him.

Her gaze stayed fixed on Burt.

"Great." Burt slapped his hands together. "Team challenge is Capture the Flag but with paintball guns. The field next to the Inn is your battleground. First team to grab the other team's flag will win a one-hour jump start. Go over to the production tent to suit up."

Storm led his team to get outfitted with paintball gear—protective mask, vest, a long sleeve shirt, and thick pants. He was then handed a paintball gun loaded with red paintballs.

His team of seven stood next to their team's red flag fixed to a five-foot pole. Rob was elected to stand guard, while the remaining team members gathered to plan their attack. About one hundred yards ahead flew the green flag of the opposition. "We should surge," he told Colleen and the other two players who were playing offense.

"Don't give them easy targets. They'll just mow us down," Colleen countered. "You three create a distraction over by that hill, and I'll sneak across enemy lines. Trust me, my plan will work."

"What makes you such an expert at military strategy?" Storm leaned forward. "Let's get to a high point and run a frontal assault. Take the advantage and overwhelm their defensive players."

"I've worked with some of the country's best soldiers. I know more about strategy than you." She crossed her arms and cocked her head.

"We're supposed to just go along with whatever you say, General Gardner?" Storm challenged. His idea would get them the win. Her idea would give the other team a one-hour head start.

"You are the most obstinate man. Why do you have to second-guess me?" Colleen ground her teeth.

Another team member, a tall Hispanic man, stepped between them. "Look, you two, if we're to win then we need to trust each other and play as a team. I like Colleen's idea…create a distraction so she can sneak over."

"What if she gets shot?" Storm wasn't ready to accept defeat—yet.

"I agree with Storm. If she is shot, we lose the one player moving toward the flag." The third offensive team member, a petite woman with short black hair, moved next to him. "Let's run all out and give 'em hell."

Colleen glared. "Give me a chance. If you see me go down then follow through with your plan. Storm the field, so to speak." She snorted a laugh.

"Fine." Maybe her idea had some merit. "But the second you're hit, we run." No one could accuse him of not compromising.

An air horn blasted—their signal to start.

Colleen waved them off and crawled around a row of bushes.

Storm led his small team in the opposite direction. They set up on a small mound and fired at the other team, who were quick and hard to hit. Up ahead, he saw Colleen's small figure working her way toward the flag. She moved too slowly. Her strategy would never work. Soon, the other team would overwhelm their defenses and capture their flag.

"We need to move," he instructed the other two

offensive contestants. "She'll never get there in time. They only have two players guarding their flag. Let's charge." Storm didn't hesitate. He sprinted across the field. The sounds of paintballs hitting the ground didn't slow him. Neither did the shouts of his two team mates when they were hit. Pain burst from his right thigh. He didn't have to look to know a green blob of paint dotted his pants. His body tensed with resentment.

With his offense tagged out, the other team set their sights on Colleen. Five pops echoed, and she was hit. Soon, a woman shot Rob, their last defense, and captured the red flag.

Game over. He'd lost. The other team would get a head start, and Storm would be stuck cooling his heels—which would be difficult when a hot temper heated his body.

Why hadn't he waited to charge like she'd suggested? Because his pride wouldn't allow him to admit her plan had a better chance of succeeding.

When he approached Colleen, he watched her walk away. Any hope for an alliance burned away like a paper heart tossed in a fire. Instead of hanging around the lobby, he went up to his room and stewed. Finally, after an agonizing three-hour wait, he walked outside the hotel for the next clue.

An airplane will be your next method of transportation. Drive to Jackson, Mississippi, then fly to St. Louis. The eight o'clock curfew is lifted for today. Take a cab to the Gateway Arch. Your instructions wait at the top. Hours of operation are seven am to five pm.

He tossed his pack into his car and jumped into the driver's seat, hoping the vehicle would make it to Jackson without breaking down. The show's producers hired a mechanic to look over the car yesterday but hadn't found anything wrong. *Why fix something that could add dramatic effect?*

He pulled into the parking lot of the Jackson airport with two other cars right on his tail. Running to the ticket counter, he glanced around for Colleen, who was nowhere in sight. After booking his flight, which was paid for by a nearby associate producer, he received his boarding pass. His flight left at seven pm and arrived in St. Louis at eleven-ten pm, which meant he'd spend tonight camped outside in the cold.

Wonderful.

****

Colleen tried unsuccessfully to sleep on the plane. Her seat was next to a suit-wearing business man who continuously showed her pictures of his cats. She knew their names, where they liked to sleep, what kind of cat food they preferred—the list went on.

Storm had chosen another flight. She'd just entered the airport lobby when she noticed him heading off to a different airline's terminal. She wanted more than anything to remain partners but didn't trust herself to maintain sound judgment. The more time she spent with Storm, the harder she fell. Deep down, under his snarly attitude, hid the boy she'd loved during their early school days. If she let her heart rule her head, she'd make bad choices, which would ultimately lose her the competition. Try explaining that to the vets who needed her retreat. *Sorry I didn't win the money. I was too busy getting a boy to like me.*

Staying away from Storm was for the best. Of course, in these crazy circumstances, the separation was easier said than done. Her plane landed in St. Louis at eleven-forty-five pm. She shared a cab with Rob and Brad, and they reached the Gateway Arch after midnight. As she climbed out of the cab, Colleen shivered. The chilly night air nipped any exposed skin.

She consulted her travel book and learned the tickets were sold at the old Courthouse a block away. She, Rob, and Brad would be first in line at the ticket window.

Colleen unpacked a thin blanket from her backpack and cuddled up on the sidewalk outside the Courthouse. She was thankful for the extra body heat of the two guys. After a battle to get into a comfortable position, she drifted off into a light sleep, dreaming of Storm and a little farm set in the Texas countryside.

Chapter Fourteen
Day 7

Colleen awoke before the sun peeked over the eastern horizon. "I need a cup of hot coffee right now." She yawned, stretching under her blanket. "Preferably black and strong enough to wake the dead."

"Forget coffee," Rob said. "Give me three energy drinks, and I'll tear up that Arch in five minutes flat."

"We don't have to climb stairs. We take a tram to the top." Colleen sighed. After spending time with Rob, she realized he wasn't the sharpest crayon in the box. But he was in good shape and kept her laughing. She could think of worse characteristics in a teammate, and then thought of Storm.

Wonder if he'd made it to St. Louis? He was probably waiting over by the Arch. Guilt stabbed her heart. She should help him instead of these guys she barely knew.

Storm's problems and stubbornness were none of her concern. She'd already paid more than her fair share for past wrongs and didn't have another pound of flesh to give.

When the ticket window opened, she bought her ticket, waited for Rob and Brad, and then the three of them sprinted to the entryway to the Arch. There, she found Storm waiting with the other contestants.

Once the group realized tickets weren't purchased

at the Arch, they all ran in the direction she'd come.

As he passed her, Storm firmly pressed his lips together and clenched his jaw.

Her team of three was first on the tram—a painstakingly slow ride to the top. When the small door finally opened, she exited first, barely noticing the sky-high view from the small windows.

On 4th Street is the Stadium Parking Garage. Inside are cars for your use. If you build it, they will come. Drive to The Field of Dreams.

"Dude." Rob clapped his hands. "I know where to go. My buddy went there last year. The Field of Dreams is in the middle of nowhere in Iowa."

Colleen pulled out her travel book and opened to the map of Iowa. She set her finger on the listing for the *Field of Dreams* movie site in Dyersville, Iowa—one of the few tourist attractions in the state.

"Do you want to follow me?" Colleen pulled most of the weight for their so-called team, which she found a positive. Let them become dependent on her for direction. In the end, the remaining contestants would be on their own. Sink or swim.

"Yeah, we'll follow you." Brad looked over her shoulder at the map and scratched his head. "When do you think we'll get there?"

"The trip is five hours, so we'll arrive around one pm." She strode toward the tram to head down. As of now, they were still the only contestants at the top, but their lead could change very quickly. *Better get moving.*

She packed her body into the steel ball they called a tram and closed her eyes, pretending she was not trapped in a space the size of a dryer drum. Colleen let herself float away from her claustrophobia and focused on the next leg of the race.

****

While Storm drove north to Iowa, he berated himself for wasting all last night freezing at the base of the Arch, only to find out the tickets were sold at another location. How could he have been so stupid? Colleen, as cool and calm as always, knew exactly where to go. Once he'd discovered his mistake, he'd dragged his numb rear off the cold concrete and ran like his life depended on winning, because in a way, it did.

After the flight and wait to get into the Arch, all thirteen contestants were now bunched together. Being one of the first to arrive at the Field of Dreams was crucial to getting ahead. He pushed down harder on the gas pedal.

During his drive through rural Iowa, the corn fields seemed to stretch to infinity. Green combines pulled large trailers, working tirelessly to reap the season's harvest. He had moments where he literally felt trapped in a corn maze. Finally, at the end of a gravel road, sat a large white farmhouse—the famed Field of Dreams movie site.

He glanced around to see other cars had already arrived, parked, and then ran over to the baseball diamond. Beside the fence sat a basket filled with white cards.

Challenge: *Hit a home run and collect a baseball to receive the next clue.*

Colleen stood at home plate, holding the bat high above her head and shaking her rear. First the pitch, then the swing—and nothing but air.

"Strike," the umpire yelled.

Her full mouth turned down on one side. As the

pitcher wound up for the next throw, Colleen dug in her heels. She swung with force and sent the baseball soaring out over the heads of the outfielders. With a hoot, she hustled around the bases.

The catcher handed her a baseball and the next clue.

Rob and Brad waited at home plate and gave her a high-five as she crossed.

The men seemed as attached to Colleen as remora fish to a shark, which spiked Storm's annoyance. Out of anyone in the competition, he should be the only one allowed as her teammate. He and Colleen shared history. Who else knew she had an allergy to shellfish and a deep fear of thunder and lightning?

Rob went next—a swing and a miss.

Colleen approached and stood beside Storm. "The ball field is so cool." Her arm swept out toward the house, ball diamond, and corn fields surrounding them.

Instead of the lush green stalks he'd seen flanking the diamond in the movie, the fall corn plants were a golden yellow. The undeniable scent of autumn hung in the air. He crossed his arms over his chest and watched as the period-dressed baseball pitcher tossed out another ball to Rob. "*Field of Dreams* is one of my favorite movies." Although, he couldn't remember the last time he'd sat still long enough to watch a movie.

Rob's next swing connected with the ball, but the bunt rolled to the pitcher's feet.

"Come on, man," Brad called from the bleachers. "We don't have all day."

"You should leave them behind." Storm pointed to the two goofs she'd teamed with. "You're in a competition, not a dating show."

She smiled and shrugged. "I have my strategy just like you have yours."

"Yeah, but mine doesn't involve tagging up with a couple of dopes." Colleen was the only one he'd consider working with, and she was no dope.

"An alliance with you would be so much better?" She stared back with wide blue eyes.

He grinned. "At least you know you could trust me."

"Ha." She laughed. "You of all people have the best motivation to throw me under the bus. I don't trust you, Storm." Colleen arched one sandy blond eyebrow. "Not any farther that I could carry you."

"Oh, that hurts." Placing a hand over his heart, he sighed. He still got a thrill from teasing her. "You did good at home plate. I don't remember you playing softball in high school."

Her gaze drifted over the baseball diamond. "That's because I didn't."

"That's right. You were more of the homecoming queen type. You wore a pink dress senior year when you were crowned." He could still picture her standing on the football field, looking like a movie star. He'd only gone to the game to catch a glimpse of her. Afterward, he found a quiet spot back home at the commune and drank himself into oblivion. "You looked beautiful."

"I thought you didn't pay attention to silly things like football games and homecoming queens." She tipped her head to look up, shielding her eyes from the sun with her hand.

Storm wrapped an arm around her waist and pulled her toward him. Her body molded precisely against his.

Every hollow inside him filled with her warmth. Holding her was like wearing his favorite pair of jeans. He inhaled and took in her naturally sweet smell, which wasn't masked by the scent of perfume or fancy soap. His body and mind buzzed. "You were the only person who captured my attention. You didn't notice, but I worshiped you."

Her hands pushed back against his chest. "I'm not falling for your trickery. You whisper sweet nothings into my ear, and I let down my guard then you pounce. You're good, Storm, but I've figured out your angle."

He'd forgotten about their kiss on the beach in California and how he'd drawn her in, only to push her away in anger. "I'm not playing. I meant what I said. You were…still are…the most beautiful woman I've ever seen."

Cheering pulled her attention to the baseball diamond. Rob finally hit a home run.

"Look, you made your feelings about me very clear back in Liberty Ridge. You don't like me. I get it. But I won't be your punching bag—someone you can use heartlessly to get ahead. Teaming up with someone to help win the competition is one thing. To use someone's feelings against them is low."

What could he say in reply? He had acted like a spoiled child that night on the beach. If he was honest with himself, he'd admit the Colleen Gardner standing before him today might look similar as she did in high school, but her heart had changed. Instead of the cardboard cut-out mean girl, she now was a multifaceted, complex woman. "I'm sorry for treating you horribly at the start of the race. I promise I'm not playing you. If we can put our egos aside, we'd make a great team."

Brad hit a homerun on the first pitch.

"Look, I got to run." As Colleen walked away, she peered back over the shoulder. "Let's see how things go. I won't rule anything out." Her hips swayed as she walked back to her car.

Brad jogged up and tossed Storm the bat. "She's a beauty." Brad's gaze stayed glued to Colleen. "Too bad for you, man. She's with us now."

Storm didn't bother answering. As he stood at home plate, irritation brewed in his gut. Could he convince Colleen of his sincerity? The odds were low.

He let the first two pitches fly past. The third he hit so hard, he expected the seams to split. The baseball arched up, and then dropped out of view into the golden wall of corn stalks.

Not wasting a second, he took the clue and ran to his car. His jumbled emotions for Colleen aside, he wouldn't allow Brad and Rob to use her and then lose her. Not on his watch. Not while he was still in the game.

****

As Colleen sat in the driver's seat of her car, she balanced the baseball on one palm and read.

Up, up and away! Picture the world from high above. Great Escapes Hot Air Balloon Company is awaiting your arrival in Sioux Falls, South Dakota. Balloons will only go up between seven and nine am and again from five until six pm.

Looked like another long drive to get to Sioux Falls. According to her map, she calculated a trip slightly under four hundred miles. A Safe House was placed nearby the next stop in the town of Brandon. She should have no trouble getting to the Safe House by the eight o'clock curfew and be on the first hot air balloon ride the next morning.

With her plan set, she put the car in Drive and took off down the long gravel road. Rob and Brad followed. Colleen let her mind drift to Storm and the way her body lit up in his arms. Surely, he toyed with her emotions. But she got an amazing jolt of chemistry every time he was nearby. Did Storm feel the attraction, too? Why had he acted so emboldened around her lately? He might sense the yearning she tried so hard to hide.

Storm was a predator, with a tiger's ability to sniff out weakness—and her biggest weakness—Storm Thompson. How would she hold her resolve until the competition was over? As she looked at the challenges ahead, she knew keeping her heart closed off was impossible.

After a five-hour drive, she arrived at the Safe House. She parked beside an old, Victorian house, which probably had been constructed at the turn of the century and lovingly restored to its original grandeur. Gingerbread trim and bright colors gave the house a fairy tale quality. Colleen pictured Hansel and Gretel running out the front door.

Inside, she was greeted with the smell of lemon wood polish and fresh-baked cookies. The entry held a grand staircase made of rich walnut, which wound to the second floor. As she followed the hostess to her assigned room, she glided her hand along the smooth wooden banister.

Later, she wandered outside for some fresh air. Wrapped in a thick, crocheted blanket, Colleen curled up on the patio swing. Outside, the air was quiet and still. The scent of autumn clung to the earth as the summer world slowly died away, making room for the rebirth spring would eventually bring.

The front door creaked, and she glanced to see Storm stepping outside. With his head down, he seemed hesitant.

He approached the porch swing. "Can I sit—"

Colleen held up her hand, palm facing out. "You say one word about this competition or high school or start giving me a hard time about anything, and I'm leaving."

Storm nodded and sat beside her. "Don't worry. I'll behave." In his hands, he held a picture of his daughter. He handed it to her.

"Must be hard to be away from her." She traced with a finger the image of the little girl with pigtails and a big smile.

He rubbed a hand down his face. "Harper is everything. I'm doing this competition for her. I need to remind myself that her wellbeing is at stake." He cleared his throat. "I don't want the way I act on TV to become a bad example for Harper."

Something she should keep in mind, as well. "The cameras catch almost everything. I'm sure someone recorded our little exchange by the baseball diamond."

"Yeah, I know, and I'm sorry, Colleen." He hesitated. "What do you think if we tried just being friends? No bad blood and no living in the past."

As much as she wanted to make peace, she seriously doubted his sincerity. Why, after so much time, did he want to mend fences? What were his true intentions? "I'm game if you are." She smiled and patted his leg. He had to believe she fully trusted him. Keep your enemies close, or something like that.

"Good." He smiled and rested an arm behind her on the back of the porch swing. "I also wanted to thank you for helping my mom. She said you went to the commune to see her."

Colleen adored Rose Petal Thompson and had been visiting her for the past year. Storm moving home to take care of his mother showed Colleen that even after everything Rose had put him through, he still loved her. Hope prevailed that mother and son could mend the tatters of their relationship.

"I visited her about once a week," Colleen said. "Rose wouldn't accept my help as a psychiatrist, but she would as a friend. I helped her in the garden, pulling weeds, and we chatted. I noticed her deteriorating. She talked to people who weren't there and had severe mood swings. Nothing I said convinced her to take medication." Common enough, in Colleen's practice, for a patient to resist change. Starting a new medication, or medication in general, was usually a tough sell. She'd done her best with Rose, but in the end, Storm's mom wasn't a patient, which meant her powers of persuasion were limited.

"She's on medication now." Storm tipped back his head and exhaled. His breath misted in the cold air. "When I found out I was chosen for the show, we met with her doctor, and she agreed to stay in a facility under professional care while I'm away. Every day I worry about her."

"In my opinion, having you and Harper back in her life gives Rose a reason to get better. She wants to make things right with you." Storm turned to face her, and his minty breath flowed over her like an intoxicating fog.

"Thank you for being her friend. She never had many real friends. Not even me, her own son."

Colleen covered his large hand with her own. With a turn of his wrist, their palms lay flush. His rough fingers snagged against her smooth skin. "Your mom has a good heart, but she wasn't a very good mother. No one blames you for wanting to get away."

The memory of her own mom's smiling face created a stitch in her chest. Her life might have been so different if her selfishness hadn't caused the car accident. If her mom hadn't been distracted by Colleen's demands from the back seat, she never would have run off the road. Her dad wouldn't have turned to alcohol to dull his pain. She would have grown up in a loving home, with a mom and dad.

Storm could never know helping others, like Rose Thompson and the veterans, was pure penance. Under her kind actions hid a tainted conscience she was afraid she'd never wipe clean.

Chapter Fifteen
Day 8

The next morning, Storm awoke feeling like he'd slept with his head stuck in a vise clamp. A deep throb pulsed behind his eyes. He rested in bed for an extra few minutes, unwilling to move and cause more pain.

When he finally rose, nausea rolled from his stomach up to his throat. He couldn't get a migraine. Not now. Rummaging through his pack, he found the plastic lunch bag his mom insisted on packing. Stored inside was a packet of dried tea leaves wrapped in cloth. When he opened the bag, a spicy scent tickled his nose. Rose might lack in many areas, but she did know natural medicine.

He descended the wide front staircase and headed straight for the kitchen. After asking their hostess for a mug of hot water, he dipped the homemade tea bag into the steaming water and inhaled. The familiar aroma of chamomile, ginger root, and lemon balm eased the pain in his head.

He hadn't experienced a migraine in a long time. The stress of the race, along with his unresolved feelings for Colleen, made him more susceptible. His first migraine had appeared in grade school. Recently, they'd all but disappeared. Storm attributed the relief to his uncomplicated lifestyle as an organic farm consultant. The fresh air and freedom had done wonders to improve his mental and physical health.

Once he owned his own farm, he wanted Harper to learn the gift of nature. She'd witness the miracle of growing something from seed to something good to eat and use the earth's resources to protect tender plants from insect damage and disease.

By the time he left the Safe House, the tea worked its magic. With his headache reduced to a shadow of its former self, he drove to the hot air balloon site. He crested the final hill, and a large field spread out, spotted with bright, rainbow-colored, hot air balloons. His stomach plunged, churning with nerves. An early morning fog rolled over the valley. Storm counted five balloons at various levels of inflation. He parked then joined Colleen, Brad, and Rob. The colorful balloon loomed high above, with a basket tethered to the ground by thick ropes. Roars from the propane burners echoed across the field.

"We're the first ones here." Colleen patted Storm's arm. "The basket can hold four, plus the balloon operator. You can come up with us."

"Are they almost ready to go?" The thought of ascending inside a flimsy wicker basket terrified him. He imagined falling to his death, and a cold sweat dripped down his face.

"The balloon dude just went to his truck to get something." Rob took a slight step toward Colleen. "As soon as he gets back, we go."

Wonder what the 'balloon dude,' as Rob so eloquently stated, needed to retrieve from his truck? A parachute? His last will and testament? Bile rose in his throat.

Their flight operator returned, wearing a wide

smile. "Can't forget the barf bags." He waved the small, paper sacks then motioned toward the basket. "Climb on in."

Storm entered into the basket. A man, whom he considered smarter than the rest of them, stayed on the grass to untie the ropes from the posts on the ground. As the balloon slowly rose, the ground underneath him fell away. Parked vehicles, trees, and people were reduced to miniature versions, like the diorama he'd made in the third grade—the one Colleen spent hours helping him construct.

With discretion, Colleen reached over and held his hand. She stood side by side and pointed to the sun hovering just above the horizon. "The view is beautiful up here. You doing okay?" she whispered.

He didn't turn, because if he did, he'd lose the composure he struggled to maintain. His fear of heights was nothing compared to the surprising strength of his emotions toward Colleen. The woman he'd dreamed about loving for so many years was right here, holding his hand in reassurance. In that moment, he was back in their kindergarten classroom—a scared little boy, too afraid to close his eyes. Colleen's warm hand soothing him. She whispered everything would be okay.

Did she realize back then how much he'd loved her? To a five-year-old boy with no other friends, Colleen had been his personal angel. As she had watched over him, her hair fell around her delicate face with an unearthly glow.

Later, her cruel teasing ripped out his little heart. Besides Harper and his mother, he didn't believe he could love another woman. Not with all his body and soul. Colleen had been the one to kill that part of him.

Was she the only one who could bring it back to life?

****

The hot air balloon ride was amazing. Colleen couldn't get over the feeling of floating through the air with the ground so far below. The cars and people looked like insects, scurrying about their morning tasks.

Now, with her feet firmly planted on the soft grass, she collected a hot air balloon magnet and a piece of paper.

The granite faces of four former US Presidents gaze over the Black Hills of South Dakota. Take a selfie with them and find the clue placed along the President's Trail.

She pulled together Rob, Brad, and Storm. "Look, I suggest all four of us stick together for this leg."

The guys nodded.

"The next group is just going in the air right now." Rob pointed up. "We'll have at least an hour jump. Let's go."

They headed toward their separate cars then drove in a convoy through the plains and alongside the rocky Badlands of South Dakota.

The landscape was desolately beautiful. Jagged rock stacked with layers of color pushed toward the sky. Lines of red, orange, and tan striped the side of each hill. How many years had they stood here, beaten down with the erosion of weather and time? She stopped at a gas station in Wall to fill up and grab a sandwich. Before hopping back in the car, she snapped a few pictures of the surrounding rock formations as a souvenir.

The prairie landscape morphed into sharp hills and valleys, tall Ponderosa Pine flanked the road. When

Colleen finally pulled into the Mount Rushmore Visitor Center's parking lot, she exited her car, causing her numb legs to rejoice. Grabbing her camera, she walked toward the granite mountain and shook out her legs. *Wake up! Time to go to work.* Her thick sweatshirt and cap protected her from the cold, mountain air, but she still couldn't stop the shivers that vibrated her body.

Storm walked beside her. His sandy blond curls poked out from underneath his knit cap, and she itched to wrap a finger around a lock and pull him close. When they got to the lookout spot, she took her selfie with the stone presidential faces looming over her shoulder. A show producer handed her the next clue.

Arrive soon at the Stockade Lake South campground in Custer State Park. This stop is a Time-Out. Last two *contestants to arrive will be eliminated.*

Colleen raced after the guys, who'd taken off at a breakneck pace. Rob and Brad drove off before she reached her car—deserters. She never went anywhere unless she was confident of her route. The trip to Custer State Park might be relatively short, but out here were a million ways to get lost.

A bang on the window startled her heart. She jerked her hands, along with the map she held. She turned to see Storm.

His mouth was set in a tight line. "A couple of fair-weather friends." He motioned his thumb toward the dust cloud kicked up by Rob's and Brad's cars. "I'm learning the method to your madness. You get your bearings before heading out. Smart."

"Thanks." *Wow, a compliment.* She glanced up to make sure the sky wasn't falling then ran a finger along a thin line on the map marking the road to Custer State

Park. "This road is the most direct route, but when you take into account the hilly terrain, I'm not certain. What do you think?"

Storm opened the door and leaned in. His face was inches from her. Inside the small confines, she became dizzy with the sensory overload. Between his sensual male scent, the heat radiating off his skin, and the small stubble lining his jaw line, she could barely breathe. His lips were so close. If she wasn't such a coward, she'd shift over to connect their lips with a kiss. She could almost taste the mint on his mouth.

"I think you're right." Storm straightened. "This other road loops around too far to the west. You mind if I follow you?"

"We're wise to stick together out here. Wouldn't want to get lost and have to spend the night with the bears and buffalo." Her solid map-reading skills didn't steer them wrong. She and Storm arrived at the campground tied for first place. Looking around at the buffalo herding in the vicinity of the contestants' cabins, she felt a shot of excitement. She loved seeing pockets of the country she might never experience otherwise.

Six cabins were available for the twelve remaining contestants. Cameras were set up inside, not only to capture any backstage drama but to dissuade bad behavior. Big brother was always watching.

"You want to bunk together? I promise not to invade your space again." Grinning, he hitched his pack onto his shoulders.

Why was Storm acting sweet and harmless? What did he want?

What did she want? In reaction to her initial

answer, warmth spread through her body. Her mind said spending time with Storm, especially at night, was not a wise strategy. But her assertive heart had other ideas. "Okay. I'm so exhausted I could sleep anywhere, even next to you." She had a comfort level with Storm she didn't have with anyone else. They might have issues, but she couldn't deny he was the only person she wanted by her side.

"I'm sure we'll have our own beds." He bumped her with his hip and winked.

She turned her head so he couldn't see her blush. Inside her chest, a warm tenderness expanded—the same deep attachment she'd only felt once before as a young girl. Darn. She'd gone and fallen in love—again.

Chapter Sixteen
Day 9

Deep snorts roused Storm from sleep well before the sunrise. Why were the buffalo outside making a racket so early? He listened for another minute before realizing the sound came from inside the cabin— Colleen to be exact. Laying on the bunk below him, she snorted again, startling herself out of her deep sleep, and then she moaned and rolled over.

He couldn't stop the laughter. Delicate Colleen sounded like a bull in heat. Last time they'd shared a sleeping space, he'd been too exhausted to notice. Now, if she didn't quiet down, he wasn't sure if he'd get back to sleep.

An hour later, bright daylight startled him awake. He didn't remember falling asleep again. Peeking over the edge of his top bunk, he saw Colleen cuddled under a mound of blankets.

She stirred and opened her eyelids. "Ugh," she moaned, rubbing her eyes. "Why do I have to see your face first thing in the morning?"

He slid to the edge of the bunk and jumped to the floor. "Princess, you don't look too hot yourself." The morning air chilled the bare skin of his chest, so he grabbed the sweatshirt he'd thrown on the floor last night. "At least, I don't snore."

Colleen bolted upright in bed, nearly hitting her

head on the beam on the top bunk. "I beg your pardon. You're the one who snores."

"No, my dear, you were so loud a group of male buffalo surrounded the cabin, looking for the female in heat."

She huffed. "You're teasing."

Her hair stuck out in gravity-defying tuffs. "Argue all you want. I have recorded proof." He pointed to the two cameras tucked in the corners of the cabin.

"I don't snore." Laughing, she climbed out from her blanket cocoon. Colleen tossed a pillow at his head, which he deftly dodged. In baggy fleece pants and a rainbow t-shirt, she looked like a preteen girl. His chest squeezed at the memory of her striding into their seventh grade classroom like she owned the world. Everyone wanted to sit beside her in class, eat lunch with her, and receive invites to her parties. Just like all the other kids, he also wanted to be in her aura.

Back in school, he was a kid figuring out where he fit into the big puzzle of life. Now, as a man, he saw her shine was an illusion. Colleen wasn't perfect. And he'd come to realize she'd be the first to agree.

He remembered when she lost her mom in the car accident. They'd been in the first grade. She'd returned to school the day after the funeral with a smile, like her whole world hadn't shattered. She'd tucked away all the pain and hid it deep inside.

After spending time with the adult version of Colleen, he saw her battle scars from childhood. He recognized the flashes of insecurity in her blue eyes, and then she acted like nothing bothered her.

If they weren't competing against one another, nothing would stop him from pursuing a relationship.

But they were competing. He would have to beat her in order to make his dream come true. When the competition ended, the bridges they'd built would blow to splinters.

His heart would remain closed. If a door opened and either of them crossed the threshold, he'd pay a high cost. One he couldn't afford.

****

Colleen did not snore. Well, she was fairly sure she didn't snore. Storm only wanted to rile her. But watching him hop down from the top bunk only wearing a pair of athletic shorts had done more to knock her off balance than any amount of teasing. The unobstructed view of his muscular chest nearly gave her fits—and his tattoo of the phases of the moon running down his spine—super sexy. Years of farm work blessed his body with angles and hard edges she'd love to explore. If he wasn't her rival.

He'd been acting very nice the past few days, tricking her into thinking he'd put aside their past. But she still possessed a nagging doubt he used her to get ahead. A strategy serving two masters—victory and revenge.

After breakfast, she walked to the bathhouse. On the way, she noticed Storm standing in a clearing and working through a yoga flow. He looked like a reincarnated demigod—skin glistening with sweat. As she watched him hold a tree pose, balanced on one leg, arms stretched up to the blue sky, she experienced a head rush, a result of her quickening pulse.

Not trusting her judgment, she turned and jogged to the bathhouse. Maybe the water would wash away not only the dirt and grime from travel, but the feelings

Storm stirred. She stood under the spray of hot water and turned her focus to the next leg of the race. The group of contestants slowly diminished with each elimination. Rob and Brad drove in circles around the Black Hills and Custer State Park until one finally stopped to ask for directions. They were too late, though, and had arrived as the last two.

After she got dressed, she returned to the cabin and repacked her backpack. The sound of Burt Blackstone's voice shouting over a megaphone made her cringe. She stepped outside to see the host standing next to the open field behind the cabins.

"This morning is another team challenge." Burt Blackstone pointed to the set-up behind him. "Each team will elect a captain, who will guide the rest of their blindfolded teammates to collect twenty-five puzzle pieces. After all twenty-five are in hand, the team will remove their blindfolds and put together the puzzle. First team to finish their puzzle correctly wins a one-hour head start."

Colleen was placed on team One.

Storm sent her a challenging but good-natured grin when he was assigned to team Two.

When the time came to elect captains, Colleen stepped back. Could she manage and motivate her team? What if no one listened and just wandered around the playing field like a flock of stoned zombies?

A woman named Mai moved next to Colleen. Her black hair was pulled up in a high ponytail. "I vote for Colleen. She's organized and loud."

Colleen protested but the sound of agreement from the rest of her team silenced her. Guess she wasn't as loud as everyone thought. *Okay, I can do this.* She climbed up a wooden ladder and stood on top of a platform overlooking the field. The flat land was divided into two sections. Her team stood below, chatting.

A bullhorn blasted. With a pounding heart and sweat dripping down her face, she yelled out directions to her five team members, who walked blindly with outstretched arms. "Amy, take five big steps to the left. There you go. Move a little faster." She took a few deep breaths. "Lenny, you're going in the wrong direction. Walk forward until you feel the tree. Turn so your back is against the trunk then keep walking forward until I say stop." Like moving chess pieces around a board. If she took her gaze off any of her teammates for a few seconds, they'd walk in circles.

The other team captain yelled Storm's name. She quickly glanced over to see him zigzagging around the field, not following directions. *Typical Storm.* Chuckling, she turned her focus back to her team.

After about ten minutes, her team had captured twenty pieces. Activity from the other side caught her attention. *Shoot.* The other team found all their pieces and ran toward the wooden platform to assemble the puzzle. Her team would lose if she didn't get them moving quickly.

Two minutes later, Team Two cheered in victory.

Which meant Storm would get a head start while she was stuck at the campground. She stomped down the platform, frustrated by her failure.

"Good try." Storm patted her on the back. "I'm serious. You did really well up there."

"Thanks." She didn't want his false platitudes. "Bet you're happy you can leave me in the dust."

As he studied her, his eyebrows lowered. "I don't want to leave you behind. You'll have no problem catching up."

She snorted.

"I'm serious, Colleen. I can't believe I'm saying this, but you make the competition fun."

"You must have hit your head last night." She crossed her arms over her chest. A strange energy tingled over her skin.

"Maybe I'm just coming to my senses." Storm stepped forward.

His eyes burned with an intensity that made her hot and cold at the same time. *Not real.* He was playing the game. Her chest squeezed tight with conflicting emotions. As his hand reached for her, Colleen stepped back. *Walk away before you say something you'll regret.* She did and left him standing alone.

Each contestant was scheduled to spend ten minutes in the confessional booth, and she made an abbreviated visit. She couldn't risk saying too much and inadvertently admitting her feelings for Storm on national TV.

At two pm Mountain Time, she ripped open the next clue.

Get ready to rock but careful not to roll. Climb the Needle's Eye. Look for the red flag and take a picture from that spot.

Looked like rock climbing was on the agenda for today—something she hoped never to do. She needed to figure out where. The weather was sunny and warm today, but with luck, she'd overtake a Storm.

****

After consulting with the Park Ranger at the State

Park's main office, Storm learned the Needle was a rock formation inside the park. The drive looked short on the map but with all the twists and turns going up the mountain, the trip took longer than he'd expected. Once he arrived, he glanced up at the tall rock standing perched next to a steep drop-off and swallowed hard. He wasn't a big fan of heights but had rock climbed before. *Just don't look down.* The climb wouldn't kill him, or at least he hoped not. The red flag stuck in a crevasse almost at the top, waving in the breeze.

While Storm stood on the safety of the pavement, the climbing instructor gave him a crash course in face climbing—showing him the equipment and safe climbing procedures. Storm changed into a thin pair of rock shoes, strapped on a helmet, and waited for the instructor to secure his harness. After one last tug on the rope secured above, he was off.

The granite face of the Needle's Eye was filled with jutting rocks, giving his hands and feet secure holds. As he moved upward, he wouldn't allow himself to glance down or, even worse, out over the rugged valley spread out far below. Heights made him dizzy. Rock climbing and dizziness did not mix well.

His legs burned with the effort of pushing the weight of his body upward. The small muscles in his feet and hands ached from the strain of grasping at the rock. Up above, the red flag waited. After about a thirty-minute climb, he reached the flag and sighed in relief. He took hold of the envelope with the next clue then hung out there for a minute to catch his breath.

The fresh air filled his lungs, helping revive the blood flow to his tired muscles. Hovering high on the rock face, he let his gaze wander to the landscape surrounding him. His stomach buzzed for a moment then settled. Granite spears jutted out of the ground like the surface of the moon.

Storm repelled down, meeting Colleen at the base. With his feet back on the ground, he unhooked then walked to where she stood. "You can do this." He squeezed her shoulder. "Take one step at a time. Before you know it, you'll be at the top."

Sweat beaded and rolled off her face. "What if I fall?"

He pinched her chin and lifted her face to meet his gaze. "If you lose your hold then hang there until the climbing instructor comes to help." Storm fought the urge to stay and encourage her to the top. He had to keep moving. With a pat on the back, he gently urged her toward the rock. After glancing back one last time, he slipped out of his climbing gear and took the next clue.

The mile-high city is your destination. If you're a fan of the Star Wars movies, you'll love where we've hidden the clue. Grow wings and fly over the Rockies.

Okay, the only thing he knew for sure was his next destination was Denver. Easy enough. The Star Wars reference and growing wings were still a mystery. He'd ask for help once he arrived.

He glanced at the Needle's Eye and saw Colleen take her first step up the rock face. She looked so determined to conquer the climb—a very different person than the girl he knew. One who had everything handed to her. Now, she struggled to overcome her fears in order to reach her goals.

Maybe he should wait. A few minutes' delay won't hurt. Harper's cute little face flashed in his mind's eye.

She cheered him on, her chubby hands clapping. The one person he couldn't bear to lose. He sprinted back to his car and started toward Denver—another step closer to the journey's end and his one-million dollar prize.

****

Colleen would never rock climb again. Her hands throbbed, her shoulders ached, and the arches of her feet cramped with evil delight. Once she reached the flag, she grabbed the clue and returned to the ground.

The instructor helped her out of the climbing equipment and gave her some encouraging words. *Save the platitudes for the next contestant*, who looked to be Lenny.

The large African American man gave her a quick wave as he ran over to the Needle's Eye.

"Good luck," she hollered. She liked Lenny. His huge smile and baritone laugh could break down the strongest of defenses. She'd even seen Storm befriend him.

Storm's armor had shown weakness to the point he'd been kind, even sweet. But his new-found civility hadn't kept him from leaving her while he chased the next clue. *All's fair in love, war—and one-million-dollar prizes.*

After climbing into the car, she turned the ignition and pulled out her trusty map. The time was now three-forty-five. After a few calculations, she decided she couldn't make it to Denver by the eight o'clock curfew. She'd be satisfied if she could get to Fort Collins before stopping for the night.

As she drove, the flat landscape lulled her into daydreaming. She pictured her veterans' retreat, built on the perfect piece of land she'd found outside of

Liberty Ridge. Imagining the soldiers she'd help, she made a mental checklist—staff to hire, ADA facilities to be constructed, and the different activities offered. The whole program was coming together—except for the annoying part about funding the project. The rise in the suicide rate for the country's veterans made her even more determined to win.

When the low gas chime sounded from the car, she jumped. *Shoot, shoot, shoot!* She was in the freakin' middle of nowhere and would run out of gas within thirty miles. Praying for a gas station sighting, she eased her foot off the pedal.

Just as she passed a billboard for a rest stop five miles ahead, she heard the chug of the car's engine, and then silence. She coasted off onto the shoulder, wanting to cry. How could she be so stupid not to check the gas gauge?

Pull yourself together. Get out and flag down a passing car. Hopefully, a kind person would take pity and stop. A scene from the horror movie *The Hitchhiker's Grave* flashed in her mind. The poor girl in the movie never stood a chance against the mass-murdering truck driver.

Colleen swallowed her fear. She stood on the side of the road for fifteen minutes before a minivan pulled over. *Okay, a minivan.* Probably a nice family. Behind her back, she crossed her fingers.

The passenger side window slid down to reveal a smiling woman. "Honey, you havin' car problems?"

Colleen looked inside to see the driver, a seemingly normal-looking man, and let out a breath. "I ran out of gas. Would you be kind enough to take me to the next gas station?"

"Hop on in," the woman said. The back door glided open, and a little boy with dark curly hair waved from his car seat. "That's Jack. I'm Monica. My husband's Travis."

"Nice to meet you." Colleen climbed inside and seat belted herself in.

Little Jack offered to share his Cheerios, which she politely declined. He started to cry, so she took a few circles of cereal out of his sticky hand and popped them in her mouth. Jack smiled, now seemingly appeased.

When they pulled to a stop, Colleen climbed out of the van. "Thanks for the ride."

"Oh, honey. We're not leaving you here. Travis, go help her get a container and fill it with gas. We'll drive you back to your car. You never know what kind of crazies are hanging around a place like this."

Breathing a sigh of relief, she followed Travis into the station. Before long, she was back inside her car with enough gas for a return trip to the station to fill up. She'd made a stupid mistake in not keeping at least a half tank of gas. In order to win, she couldn't make another.

After refiguring her distance and time, Colleen realized she'd only make it to Cheyenne by eight. Luckily, a Safe House was nearby. She decided to stay there for the night and save money. Tomorrow, she'd have to make up the lost time.

The Safe House was a rustic lodge, featuring a large moose head hanging on the stone wall of the lobby. She checked in then went to find a nearby restaurant. When she entered the fast food establishment, she saw two other contestants sitting in separate booths and decided to join Niko. From the interaction she'd had, Colleen knew he was Puerto Rican and had a great sense of humor. She went to order, waited for her food, and then took a seat across the table.

Niko smiled as she sat. "Hello, darling. Good to see a friendly face out here in the wild, wild west." He waved his hand around the room filled with glassy eyed animals.

Someone around here must love taxidermy. "They're kind of creepy, huh? How was your day?"

As they chatted, she grew sleepy, and fatigue crept into every bone in her body. The rock climbing and stress of running out of gas on the interstate had taken its toll.

After dinner, she headed straight to bed. Setting her alarm to the ghastly time of five am, she moaned then burrowed under the covers. She thought of Storm and her time with him in the cabin. Did she really snore? Of course not. He was such a tease.

The constant adrenaline rush over the last nine days had taken a toll. She was overtired but couldn't fall asleep. What if she became physically unable to keep up and quit? How would she go home with the knowledge she'd failed? She had to find a way to power through the tough times when a little voice inside her head sounded, telling her to take the easy route.

Could she fight the urge to give up until the very end, while each day with each challenge, the temptation grew stronger?

Chapter Seventeen
Day 10

Whether he liked it or not, Storm was on his own now, staying at a cheap motel outside Fort Collins, Colorado. Last night, he'd dreamt about his daughter. She'd been a little older, maybe ten, riding a white horse.

While he watched her ascend a hill, Harper turned to wave. All around lay acres of farmland, ripe and green. Colleen approached and took hold of his hand. Even though he was lost in a dream, she felt solid and real. He sensed an intense familiarity, like the farm, Harper, Colleen, and him were all pieces which belonged together.

Ridiculous notion. He scolded himself as he loaded his pack into the back of the car. But was it really? After the competition was over, and they were back in Liberty Ridge, how would their relationship transform? He and Colleen started out as friends then grew to be enemies. They'd grown apart with age and distance. Now, he found himself forced together with her, for better or worse. Suddenly, anxiety burst in his gut. He wanted to finish this competition and get home—buy his land, start his farm, and get custody of his daughter.

What about Colleen? Could he win her heart in the process? Or would they be destined to stay forces always working against one another?

On his way out of the motel, he made a few inquiries about the clue. The guy at the motel's front desk had no idea what—*Grow wings and fly over the Rockies*—meant. Once he got closer to Denver, he'd have to ask someone else.

The drive into Denver lasted a little over an hour. Not too much time to think about Colleen but long enough to start missing her. He stopped at a gas station off the freeway. After making the rounds to all the store workers, he was stopped by an elderly woman.

"You want the Air and Space Museum." She pulled out a tourist brochure from the rack by the front door. "They call it Wings over the Rockies."

Jackpot! "You're an angel. Thank you." Storm kissed her soft cheek. Now, how did he get there? He'd never missed the convenience of his cell phone more. After purchasing a map of Denver, he charted the fastest route. He arrived at the front door at seven-thirty am. Unfortunately, the doors were locked. The sign of the museum stating they opened at ten made his heart sink. Every time he got ahead, something halted his progress. He kicked a concrete planter and earned a stubbed toe in the process.

The cold weather didn't stop him from holding his place at the front of the line to get inside. As he waited, he watched with growing frustration as other contestants arrived. With the timing of the challenges ensuring delays, he'd never get a good lead, which burned his temper. He needed to develop a strategy to gain on the pack and stay ahead. Coming in second place would not be enough—not for the size of his dreams.

****

As usual, Colleen researched the night before. She knew the Air and Space Museum didn't open until ten am, so she didn't rush. She knew exactly where to go and had an easy time finding the next stop. She'd even borrowed a cell phone with WI-FI from a friendly teenager at a fast food restaurant and pulled up an interior map of the museum, and then memorized the path to the X-Wing fighter.

When she arrived, she noticed Storm sitting in front of the closed doors—arms crossed and a deep scowl on his face. "Good morning." She got in line. "How long have you been waiting?"

"Too long," he mumbled. "So much for my lead."

"This building is big. You still might be first out the door." Not likely, but she wanted to boost his spirits.

Storm narrowed his eyes. "You know where to go once we get inside. Don't you?"

She turned away her head. *Sorry, buddy. I'm not giving up my secrets. Not even for you.* A short, guilty spell had her second guessing her unwillingness to help. She brushed it off, reminding herself of the veterans needing her help—the only reason she competed in a crazy reality TV show.

A tall man finally appeared on the other side of the doors and unlocked the entrance. Everyone made a mad dash inside. While the other ten contestants scrambled with maps, Colleen slipped away. When she heard the sound of footsteps behind her, she didn't have to look over her shoulder to know who followed. After a power walk that left her short of breath, she found the replica X-Wing fighter and grabbed the envelope.

Hang on tight. The Taos County Fairgrounds is

your destination. A very angry bull is the key to unlocking the next clue.

Her stomach lurched.

Please, not bull riding.

"Sweet," Storm hollered. "I bet we are going bull riding in Taos."

Instead of celebrating with Storm, she wanted to cry. Watching a sexy cowboy ride a kicking bull was one thing. Riding one herself while hanging on for her life was another. She caravanned with Storm to Taos. Why not? Plus, the security of seeing Storm in her rearview mirror helped ease some of her fears.

They pulled into the Taos County Fairgrounds around three-thirty pm. Except for several trucks and livestock trailers that surrounded a white, metal fence, the place was empty. Through the bars, Colleen could make out the undeniable shape of cattle. Her stomach twisted into a slip knot. This challenge was it—the end—the day she'd die.

****

As they walked toward the pen, Storm watched Colleen's face pale.

"I'm going to die," she said with a crack in her voice.

"Maybe get bruised up a bit but you'll survive." Not very reassuring but the best he could come up with on the spot.

"You're not helping." Colleen leaned against the fence, resting one foot on the lowest rung. "I'll go first because if I don't, I'll get seriously sick."

"Don't toss your cookies on my shoes." He stepped away. "Promise you'll wait once you're done? You can watch me set a new world record."

She set a hand on her hip and laughed. "What…the world record for the shortest ride?"

"I bet I stay on longer, princess."

Straightening her spine, she poked a finger at his chest. "You're on. Loser does the winner's laundry at the next Time-Out stop."

They shook hands, and Colleen strode over toward the cowboys to get geared up.

Storm stood off to the side and observed. Colleen's wide blue eyes were filled with either excitement or fear, or maybe a combination of both. She looked fierce underneath the helmet and mask, and her gaze stayed fixed on the bull being led into the chute.

While walking toward the platform, she turned and smiled.

His common sense was flooded with an overwhelming desire to hold her close and provide comfort. Every day, she'd done something that totally amazed him. A stunning realization forced him to physically hang on to the pen rail for support. The truth hit as strong as a wrecking ball and as softly as the leaf of a lamb's ear plant. After all this time, his heart had stayed loyal to Colleen. He had never stopped loving her.

****

Colleen couldn't stop her legs from quaking as they wrapped around the wide body of the bull.

The cowboys promised the animal was relatively tame.

If she followed their instructions, she wouldn't get hurt. *Yeah, right.* At that moment, she felt as safe as a seal swimming with sharks. She harnessed all the adrenaline pumping through her veins, sending it to her arms and hands. She'd need the strength to hold on for as long as possible, because she had to beat Storm.

Three cameramen, along with the camera strapped on her helmet, were ready to capture her terror for the world to witness. Underneath her body, the bull shifted and grunted. Its foul odor fueled her nausea.

A cowboy on her right tightened the rope around the bull's stomach then wrapped it around her gloved right hand.

Sticky rosin coating kept the rope from sliding out of her grasp.

"You got this." The cowboy tipped his black Stetson and winked.

She forced back the tears threatening to break free. *Time to put up or shut up.* "Let's do it."

In response to the nod of her head, they opened the chute door.

The entire ride passed in a blur. The beast underneath her bucked, kicked, and shook its head, but she refused to let go of the rope. The bull gave a huge leap, sending her flying through the air. She landed on packed dirt. All the air exited her lungs with a *humph*, and she lay stuck on her back like a beetle. Out of the corner of her eye, she saw a rodeo clown chase the bull. The world around her spun. Someone took her hand and pulled her back onto her feet. The ground beneath her swayed. Somehow, she weaved her way back to the fence and crawled through to the other side then collapsed into Storm's embrace.

He wrapped his arms around her, holding her close. "Good job, princess. Eight seconds. That time will be hard to beat." Storm unhooked her helmet and slid it off her damp hair.

He kissed her tenderly on her forehead, and she wished he'd move his lips a little lower. "Thanks." She reluctantly stepped away. "You better hurry up and take your turn. I heard another contestant was already here. Right now, we're numbers two and three."

Storm nodded then strode over to the cowboys. "Let's ride."

She gripped the rail to steady herself. Exhilaration replaced her earlier fear. *What a rush!* She couldn't believe she'd actually ridden a real bull and stayed on for longer than a millisecond.

She watched Storm get the same training session— Bull Riding 101. As he walked over to the shoot, he moved with a distinct swagger she classified as male pride. Wouldn't want to look scared in front of the other guys. After all, they were real cowboys—men who breathed life into women's fantasies. Big hats and even bigger belt buckles. Before turning her attention back to Storm, Colleen sighed.

He climbed on top of the bull.

From what she could see, he struggled to get a good hold on the rope.

Finally, the chute opened, and the bull took off. It kicked once, and then twice.

Storm went flying like a clumsy trapeze artist. His body hit the ground with an audible thud. He rolled over and groaned.

Watching from the other side of the fence, she cringed. A billowing dust cloud drifted her way, along with the sound of Storm's cursing.

Looks like I just won myself a laundry maid.

"Two seconds," the cowboy holding a stopwatch called out. "No shame, though. My first ride lasted less than that."

Storm eased upright and hobbled toward her. "The stupid rope slipped right out of my hands. They set me up."

"Oh no, you don't. You lost fair and square." She wagged a finger.

His scowl cracked to a grin. "I look forward to washing your undies."

Warmth crept up Colleen's neck and onto her face. "They're recording us, don't forget."

"I didn't. Just feeding the beast, so to speak." He winked. "Why do you think they cast us? They knew we had a history."

"I doubt anyone back home thought we'd end up working as a team. Maybe murdering each other, sure. They'll be shocked when they watch the show." Would they ever. She could just picture all the people in Liberty Ridge witnessing Storm and Colleen grow closer with each episode.

An older man wearing overalls covered in dust handed them the next clue.

Storm opened his envelope. "Let's see what torture awaits us."

****

The New Mexico flag is decorated with the Zia sun symbol. This symbol's home is your destination. Purchase a piece of handcrafted pottery from a local artisan. The pottery must display the Zia sun symbol.

While Colleen ran to her car, Storm was left scratching his head, confused by the clue. He cursed under his breath. She took off on him. Which, he guessed, would only be fair. He'd left her behind more times than he could count. His frustration turned to shock when she strode back, holding a thick book.

"My little secret." Grinning, she cracked open the book. "Let's look at the New Mexico tourist section and see if we can't figure out this clue."

So, a tourist book was her super power. No hocus pocus—only a smart understanding of the phrase "always be prepared." As she thumbed through the worn pages, he peeked over her shoulder. Even in grade school, she'd been a smarty-pants.

"Here." She pointed to a tiny dot on the map. "The Zia Pueblo is a little north of Albuquerque."

His gaze followed her finger.

"I don't know if we'll make it by curfew," Colleen said. "Depends if the terrain is smooth or hilly. Once we're there, we still have to buy pottery. What do you think?" Colleen's blue eyes peered upward. "Should we push it or find a place close by to stay the night?"

"I want to do as much as possible today. If we wait, we run the risk of falling behind."

"But what if curfew comes with no hotel in sight? We'll get a time penalty tomorrow."

He wasn't one-hundred-percent sure, but his gut told him to push on. "Let's drive to the Pueblo. Is a Safe House nearby?"

"No." Colleen blew out a breath and combed back her bangs with her fingers. "We'd need to find a motel."

"Let's go." His jaw clenched as he took her arm. "We're wasting time." Storm drove in the lead, and Colleen followed. He pushed the speed limit. As he drove past the entrance sign for the Pueblo, he glanced at the clock in his car. Thirty minutes until curfew. They had to act fast.

The Zia Pueblo blended seamlessly into the rocky landscape. If he hadn't been paying attention, he would have missed the main road leading in. Storm parked next to an adobe building with the Zia sun symbol attached to the exterior wall.

Two Zia Pueblo natives greeted them.

After a warm welcome, he and Colleen were escorted to a covered area displaying many beautiful pieces of pottery. Each piece was uniquely crafted and decorated, and all possessed a deep, rich red color. One of the artisans explained the color was a result of the special clay found in the region.

After a brief search, Storm picked out a jar to purchase. The piece had two large Zia sun symbols— the image of a roadrunner decorated the center of each sun. He glanced over to find Colleen still shopping. "Come on. Time to get moving."

She finished her conversation with the artisan and paid for the earthen jar. "Okay, I'm ready."

Storm checked the time. He should have listened and not pushed their luck. Too late now to second guess. Annoyance and anger sent his heart beating at an unnaturally rapid pace. He couldn't risk a time penalty and fall behind. Not now, after he'd come so far

****

By the time she'd purchased her pottery, Colleen fretted, her optimism out of gas. "We'll never find a hotel in time." She stood by the open door of her car.

The orange globe of the sun dipped low, hovering just above the horizon. Night animals yipped, ready for their chance to rule the desert.

Storm scowled. "Just drive. I'll follow you. Stop at the first place you see. I don't care how seedy it is."

Colleen drove along the dusty road and passed a beautiful whitewashed church she missed entering the Pueblo. Other than the church, most of the other buildings looked the same. She couldn't make out any other landmarks to help guide her back to the freeway. Unlit street signs were her only direction. Most intersections didn't even have signs. She tightened her grip on the steering wheel. How in the world did she get back to the highway?

Storm honked from behind.

She pulled over. As he approached, she rolled down her window.

"We've been driving around in circles for the past ten minutes," he said. "Do you know where you're going?"

Flustered, she reached for the map of New Mexico. "I'm sorry. I thought we were heading toward the freeway."

Storm kicked at the tires. "*Ugh.* I'll find someone and ask directions. We've wasted enough time." He walked along the gravel shoulder about a hundred feet until he waved down a passing truck.

The driver gestured with his hands.

Storm ran back to his car. "Follow me." He performed a U-turn on the road and took off.

She stepped hard on the gas, trying not to lose him. By the time she got back on the freeway, Colleen knew they wouldn't meet curfew. They were still too far out in the sparsely populated desert. But as the night sky opened above, she sighed, her stress evaporating. From behind the windshield, she soaked in the breathtaking view. Without the interference of city lights, a bounty of stars burst forth through the blackness. For a moment, she forgot about the competition, her worry over raising money to start her retreat, and her conflicted feelings about Storm. She enjoyed the peace. Tomorrow would be the start of another day's problems. She wouldn't let those worries bother her—at least not for tonight.

Storm found a little motel around eight-thirty and pulled in.

She followed.

Today's cameraman handed her a note, stating they were both penalized with a two-and-a-half hour delay tomorrow morning.

Both she and Storm checked into the motel, and the college-age woman behind the desk handed them each key-cards to their separate rooms.

Without a word, Storm marched away.

Guilt bubbled inside over becoming lost at the Pueblo. In her opinion, though, they never had a chance at reaching a hotel by curfew. Colleen entered her room and tossed her pack on the bed. "I'm so happy to see you." She flopped down on top of the burgundy bedcover and laid back. A knock sounded on her door, and then it swung open. Lesson learned. *Next time, lock your door.*

Storm entered. "After today, we're both out of the competition." His face flushed red.

His dark mood was a perfect manifestation of his name. "Aren't you being a tad overdramatic?" She was in no mood. After getting into a sitting position, she tipped her chin to meet his gaze. "We weren't eliminated, just delayed."

"You should have admitted sooner you were turned around." He towered over her.

Her temper rose, ready to clash with his. "You were the one who insisted we push on and go to the Pueblo tonight." She stood and jabbed a finger into his chest.

Storm took a step in retreat. "I remember, but we wouldn't have missed curfew if you hadn't gotten us lost."

Taking a step toward him, she placed her hands on her hips. "You have all the answers, don't you?"

Storm moved fast, trapping Colleen between his body and the wall. "I trusted you, which might be a mistake. I should have kept with my first instinct to do this competition alone."

"Fine." She set her palms on his chest and pushed. "Honestly, I don't trust you either. We're both playing to win, but I would never do anything purposely to hurt you. Unlike you, who loves watching me suffer."

He blinked. "That's not true. I don't want you to suffer."

She would not be drawn in by his softened tone and fooled. Storm needed to win at any cost—even using her to get ahead. "Sure you do. You've even told me as much." Colleen sagged, her earlier bravado deflated. "You said you hate me. Remember?"

He grabbed her arm and pulled her toward him. "I don't hate you. My feelings are quite the opposite." Tucking a strand of her short hair behind her ear, he let his fingers linger then drew a slow line down her neck.

Her brain flashed a warning—his actions were only a play at seduction. Nothing about this moment was real. Storm didn't want her, not in a meaningful way. She took a step to the side.

He followed.

A dance which would not have a happy ending. When he tipped down his head to kiss her, she frosted over with cool indifference in protection of her tender heart. The contact with his lips sparked a fire, quickly melting her resolve.

"What's the matter?" Storm whispered in her ear. "Tell me to stop, and I will."

His warm breath made her shiver. The stiffness in her body faded, and she leaned into him. She wrapped her arms around his neck. A deep groan rumbled from his throat. The ice around her heart broke away in large chunks, leaving it exposed and vulnerable.

Footsteps sounded from nearby. Colleen glanced over to see a cameraman standing at the open doorway, filming. Panicked, she pushed Storm away. Frustration sickened her stomach. "Get out," she yelled to both the cameraman and at Storm.

The cameraman disappeared down the hall.

Storm stayed as still as a sculptor made of sand.

"Colleen…I'm not sorry for kissing you."

She put up her hand to stop him from saying more. "How could you go from loathing to lusting in only one week? I'm sick of being used as a pawn in your game."

"We're both playing a game here, don't forget." He hooked his thumbs in the front pockets of his jeans. "But I'm not using you. I'm not a heartless monster."

"No? Do you still think I am?" Hot tears welled in her eyes and blurred her vision.

"You're not only beautiful, but you are the smartest person in this competition. We've both made mistakes in the past—hurt each other when we were immature kids." He took hold of her hand and brushed his lips across her knuckles. "I'd like to start over. A fresh beginning."

"A fresh beginning?" She considered the concept as probable as both of them winning the competition. "I want to win the money and open my retreat. You'll work to make sure I don't succeed. One way or the other, one of us will lose out on our dream."

He dropped her hand. "Then I guess I'll say goodnight." With his head and shoulders hunched low, Storm headed out the door.

She started after him, but good sense kept her inside her motel room. If Storm knew how much she cared, that she'd fallen in love, he'd use her feelings as weapons. Over the years, the wall standing between them had grown. Stones of betrayal and unkindness heaped on one another and set with mortar of distrust. She'd need a lifetime to disassemble the damage done.

On the other side of the motel room wall, she heard the shower start. She imagined Storm standing under the hot spray. Her pulse quickened, and her body warmed. Now, she needed a shower, too—a cold one— then find a cheap place to eat, and finally go to sleep. Tomorrow would be another long day.

Would Storm stick with her or go off on his own? Either way, she'd be fine. While he played his games, she played her own. *Let him break down my defenses. Eventually, he'll learn I have a will of steel.*

Chapter Eighteen
Day 11

The following morning, Storm opened the next clue.

Train or Bus? Travel from Albuquerque to Flagstaff on either a train or bus. Time-Out stop is at The Hotel Weatherford in Flagstaff. You will receive another car tomorrow morning at the hotel. Last four contestants to arrive will be eliminated. The curfew for tonight is lifted.

"Do you have a computer with Internet I could borrow?" Storm asked the ancient man behind the motel's front counter. His milky blue eyes stared back like Storm had dropped from an alien spaceship.

"We don't got no computer here, son. Got no use for 'em."

Storm walked outside to clear his head with fresh morning air. Since he couldn't leave until eight-thirty, he planned on using the extra time to research the bus and train schedules. But with no computer and no Internet, he was left stewing over his latest row with Colleen.

That kiss—he couldn't get the taste of her out of his head. And the way her pretty blue eyes had gone ice cold when she'd pushed him away. A fine line separated love and hate, and he smudged the boundary over and over again. He'd let his own pain taint his view of Colleen. Instead of seeing the woman she'd grown into, he only saw the spoiled, mean girl she'd been. Now, he might be too late. Colleen didn't trust his motives—and rightly so. They were competing against one another. From her perspective, his kindness was a sleight of hand trick.

He had to make up for his earlier bad behavior. But how? Flowers—diamonds—a puppy? He'd need more than grand gestures to win her guarded heart. Shaking his head, he opened the door and stepped back into his 1960s motel room. The interior smelled like stale beer and old cheese, and the curtains would have looked good back in the Jungle Room at Graceland. Last night, he'd slept on his own blanket, not trusting the cleanliness of the sheets.

With his pack in hand, he closed the room and headed to his car.

Colleen stood ahead, with her backside leaning against his driver's side door.

"Mornin'." He nodded and opened the door then tossed his pack onto the back seat.

"Sorry for losing my cool last night." She pushed off from the car. "Anything they record can be aired on the show. I don't want people back home watching us make-out."

Storm scratched at his chin and laughed. "You certainly have a way of putting things."

"I'm not being funny, Storm. I have to live with those people. Once we get home, I don't want to become the talk of the town…again."

"Honey, hate to break the news, but you already are." Storm had seen the men in Liberty Ridge follow Colleen with interest.

She wandered over to her car parked a few spots down. "I'm also sorry about getting us lost last night. I hope we can catch a train or bus and make up time."

"The roads were dark and unfamiliar, which was not your fault. You did the best you could." He reached out, taking hold of her hand.

She slipped it out of his grasp. "We can leave now. I'm stopping somewhere along the way to see if I can borrow someone's WI-FI connected device, or maybe I'll find a library with public internet and hop online to check out the schedules. You're welcome to stay with me or go off on your own. I don't care."

Fortunate for him, Colleen had a forgiving nature. "I'm hurt." He dropped his smile to a frown. "You think you can get rid of me so easily?"

Her stoic face broke into a crooked smile, and she punched him lightly on the shoulder. "Yeah, right."

If he had anything to say, she'd never cut him free.

****

After an hour's drive, Colleen stopped at a coffee shop, looking for a kind stranger who'd let her borrow their Internet access. As long as she was there, she might as well order a latte for the road. The rich aroma of ground coffee wrapped around her like a comforting blanket. Finally, after ten days of sludge coffee, she had a little cup of heaven warming her hand.

While she was at the counter, Storm gained the temporary use of a college girl's laptop. He put those sweet talking skills to good use.

Once she was seated beside him, she watched Storm pull up the website for the train.

"Only one train leaving today and not until two in the afternoon," he said. "Looks like the trip takes five hours. We would arrive in Flagstaff at seven pm."

"That's a long wait. Check out the bus schedule." Colleen took a sip of her coffee. *Yum.* A welcome caffeine hit tingled her brain.

"Okay…the bus has more departure times. The next one to Flagstaff leaves at noon, but it takes six hours. If we take the bus, we'd get in an hour earlier, even though the trip takes longer."

Storm beamed like a student wanting a gold star from his favorite teacher. She patted his hand. "The bus it is. We have two hours to kill. How about we drive to the bus terminal and buy our tickets then head to Old Town Albuquerque for some shopping?"

"Shopping? You want to go shopping?" One eyebrow arched high on his tan forehead.

"Sure. You can buy something for Harper. Maybe a piece of jewelry or a handmade toy."

He slid the laptop back to the teenage girl and stood. "Thank you." His gaze turned back to Colleen. "Fine, but we'll need to keep track of time. I won't miss our bus."

She clapped in excitement. Good coffee and shopping all in one day. After so many days pushing her body on the road, she needed a lift. She was still recovering from the rock climbing and bull riding. A six-hour bus ride would feel like heaven.

After a stop at the bus terminal, she made the short drive to Old Town Albuquerque. She parked in front of a beautiful, old, Spanish Mission-style church—*San Felipe de Neri*—and took several minutes to appreciate the history and architecture of the building.

She waited for Storm to join her. A short walk brought them to a shaded walkway, where vendors spread their wares on blankets covering the sidewalks. Turquoise and silver jewelry, pottery, and hand-woven baskets made Colleen stop at every vendor to gaze at the gorgeous display. She held out a turquoise ring and a silver bracelet toward Storm. "Which one should I get?"

He shrugged. "Get both—problem solved."

"I don't have enough money for both. Don't want to run out of cash before the finish line."

"Would hate for that to happen."

Colleen didn't miss the sarcasm in his voice, and his grin hinted at teasing. "I think I'll get the ring." She pulled out a twenty and a ten from her bag and handed the bills to the Native American woman who sat nearby on a small chair.

She slid the ring onto her index finger, and it fit perfectly. The gift would be a reminder of a perfect day spent with Storm. She hadn't seen a cameraman lately and breathed a sigh of relief at the freedom, however short lived. As they wove through street vendors, he took hold of her hand. Right now, she didn't care if their relationship was an illusion of smoke and mirrors.

He was distracting her while he pursued what he really wanted—the prize money—and she didn't care. For these few hours, she'd play pretend. She and Storm would be just another couple, enjoying the fall weather and shopping in Old Town Albuquerque.

"You want to get some food?" Storm halted in front of a store's sidewalk display. He picked up a large sombrero and set it on his head. The red rim of the hat hovered over his face. Small, colorful balls swayed with his movements.

"Sure." She giggled. "You should buy that. For

some reason, it suits you."

He took off the sombrero and placed it back on the table. "I think not. Although, a wide brim hat would keep the sun off my face and shoulders when I work in the fields."

"Farming seems to be in your blood."

He gazed off across the courtyard. "Farming is my future. Not just for me, but for Harper, too. I want to give her the life I never had."

"In the commune, you grew up with farming and gardening." As she walked, she inhaled the spicy aroma of southwestern cooking.

"My childhood lacked security. All that free living and love is good, unless you're a kid in need of structure and rules. I lived with the constant threat of upheaval." He hunched his shoulders and lowered his head. "I'm honestly shocked the commune waited so long to kick out my mom."

Colleen followed her nose to the *Hacienda del Rio Cantina*. "Growing up, I envied your life. Your mom loved you without conditions, unlike my father."

"Your father pushed you, because he wanted what's best." He held open the wide red door as she entered the restaurant.

"I guess the grass is always greener on the other side."

The hostess led them to a small table on the outdoor patio.

"I want Harper growing up with the knowledge she's loved. The farm will help me build a real home."

Spread across the adobe wall of the building was a lovely painting of early settlers and their livestock. Colorful flowers hung in baskets from the patio overhang. She accepted a menu from their server. "What about Harper's mom?"

"Val is pursuing her own dreams. Thankfully for me, she can't take Harper to Brazil. After she moves back to the US, then who knows what will happen. I know a judge will be more favorable to grant me permanent custody if I can prove to be the more stable parent."

His plans for the future gave Colleen something to chew on, besides the chips and salsa on the table. What would happen if Storm didn't win the money? Would he lose the chance to raise his daughter along with his dreams of owning a farm? Guilt seeded at the thought of going after the same prize money to fund her own dreams. She couldn't let doubt take root. The veterans needed her retreat. She would save lives, which was just as important as Storm's desires, if not more. "Any judge would be a fool not to see what a wonderful father you are." She scooped a chip into the salsa bowl and took a bite. Spicy heat warmed her tongue.

His eyebrows lowered, causing a crease to form between them. "If I am homeless, I will have no shot at being awarded custody. When I get back home, I'll almost be out of savings."

She glanced down at the menu, not missing the determined expression on Storm's face. The blond scruff on his face couldn't hide the firm set of his lips—the lips that made her weak in the knees with memories of their kiss. He'd do anything to win, including lead her on and break her heart.

Which would not happen. Colleen had too much at stake.

****

Storm made an excuse to sneak away, saying he needed the restroom. He left her smelling the bougainvillea in the courtyard. Earlier, he'd seen a necklace he wanted to buy Colleen as a gift for when they returned home. The necklace had multi-strand copper wire decorated with delicate turquoise stones and metal workings. Along with the necklace, he purchased a pair of tiny silver earrings for Harper and a bracelet for his mom.

"Beautiful pieces for a beautiful woman. I saw you together earlier." As the artist wrapped up the items, the metal bracelets decorating her wrists clinked. "You two looked so much in love. Are you on your honeymoon?"

Heat spread along Storm's neck. "No, we're not." He imagined spending lazy mornings in bed with Colleen as his new wife, his lover, and the mother of a child they'd create together. *Geez, get a grip. Slowly step away from the cliff.* Only last week, he couldn't stand her presence. The stress of the competition must be getting to his head. What other excuse was there?

With a bag full of newly purchased jewelry in hand, he found Colleen over by the gazebo. A small Mariachi band played. Storm stayed back and watched as she swayed in time to the strong beat of the music. A little girl ran onto the makeshift dance floor, and Colleen reached down to pull the toddler up into her arms. The girl's mother laughed as Colleen spun.

Giggles filled the air, making his heart ache for Harper. He missed the sounds of his own daughter's belly laughs.

The woman he currently watched was the Colleen Gardner he'd known in primary school—the little girl with a crooked smile and pigtails. A child with a heart big enough to include a shaggy, scared boy who'd absolutely adored her. To this day, she still cared for those in need and held a deep passion for her work.

After the competition was completed and they were home in Liberty Ridge, he'd sit her down and have a heart to heart. Hopefully, she'd forgive him for winning the money. Her rich dad could supply her with whatever funds she still needed. Everyone in town knew Clive Gardner was loaded. Someway, somehow, he'd figure out a way to have it all. His daughter, his farm, and Colleen by his side.

Once he slipped the bag holding the jewelry into the front pocket of his shirt, Storm strolled over to Colleen. "Our bus leaves soon." He hated seeing her dance come to an end, but time was money.

She tipped back her head to the sky. The sunshine highlighted golden streaks in her short hair. Handing the little girl back to her mother, she turned to face him. "How about we quit and stay here?" Then, she laughed. "I'm so tired of this rat race."

"Come on." He took hold of her hand and pulled her close. So close, he inhaled the citrus scent of her hair. "You're not a quitter, and neither am I. Let's get back to the bus station."

"Fine." As she followed, she dragged her feet. "When you said you had to go to the bathroom, I thought you took off in hopes I'd miss the bus."

What? He wouldn't do something so cruel. At least, not anymore. "*Oh*, come on. That hurts. Don't you trust me?"

One eyebrow arched up over a blue eye. "I'd be a fool to trust you."

He wanted to deserve her trust but had no idea how

to win it—a tricky tightrope to navigate. "You can trust I won't play dirty. You mean too much to me."

They walked in silence back to their cars.

Colleen opened her door then hesitated. "You're good, Storm. I'll give you credit. I might fall for one of your lines if I didn't know you better."

Her smile held a touch of sadness, which dampened his good mood. Maybe once the craziness of the competition was over, he'd have a chance to prove himself. Until then, all he could do was keep moving toward the finish line.

****

Two hours later, Colleen sat on a commercial bus, headed to Flagstaff, Arizona. Storm claimed the seats on the other side of the aisle and currently slept.

No other contestants boarded the bus. Had everyone else taken the train, thinking the ride would be faster? Some might have taken the early departure, the one she and Storm missed because of the penalty, but she hoped not.

Back at the Albuquerque bus station, she'd made a reservation for a cab to meet her in Flagstaff and take her to the motel. She'd share the ride with Storm, since he'd offered to split the cab fare and her cash supply had grown light. With the last four to check in eliminated, Colleen needed every advantage. She wasn't ready to go home.

She drifted into sleep. In her twilight dream, Storm stood before her, talking about love and trust. His words were solid and real, without any hint of deceit, which meant their conversation was definitely a dream.

A clatter sounded from inside the bus, and she roused back into reality. She gazed over at Storm.

Could her dream of a future with him ever come true? She shook her head, banishing the foolish thought. Storm's young life molded him into a man who was rock solid in his resentment. Her life didn't hold enough minutes needed to chip away his shell.

The sparkle of city lights marked their arrival to Flagstaff. With a stroke of good luck, their bus arrived ahead of schedule. As soon as the bus parked, she grabbed her pack and exited. Her cab waited ahead by the curb. Good fortune was smiling on her today. She sprinted toward it with Storm right on her tail.

"The Hotel Weatherford." She closed the car door behind her. "Please hurry."

Once Storm was seated in the backseat, the driver hit the gas.

The force pushed back her body. Colleen whispered a prayer they wouldn't arrive last.

The cab pulled up in front of the hotel lobby. The second the vehicle stopped, Colleen jumped out, sprinted inside, and over to Burt Blackstone.

"You are second and third to check in. Congratulations!" Burt motioned them to move to the side.

Her heart soared. The mistakes made yesterday hadn't beaten them.

Other contestants arrived shortly after. All the remaining contestants were informed this Time-Out stop would be shorter than normal—only twelve hours instead of twenty-four.

Since she'd arrived at six-fifteen pm, she'd leave tomorrow morning at six-fifteen. Adrenaline created by the race buzzed her body. Not ready to sleep yet, she left her room and went down to Charlie's Grill, the little restaurant inside the hotel. She picked a table set in front of the stone fireplace. The heat radiating from the fire nipped the chill out of the air. While she waited, she watched the flames dance above the logs. Between the smoky smell, the crackling sound, and a comfortable warmth, she slowly became hypnotized.

What surprises were in store for tomorrow? If she had to guess, she'd say they were probably heading to the Grand Canyon. She could do some research of other possible destinations. Colleen flipped open the menu and browsed the selections.

Eight contestants were now left—all of them good competitors. She'd been sad to see Mai sent home and would miss her friendly smiles. Out of everyone on the show, maybe besides Storm, she was the one Colleen liked the most. The remaining eight inched toward the west coast—the journey's end. Soon, the gloves would come off. Sure, Storm played nice now, but his gracious mood wouldn't last.

He'd split off in an attempt to beat her, which would hurt. She'd gotten used to the nice version of Storm. The one so much like the little boy she'd known back in Liberty Ridge, before her mean behavior ruined their relationship forever.

Storm slid out a chair and took a seat. "Mind if I join you?"

"Sure. I already ordered. The Navajo Tacos look really good."

He waved over a server and ordered what she'd suggested. "This place is cool. We should come here next spring."

"We?" Her jaw dropped. "When did you and I turn into a we?" His cocky grin was hotter than the nearby fire, making sweat bead on her brow.

He wiggled his eyebrows. "Never know. Stranger things have happened."

Strange indeed she would even consider traveling with him outside the show. But as she imagined the fun they could have together, the idea no longer seemed so crazy.

Chapter Nineteen
Day 12

Storm woke up with a jolt. Opening the curtains to his hotel room, he looked out over a dark street. Inside his mind, the clouds of his earlier dream dissipated—a dream which had been more of a nightmare. Harper was lost inside a large garden maze, and her cries echoed through the area. He searched for what seemed like hours, unable to find his baby girl.

Out of the mist, Colleen appeared, beckoning him. The temptation to follow Colleen away from the cries of his daughter grew strong. He was forced to choose between two conflicting halves of his heart. In the end, he left Colleen standing alone in the garden and found Harper lying cold in a flower bed.

Coming into a sitting position in bed, he rubbed at his face. Was his subconscious announcing his foolishness? He was convinced he could have everything he wanted—win the money to make his dream a reality *and* Colleen's heart. A million landmines were placed along the way. One wrong move and any hope of being with Colleen died. She didn't trust his motives. To win the competition, he might end up justifying her feelings.

Would he be forced to choose one or the other? Maybe. And if push came to shove, he'd place Harper first every time.

After a shower, he dressed and went downstairs to the lobby for a quick breakfast. At seven-fifteen am, he stepped onto the mat next to Colleen, and the host handed them their clue.

The Colorado River carved this natural world wonder. South Rim Village is your destination.

Colleen jumped. "I knew we'd be sent to the Grand Canyon. It's only an hour and a half drive to the South Rim."

He ran over to the new car he'd been provided and discovered one of the staff placed inside a hiking pole, water bottles, salty snacks, a flashlight, a small first aid kit, and a plastic, zip lock bag—all the makings of an awesome hike. Storm arrived at the Grand Canyon at nine. He grabbed his gear and raced over with Colleen to the Village to find the next clue. Signs led him to the Kolb Studio—a brown wood building constructed on the canyon's ledge. Inside, he found a wicker basket, which held six envelopes. Someone else had arrived first.

"Lenny must still be ahead of us." Storm pulled out the card.

Hike the Bright Angel trail to the Phantom Ranch. For safety reasons, you must embark on your hike before noon, otherwise wait until six am the next morning. Bring along the items located in your vehicle. Sunset is at five-fifty pm.

He placed his heavy backpack over his shoulders then helped Colleen with hers. With all the extra gear, the pack must now weigh thirty pounds. A short walk brought him to the Bright Angel trailhead. For the first time, he took a good look over the edge of the canyon. His heart hitched. The image spread out before him resembled a painting. Swirls of orange, red, rust, and brown decorated the rock in horizontal gradations. The bottom of the canyon seemed incredibly far away. He tracked his gaze along the ridge for as far as he could see. The landscape was breathtakingly big and beautiful.

"You won't push me over the edge, will you?" Colleen leaned forward, peering over the drop off.

"Maybe back when we were sixteen." He laughed and took hold of her hand, which felt warm and solid in the vastness of their surroundings. "Remember the time you convinced everyone in our American History class I had a fear of speaking in public and I silently farted when I talked because I was so nervous? For the longest time, I couldn't figure out why everyone in class laughed whenever I answered a question."

As she giggled, tears rolled down her face. "Oh, Storm. I forgot about that prank."

"Your word was law back then." He swiped a thumb over her cheek, cleaning off a damp tear. "We were such troublemakers, you and I."

"Thankfully, we can finally look back on those days and laugh. But you still didn't answer my question. Am I safe with you now?" Taking a step back, she kept hold of his hand and glanced up.

"You're safe. I promise." Storm squeezed her hand and stepped onto the trail, which snaked down the side of the steep rock face. He shifted his gaze between the path below him, the view around him, and Colleen's pretty face. As they dropped in altitude, the temperature steadily grew warmer. After hiking for an hour, he suggested they stop for a drink and brief rest.

He shrugged off his jacket, sat on a small bench set

off to the side, and enjoyed the view. "God's paintbrush."

She wiped off her face with the sleeve of her shirt and pointed to a cliff face to their left. "Look—mountain goats."

Several white animals stood on impossibly small rock outcroppings. Nature and its ability to adapt never ceased to amaze him.

Condors floated above, riding warm air currents.

A bird's view of the canyon would be both magnificent and terrifying. Noticing the sun's high position in the sky, Storm pushed onto his feet. "Time to roll."

Someday soon, he'd reclaim a life existing in harmony with nature. Witnessing the beauty of the world over the last twelve days only fueled his craving.

****

By the time Colleen stopped for a break at the Indian Gardens, a little oasis in the otherwise barren canyon, she was exhausted. She sat in the shade of a Cottonwood tree and rested her shaking legs. The water in her canteen was now warm, but the liquid still refreshed her dry mouth and throat. "How much longer?" She glanced over at Storm, who sat beside her.

He ripped off a piece of beef jerky with his teeth. While chewing, he opened the trail map and spread it over his lap. "We're about halfway to Phantom Ranch. The worst is behind us."

"I hope so. I don't even want to think about the return climb." She pulled out a bag of trail mix from her pack, shook out some, and popped a handful into her mouth. The salty sweet flavor satisfied her hunger.

Storm stood and held out his hand. "Let's get

moving. We might not have to hike back up. The Colorado River is another way out."

Fear replaced exhaustion. "I don't know what would be worse—hiking out of the canyon or whitewater rafting?"

"I'd vote for the rafting. The trip's a total rush."

"You said rock climbing would be fun, and I still have nightmares." Colleen lifted her pack and set it on her shoulders—an added weight for her already tired legs. What qualified as a rush from Storm proved terrifying for her.

Once past the Indian Gardens, the trail eased. After a short uphill climb, the trail snaked back and forth in a valley created by tall canyon walls, which rose high above on either side.

She walked with Storm in mostly silence—an unspoken treaty, of sorts. She knew their time working together was coming to an end. Soon, every player would compete solely for their own best interests.

Despite their renewed friendship, an emotional distance had developed, like a river carving out a canyon. With the pressure of the contest, erosion was inevitable. All she could do now was enjoy the time she had together. Maybe once they returned home, they could build on what they'd started. Unlikely, though, if she won the money and Storm lost out on building his dream farm. Surely, he'd resent her even more if he also lost custody of his daughter.

When the Colorado River came into view, she exhaled a deep sigh of relief. She wanted to burst out into the Hallelujah Chorus when she saw the Phantom Ranch appear over the bridge.

With each step forward, she gained a renewed

energy, like a light bulb given a jolt of electricity. Her skin warmed with the glow of the red and orange rocks all around her. Tipping her head to the sky, she spread out her arms and turned in a slow circle. *Look how far I've come.* Canyon peaks and spears rose high above, like they attempted to punch holes into heaven. Tall Cottonwood trees loomed over stone buildings—their leaves golden with the change of seasons.

She practically skipped down the trail toward the Phantom Ranch, while Storm lagged behind. His laughter was contagious. She stopped and waited in front of a large sign—*Phantom Ranch Welcomes You.*

A red flag marked their clue.

Welcome to the Phantom Ranch at the bottom of the Grand Canyon. Your accommodations are in the dorm. Rest and eat. At six am tomorrow, be ready to leave.

Colleen checked her watch—two-thirty pm. Plenty of time to eat and rest. Thank goodness.

Inside the dorm, she found Lenny sleeping on the bottom mattress of a bunk bed. Tomorrow, she vowed to be the leader at the end of the day.

Chapter Twenty
Day 13

The next morning, cold mist enveloped the bottom of the canyon. Storm sat outside, the heat from his cup of coffee warming his hand. Around the camp, he heard the sounds of life—a clank of a pan, shoes walking over gravel, laughter floating through the air.

His breakfast had been large and hearty, which made him assume today would be even more grueling than yesterday.

At six am, all eight remaining contestants received their envelopes.

When Storm read his clue, he inwardly groaned.

Hike back up the Angel Trail. The South Rim Visitor Center holds your next clue. Along the way, take a picture of a mountain goat, a condor, and the Colorado River. Fill your water bottles and bring food for the journey.

On the hike out of the canyon, he strived to get out ahead of the pack. Luckily, Colleen was up for the challenge. He didn't want to leave her, not yet. Delay for as long as possible—that tactic formed his plan.

He hiked alongside Colleen through the mist until the sun shone bright enough to burn off the fog. The air temperature climbed with the sun. At their steady pace, the hike was long and grueling. After an hour, he suggested they stop and rest, but only long enough to eat a protein bar and take a drink. He couldn't risk being passed by other contestants.

He took the required pictures, which was the easiest part of their task. Both he and Colleen pushed their bodies hard. Using their hiking poles, they navigated up the steep grade. Every so often, Colleen would rest her hand on his arm, and he'd craved the contact. Those brief moments didn't last nearly long enough.

After eight hours of hiking, Storm crested the ledge of the canyon. He took a moment to glance down at everything he'd conquered. His legs were about to give out, but he still felt like the King of the Canyon.

"Storm, come here for the next clue," Colleen yelled.

He jogged over to join her and accepted the paper from her hand.

Take a trip to the Eiffel Tower. Ride to the top that overlooks the Strip. Search from above for the red flag that marks the location of your clue.

"We're going to Vegas, baby." He lifted Colleen in his arms and swung her around. A renewing surge of energy filled him. "How about we get hitched? You know what they say…what happens in Vegas—" As soon as the words left his mouth, he wished to take them back. Underneath the teasing tone was truth. He wanted her, more than he cared to admit.

"Won't stay in Vegas." Frowning, she reached over and pinched his lips together. "Nobody is getting married on this trip, unless you propose to a showgirl."

He imagined Colleen dressed in a showgirl outfit, causing his heart to palpitate. After day dreaming about Colleen for the entire four-hour drive to Las Vegas, he finally approached the Strip. The action reignited his exhausted body and mind.

Did he have enough time to find a parking structure, to walk to the Eiffel Tower, and then find the next clue before curfew? Neon lights chased away the darkness of night, which created a pseudo daylight. He parked and walked with Colleen to the structure. After taking the elevator to the top, he stood on the observation deck and searched the sparkling city below for the next clue. Both he and Colleen looked for fifteen minutes with no luck. His anxiety grew by the second. Time was running out.

He raked his gaze over buildings, sidewalks, lit billboards, and even pedestrians below. *Where the heck was that stupid flag?* A flash of red caught his eye. *Finally!*

For a second, he considered not sharing his find with Colleen. At this point in the competition, he shouldn't help anyone, least of all his primary competition. But what kind of man would he be if he ran off without her? "The flag is on that castle turret."

"The Excalibur Hotel. We'll have to run to get there before the curfew." Colleen sprinted back to the glass elevator.

Once his feet were firmly back on the terra firma, he darted down the sidewalk. He weaved in and out of the pedestrian traffic clogging his path. Time was ticking away like a bomb.

At the escalator outside the Excalibur, he bounded up the moving steps then across the bridge leading to the hotel. Colleen's footsteps sounded from behind.

"Do you see the clue?" He adjusted the straps of his backpack to keep it from slipping off. While running, the heavy sack bounced on his back, practically knocking the wind from his lungs.

"No." Colleen sprinted alongside him. "Maybe the clue's in the hotel."

Inside the lobby, he found the space huge and overwhelming. The loud noise of multiple voices echoed through the air. Storm spun in a desperate search for a red flag.

Colleen approached the information desk and spoke with one of the well-dressed women behind the counter.

Smart woman, which made him almost as smart for staying with her.

After a minute, she ran back. "We have to go to the Tournament of Kings. What if they make us joust?"

"That would be awesome." He followed her to the doors to the tournament hall and found a red flag marking their next clue.

Tonight, ye shall joust. Better yet, a champion shall joust in your place. Pick a colored ribbon at your table. Once your color's champion has won a jousting match, you receive your next clue. Rooms are booked for all contestants at the Excalibur Hotel. Be ready to leave by six tomorrow morning.

"Come, my fair maiden. Let us partake in some food and sport." His English accent bordered on hideous.

Smiling, Colleen rested her hand in the crook of his arm. "Yes, my brave knight. I am so very famished."

Storm bent to kiss her hand, and his lips sparked on contact. The rest of his body caught fire at the heated look in her eyes. Out of the corner of his eye, he saw the cameraman standing off to the side. If they weren't being filmed at the moment, he'd do more than kiss her hand. Too bad. Guess his willpower had to last a few days longer. Once the show concluded filming, he planned on showing Colleen how drastically his feelings had change course, like a ship heading home.

Chapter Twenty-One
Day 14

The next morning started way too early. Now, she stood under the dim light of the sunrise and enjoyed the stillness of the strip. No hustlers, no tourists, and no cars rushing back and forth to ruin the beauty of the city. She stood between Tammy, who continuingly snapped the gum in her mouth, and Storm, who rubbed sleep out of his eyes.

Last night, she'd realized the time had come to end her alliance with Storm. His comment about them getting married in Vegas had been the last straw. Her mind automatically jumped to answer yes. For a split second, she thought he might be serious. Of course not. He was only playing her. A simple tease sent her heart soaring and crashing within moments. All the time spent together, the long talks, and the hand-holding had weakened her resolve. She would break off her partnership and strike out on her own. If she pulled off the bandage now, she'd save herself a lot of pain later on. While she waited impatiently for the clock to reach six am, she studied the clue.

Fly to The Golden City. The Dragon's Gate is the location of your next clue.

Since she'd done some research the night before, Colleen knew the first flight out to San Francisco wasn't until ten am. She'd reserved tickets for that flight.

Storm approached. "Did you look into flights already?"

"Yes." She didn't miss the sidelong look Tammy gave her. Talk about shooting daggers. Tammy tried hard to get Storm over to her camp. Colleen couldn't blame any woman for wanting Storm.

"So…you gonna tell me?" He nudged her side with his elbow.

Storm's flirty smile produced fluttering in her chest. "No." She forced out the word.

His eyebrows lowered over his eyes. "Why not?"

"I think separating is for the best." She needed to gain control of the situation. Her emotions were too vulnerable right now, and she couldn't let Storm prey on them.

"Fine." He pulled the straps of his pack and shrugged his shoulders. "You're making a mistake but whatever."

Regret weighed on her heart. "We both knew we'd part ways eventually, so don't pretend like you're hurt. I'm not buying your act."

"You think I was acting?" He turned to face her and glowered. "Seriously?"

"Before the competition started, you couldn't stand being in the same room with me. You hated me. I don't think your feelings changed. You became better at hiding them to suit your purpose." Colleen looked at her watch. *Come on.* These final moments before leaving were the longest minutes of her life.

Storm's face hardened. "Don't you dare accuse me of using you to get ahead. I thought we had something good between us."

"Anything good between us died when we were younger. I know nothing I ever say or do will redeem me in your eyes. I've accepted that fact." She turned and wiped away a tear from her cheek. Her throat burned with pent-up sorrow.

He strode to the other end of the line of contestants, running his fingers through his overgrown hair.

While he mumbled something she couldn't understand, she stuffed her hands in her pockets and let him go. In order to win, she'd remove all distractions, and Storm proved to be the biggest one.

****

Storm's blood boiled. Why now, after everything they'd been through together, was Colleen pushing him away?

She took her own cab to the airport, not bothering to even ask if he wanted to share the ride. Yesterday, he'd noticed her emotionally withdraw. He'd assumed she was just tired after the long hike up the Grand Canyon.

Nope. She wanted to dissolve their partnership. And he had believed they were finally making some headway in their relationship. He'd been stupid enough to think Colleen would want to deepen their friendship once this competition was over.

With one sharp look from her, he'd been transported to an insecure boy. He remembered the pain of being mocked by the one person he'd loved most. He wasn't good enough for Colleen Gardner, the daughter of the town's richest man. Even if he won the million dollars, he'd still be only a lowly farmer. She'd gone to an Ivy League college and now worked as a very respected psychiatrist. What did he have to offer?

Besides a plot of dirt, and only if he beat her to win.

They were racing across the country for money, not on a dating show. So, why did her rejection still hurt?

He lucked out at the airport with getting a ticket. Both he and Colleen, along with the two others in the lead, were on the same flight. Once the plane landed and taxied to the gate, he ran through the San Francisco airport and outside to the pick-up area to find a taxi to take him to Chinatown. He darted to the first open cab and jumped inside.

His cab driver navigated the streets like an Indy racer, and Storm arrived at the Dragon's gate in record time. He tossed his cabbie enough money to cover his fare plus a tip and jumped out.

The jade green tiled roof of the gate held two golden dragons, slinking toward one another. Propped next to one of the gate's pillars was a red flag marking the next clue.

Go to the Hang Ah Tea Room. Ask for the Great American Scavenger Hunt Special. Once you eat and drink everything served, you will receive your next clue. Bring along a pair of chopsticks from the Tea Room.

After asking ten people for directions, he was finally pointed toward the Hang Ah Tea Room. Sweat dripped down his face. Panic made him jittery. By the time he found the tea room, he was exhausted.

Inside, the small space was empty of other customers. Perfect. Nothing felt better than being in first. He sat and ordered what they'd been instructed. His wait wasn't long, and soon his meal was placed before him, along with a cup of strong tea. The plate held a steamed roll filled with meat, a chicken dish covered with a spicy sauce, seasoned greens, and a noodle soup on the side. He ate with a fervor, savoring the array of spices. Intense flavors danced on his tongue. As Storm took his last bite, he was handed the next clue by the server.

Colleen, who'd arrived after him, still struggled to finish her food.

She sat slumped forward in her chair with her head resting on her hand, looking like her stomach was about to burst. A small bite of sympathy made him hesitate. Should he be the bigger person and wait?

No. He couldn't afford to lose any time. As he pushed back to stand, the chair legs scraped over the floor. He grabbed the chopsticks needed for the scavenger hunt. After he walked outside, he inhaled a deep breath of deliciously scented air then read the clue.

Ride a cable car to Fisherman's Wharf. Take one of the show's cars, which are parked somewhere along Van Ness Avenue. Drive to Monterey. Check in to the Monterey Plaza Hotel. This check-in is a Time-Out stop. The last four contestants to arrive will be eliminated.

Storm turned his attention to locating a cable car stop, ensuring he stayed ahead of the competition.

****

Just when Colleen didn't think she could take one more bite, another contestant entered the restaurant. With a feat of barbaric willpower, Colleen stuffed the last helping of spicy chicken into her mouth. Heat burst from every taste bud—a fire that water alone couldn't quell. The tea balanced out the heat, and she chugged the remainder left in her cup.

The server handed her the next clue. Storm and Lenny were long gone. Of course, the guys could stuff themselves without a problem.

After reading the clue, Colleen asked an elderly Chinese woman where she could find the closest cable car stop. She wanted to run, but the food weighed heavy in her stomach. If she bounced, even a little, everything inside would come up and out. Although, after throwing up, she might feel better.

The cable car ride was a rush, and she glided over the steep hills of San Francisco. She hopped off at Fisherman's Wharf stop and asked for directions to Van Ness Avenue. Two of the eight cars were already gone, which meant Storm and Lenny had left.

Tammy, a petite young woman with long brunette hair, was right behind her.

Her trip to Monterey had to go without incident. She checked her gas gauge, wanting to avoid running out of gas again, and then studied her map. The trip would take two hours, putting her in at about two-thirty. Not bad, but still not good enough to be in first place.

She couldn't waste any time on the next leg of her trip, vowing to beat Tammy to the Time-Out stop.

****

Storm stood on the balcony and watched the churning Pacific Ocean. The sound of crashing waves helped release the extra adrenaline from his body. He pushed hard to come in first. Now, he was at a nice hotel room for the night, determined to avoid Colleen.

Four more contestants had been sent packing earlier today. Not that he didn't feel a little sympathy, but losing was part of playing the game. He couldn't believe the end was in sight. In only a few more days, he would cross that finish line as the winner. Then he could start making real plans, not the pie-in-the-sky dreams which had carried him this far.

The sun was setting over a blanket of fog hovering over the ocean. A gray hue overcast everything that earlier had been kissed by the sun. The water looked like liquid silver, shimmering as the waves swayed to nature's music.

For dinner, he ordered room service then practiced a few yoga poses, needing desperately to stretch his hips, back, and leg muscles. Every part of his body carried tension. No surprise after all the stress he'd endured over the past two weeks. Only a few more days and he'd see Harper again. Per show rules, he'd had no contact with her since the evening before the first day of the competition. He missed his daughter with an increasing ache, which stoked his desire to win. Nothing and no one, not even Colleen, could stand in the way of fulfilling his dream.

Chapter Twenty-Two
Day 15

After a good night's sleep, Storm ordered breakfast served in his room. He ate, and then sat in a small sectioned off area alone and recorded his confessional video for the show. The whole idea of talking to a video camera about his experiences was asinine, and he would not spill his guts on national television. He stuck to topics like strategy and where he thought they'd be sent next. As far as he was concerned, Colleen was no longer a topic he'd discuss.

He wondered what she'd said during her video confessional sessions. Anything about him? He hoped not. Once the show aired, he'd have to answer enough questions back home without either of them adding fuel to the fire.

After being stuck inside his room for most of the morning, he escaped to the cool air outside. He had four hours to kill before he could set off again. With a fifteen-minute lead on Lenny and a thirty-minute lead on Colleen, he needed to focus on staying ahead.

While he walked along the large balcony hovering over the ocean, he made an effort to mentally relax—let everything go and simply focus on breathing. He glanced down over the rails and watched the surf pound the rocks below with rhythmic power. About a half-dozen sea lions frolicked in the water, while two lounged on a boulder to his right.

For about an hour, he watched gulls circle through the air before diving into the ocean like tiny missiles. The breeze covered his face with ocean spray, and he licked his lips, tasting salt water.

For the past several years, while working on organic farms, he'd spent a lot of time in Northern California but farther inland. He liked the coast, though, and enjoyed the pull of the ocean.

At eleven am, he lined up with the last four contestants for one final team competition.

"Storm and Colleen, you're Team Fire," a producer announced. "Lenny and Tammy make Team Ice."

Great. Of course, I'd get teamed with Colleen. More fireworks for the TV audience. The show loved to create drama. Storm followed the small group down to the sand. Two yellow boats were beached at the waterline. Each boat had two benches inside, along with two sets of oars.

Burt stood before them, as well groomed as ever. Even his purple tie was unwrinkled and perfectly straight.

"This challenge is called *Row, Row, Row Your Boat*." The host smiled broadly. "Each team will row out to the buoy, collect the item tied to it, and row back to shore. First team back gets a thirty-minute head start."

His frustration over losing his lead crashed inside him as powerfully as the waves breaking on shore. Storm held the boat steady as Colleen boarded. "I'll row for power, and you steer. Don't screw this up. We need this win."

She gritted her teeth. "You don't think I know that?

I have just as much riding on this as you do."

She raised an oar like she was ready to whack him over the head. He grunted but held his tongue. With a rich daddy, she didn't need the prize money. The horn blasted, and Storm pushed their boat into the surf. He hopped onboard.

Colleen shouted encouragement into the wind.

Luckily, the Pacific Ocean was fairly calm, and they had no trouble moving over the breaking waves. His biceps burned with each stroke through the resistant water. They flew toward the buoy. Colleen made adjustments to keep them on a straight course.

The other team appeared to be drifting off. *Good.* If he and Colleen kept up their fast pace, they'd be back on shore before Team Ice arrived at the first buoy. They established a good groove, with each stroke of the oar sliding through the water in sync.

As soon as the front end of the boat touched land, Storm stepped from the boat and pulled Colleen up and out.

She wrapped her arms around his neck. "We did it," she whispered into his ear.

He felt the beat of her heart against his chest and a familiar magnetic pull, which left him longing to toss away everything for a future with her.

With that thought haunting his mind, he knew the time had come to completely let her go.

****

Drive to the home of the Joshua Tree. You'll find the clue at the Visitors' Center.

Colleen headed east to catch Interstate 68, then hooked over to the 101, which took her south. She drove until seven-forty-five pm then checked into a seedy, suburban LA motel. Tammy was right behind her. The little sneak must have driven like Kyle Busch to make up the thirty-minute delay.

Not only was Colleen's body tired, but her will to continue drained out of her like sand in an hourglass. Soon, she'd have nothing left to see her through to the end. She'd lose, and so would the men and women who required her help.

The person she needed was Storm. His companionship gave her strength. Now, they avoided one another, and the emotional distance took a toll. She'd let him into her heart when all along, deep down, she knew his offered friendship wasn't true. Storm only used his charm as a strategy to get ahead. She fooled herself into thinking he wanted to be friends after the competition was all said and done.

Just remember who you're really doing this for. The veterans you will help need you to stay strong.

A knock sounded on her door, and she pushed herself off the bed to stand and answered. She opened the door to find Tammy lurking in the hall.

"How are you holding up?" Tammy cocked her head.

"I'm feeling good." She'd spare her the truth. "How about you?"

"I'm good, too. Why aren't you with Storm?" Tammy smirked. "I thought you two were some unbreakable duo."

Colleen peered over Tammy's shoulder to see a cameraman standing close enough to capture the action. Keep the conversation light and happy. "We're in an individual competition."

"He is so hot." Tammy sighed and leaned against

the doorjamb. "Did you guys hook up?"

"No." Her words came out too fast and hard. "Of course not."

"Everybody thought so, you know. Since you guys grew up together. I didn't think people were supposed to know each other before the competition. But hey, I'm sure the sexual tension will make for great TV."

She didn't want to consider the personal fall-out once the show aired. "What happened between Storm and I is really none of your business."

Tammy leaned forward. "You should have hooked up. I would have. Maybe I will."

"Over my dead body." Colleen shut the door and slid the chain lock into place. An intense jealousy rose from the tips of her toenails to the ends of her hair. Her body surged with new energy. Tammy fueled the dying fire of her competitive nature.

These final days, she'd give her all. The reality of her veterans' retreat was so close, all she had to do now was reach out and take the prize.

Chapter Twenty-Three
Day 16

Storm turned up the radio volume. *Highway to Hell* blasted out of the car's speakers. The landscape through Joshua Tree National Park was barren and dry. Amazingly, though, life thrived. The plants growing in the area were hearty stock and found substance in the rocky soil. He considered the local vegetation kindred spirits, since he'd been toughened by the elements, as well.

By the time he arrived at the Visitor Center, he'd flipped his anxiety to exhilaration. The red flag marking the clue waved in the brisk breeze. Even in the desert, the early morning had a cool bite. Storm parked, exited his car, and walked over to discover what came next.

Horseback or Hike. Take your camera and travel through the park. You must photograph these six animals: Rabbit, Roadrunner, Scorpion, Quail, Snake, and Lizard. If you choose to go out on horseback, head to the Black Rock campground and get outfitted with a trail horse. Make sure to bring along water. Once you've photographed all six animals, check in at the Black Rock campground. Last two contestants will be eliminated.

Storm stood for a moment of uncertainty. If Colleen were here, she'd know which method to choose. After a mental argument, he decided to search on foot. Horseback would give him a better vantage point, but he might miss the small ground animals. Plus, he enjoyed hiking. He'd get the required pictures and be the first one into camp.

But after the first hour of searching and spotting no animals, he second-guessed his decision. At this rate, he'd be wandering around all day. Colleen, Lenny, and Tammy were likely here. He bet Colleen had a solid plan to complete their task in record time. She excelled at being well prepared.

He and Colleen made a good team. She brought out the best in him and always rose to his challenges. If they would have stuck together a little longer, he'd be guaranteed as one of the last two contestants standing. He kicked at the pebbles on the ground and grunted. The way his luck was running, he'd check in after sundown.

****

Colleen slid her foot into the stirrup and pulled herself onto the horse. Riding was the better option. In her opinion, walking ate up too much time. Up here, she could scan the ground for movement. She had good eyesight, aided by the pair of binoculars she'd purchased at the Visitor Center. She'd also taken the time to talk with a Park Ranger about the habits of the animals she needed to photograph– where they could be found during the day, what they liked to eat, and the best trail to utilize.

The ranger handed her a map with circled areas indicating spots to check out first.

She might be the last one to head into the park, but the time with the Ranger was well spent.

Knowing Storm, he had run out into the desert

without much thought to research. During her drive that morning, she'd worried breaking their alliance had been a mistake. With this task, two pairs of eyes were better than one. If Colleen won, and she planned to, he'd resent her for stealing his chance at a life on his own farm with his daughter.

She hated the fresh doubts popping up like fire ants out of the ground—and the sting was just as painful. If only the show gave two large cash prizes, so both she and Storm could walk away happy.

Riding down the trail, Colleen gave her horse a gentle nudge with her heels. She gripped the pommel and reins with one hand and swayed with the rhythm of the horse. In her other hand, she held the binoculars to her eyes. She jumped when a covey of quail scampered over the hill, heading right toward her.

Letting her binoculars hang from her neck, she picked up the camera, zoomed in, and took the shot. *Yes, one down…five more to go.*

The sound of crunching gravel made Colleen turn her head. *Darn.* Tammy rode right behind her with camera in hand.

"Is this your strategy?" Colleen shouted over her shoulder.

The quail scattered with the noise before Tammy could get her picture.

"Follow me all day? Can't you manage on your own?"

"Don't think so highly of yourself." Tammy twirled her brunette pony tail around her hand. She thumped the animal with her booted feet.

Her horse bent its neck back and nipped her on the shin before taking off at a fast-paced cantor.

With a shriek blended with a few curses, Tammy passed Colleen on the right and disappeared down the trail.

Good riddance. Adjusting her baseball cap, she scanned the terrain for signs of wildlife. During the next thirty minutes, she photographed a rabbit and a roadrunner. She'd have better luck finding the smaller animals, like the snake, lizard, and scorpion, on foot. She tied up her horse and stepped very carefully through brush and over rocks. Joshua Trees sprouted out of the dirt like ancient statues, arms reaching up to the sky.

Every stone she overturned, she felt her heart leap in her chest with anticipation and fear. Under one rust-colored stone, she found a small, yellow scorpion. It skittered backward, toward the dark safety of the rock. A chill ran through her spine as she quickly took the picture before letting the rock fall back in place.

Lizards darted over the desert floor like mice in a barn, so finding one was easy. The only animal left to photograph was a snake. *Gross.* She hated snakes with a passion. During her freshman year of high school, Storm put a Rat Snake in her locker. When she'd opened her locker door and saw two black eyes staring back, she'd screamed. Thankfully, her boyfriend protected her from the vicious thing. Now, she had no boyfriend to help—only girl power to get the job done.

By ten-forty-five, Colleen had all six pictures. She hustled back on her horse and galloped to the Black Rock stables. Once she arrived, she hopped down, and then sprinted over to the check-in spot. She didn't see anyone else there, besides the show's host and several cameramen. Colleen stopped before him, and her stomach lurched with fear. Just because she hadn't seen Lenny, Storm, or Tammy didn't mean they hadn't arrived already. For all she knew, she'd come in last.

"Congratulations." Burt clapped his hands together. "You're in first place."

"Seriously?" The weight of stress released from her body.

Burt smiled and shook her hand. "You'll stay at the campground tonight, along with the second finalist. Go find your tent and get a bite to eat. Good luck with the final leg of *The Great American Scavenger Hunt*."

After shaking hands with Burt and smiling for the camera, she blew out a long breath and went to get her pack from her car. *Yes, I did it!* Now, who would be her competition? *Please let that person be Storm.* No one else on earth she'd rather be with than Storm. He deserved the chance to win just as much as she did. Conversely, she sickened at the thought of beating him for the prize.

****

In his head, Storm could hear the countdown tick-tock of a clock. He had to find one snake—that's all, then he could head back to the campground and check in. But time was running out. Glancing upward at the sun, he judged the time hovered around noon and tensed. He had to hustle.

A few minutes ago, he'd noticed Lenny picking through a rock pile. He'd also talked to Tammy. She'd told him Colleen was on a horseback, riding one of the other trails.

Storm kicked a rock then heard a rattle in reply. *Finally.* He jumped back and maintained about six feet of distance between himself and the snake. The serpent poked out its head a couple inches, but it was long enough for him to snap a photo.

Running like the devil was on his heels, he started back toward the Black Rock Campground. The sound of heavy feet crunching on the gravel behind him sent another shot of adrenaline. When he turned, he saw Lenny closing the distance. The whole challenge came down to a flat-out foot race. Storm's lungs burned, and sweat dripped into his eyes, but he didn't slow. He rounded a curve, and Burt Blackstone came into view. He heard Lenny breathing hard right behind him.

With strength formerly unknown, Storm surged forward—thirty feet, twenty, ten, five more feet. He got to Burt, beating Lenny by a mere two seconds.

"Congratulations." Burt slapped Storm's shoulder. "You are the second contestant to arrive."

He let loose a loud shout of victory.

"We have a tent for you at the campground. You'll stay there overnight and depart twenty-four hours from now. Rest up and good luck." Burt reached out and shook Storm's hand.

Burt turned to Lenny as he stepped forward. "I'm sorry, big guy. For this challenge, you came in third." He patted Lenny's broad shoulder. "You've been eliminated."

Storm carried his pack to where two tents stood. He was shocked to see Colleen standing beside one, brushing out her hair.

When she glanced his way, she gave a wide smile. "Can you believe it? Just you and me, Stormy."

"Seems like we were meant to end this race together." Memories of his young love rushed over him like a crashing wave. After everything they'd been through together since childhood, how could he not still love her?

She was the reason no other relationship ever lasted. Even Val, who'd come the closest to winning his heart, fell short. Storm put Colleen up on a pedestal and there she stayed, protected like a priceless jewel in a museum.

Now, they'd compete head to head. He pulled out his picture of Harper from his backpack. Focusing on his little girl would get him through the next few days.

****

Colleen pulled her sleeping bag to lie out in the open. Her body was snug and warm while she admired the brilliant lights above. Tonight, the stargazing was out of this world. A comet shot across the sky, before disappearing as quickly as it materialized. She'd never seen such a magnificent display. No wonder festivals were held here in celebration of the night.

Storm appeared from his tent and set his sleeping bag on the ground beside her. They lay in silence.

The yips and howls of nocturnal animals made up for their lack of conversation.

Storm cleared his throat. "How are you holding up?"

Was he wondering because he cared or if he searched for weakness? She hated not trusting his motives, but she couldn't let down her guard. Not when she was so close to the finish. "I'm feeling strong. The race is almost over. I bet you'll be happy to see Harper again."

"I miss her." Storm sighed. "These past few weeks have felt like an eternity. I can't believe we started in DC, and now we're sleeping in the California desert.

Crazy."

"We're crazy for doing a reality TV show. If I could go back to change my mind, though, I'd sign up all over again. I've learned a lot about myself during this trip."

"What did you learn?" He faced her with his head propped on his hand.

She rolled to her side and rested her gaze on him, who fascinated her as strongly the stars above. "I'm stronger than I thought. Growing up, I always felt an undeserved privilege for being Clive Gardner's daughter. People didn't expect I worked hard to get what I wanted. But I did, especially for my dad's approval."

Filtered light from inside the tents cast his features in shadow. "From my viewpoint, you had the perfect life."

"I know. My dad excels at putting on a show. He's a drunk, and nobody but me ever saw that side of him. You want to know the worst part? I made him that way." A swell of emotions burned her chest and throat. Unburdening her soul felt so freeing. The cameras were put away, and they were finally alone. Unless she counted millions of stars.

"I never knew your dad is an alcoholic." Storm moved closer and wrapped his arm around her shoulders.

She rested her head on his chest, enjoying the strong beat of his heart. "How would you? His drinking isn't something I shared with anyone. He started abusing alcohol after my mom died, because he couldn't cope with the loss."

"I remember how devastated you were during that

time. I'd find you off by yourself crying in the school field at recess. I wish you would have confided in me."

Colleen choked back tears, but they spilled out anyway, running down her cheeks onto his T-shirt. "The car accident that killed my mom was my fault."

He rubbed a hand over her arm, which rested outside the sleeping bag. "What do you mean, your fault? You were just a little girl."

"The morning of the accident, we were on the way to school. I'd forgotten my special pen and was having a fit in the back seat. Mom told me she wasn't going home to get it, and I screamed and cried like a spoiled brat. She turned to face me only for a second," Colleen said between sobs. "She lost control of the car. She died, because I wanted a stupid pen."

"I'm so sorry." Storm held her close and stroked her hair.

"My dad changed after my mom's death." She melted into him, absorbing the comfort he offered. "I know he blames me."

"You've shouldered the blame for so many years." Storm sighed. "Your dad chose to medicate himself with alcohol. And the car accident was just that…a tragic accident."

Colleen pulled away, but Storm's strong arms tightened. "I wish I could go back in time and fix my mistakes. I'm so sorry, Storm."

"I forgive you," he whispered. "Will you forgive me?"

"Of course." His kind words released a whole new round of tears. She peered at Storm, whose soft gaze rested on her. "You're a really great guy."

"I've been told that once or twice." He leaned close

and gave her a gentle kiss on the temple. "Come on, let's go inside our tents and get some sleep. I'll need the rest in order to beat you."

"Ha. No way am I letting you." Her pride rose.

"I'm up for the challenge." Storm slowly stood.

She recognized the wickedly teasing grin on his face. Raising herself on tiptoes, she planted a soft kiss on his scruffy cheek. Sparks sizzled in the dark. "You better bring everything you got. I won't go down easily."

Chapter Twenty-Four
Day 17

"This competition has been such a great experience," Colleen told the woman conducting the interview. She sat on a hard, folding chair, across from the video camera. Above them stood a portable canopy for shade. The sun warmth helped remove some of the chill from the air. Doing these interviews was as enjoyable as a trip to the Department of Motor Vehicles—a necessary evil.

"Do you have any doubts about competing against Storm, one on one?" The interviewer took an offered bottle of water out of the hand of one of the production assistants. With long fingers tipped with hot pink nails, she twisted off the cap and took a drink.

"He's a strong competitor, but so am I. We have different styles. When we work together, we complimented each other. Only time will tell who'll come out ahead."

The woman pushed up her purple framed glasses to the bridge of her nose and glanced at her notes. "The dynamic has been interesting to watch. Do you see a future together?"

In her dreams, but she wasn't sharing her secrets on national TV. She relaxed the muscles in her face so not to reveal her unsteady emotions. "A future? As in dating? I'm not thinking about my love life right now."

"You want to build a retreat for veterans suffering with PTSD and other service-related trauma. Is that what's pushing you through each challenge?"

"Yes." Colleen leaned forward. "I've worked for the past year to raise the money for construction. Winning would guarantee the doors opening soon. The men and women who've served our country now find themselves underserved by the government. I've seen firsthand how therapy can save lives. Making this retreat a reality means everything to me."

"What if you don't win?" A gust of wind blew the woman's black hair over her face. She brushed it back before returning her attention to Colleen.

"I'll double my fundraising efforts, but every day that passes, more vets go without lifesaving help. Which is why I need to win." She allowed emotion into her voice, needing to convey her passion and commitment. If she didn't win, she'd use the publicity from her participation in this event as a new opportunity to raise money. Looking into the camera, she smiled. "If viewers would like to donate, please visit my professional website for a link. A quick web search of my name plus veterans will lead you to the site."

"Thanks, Colleen." The interviewer reached over and shook her hand. "Good luck."

Colleen left in search of a quiet spot to collect her thoughts. In two hours, she'd set off for the final leg. She spent about thirty minutes strolling around the area, enjoying the beauty of the desert. Lizards scurried along the desert floor, over rocks, and up Joshua trees. They looked so busy, like tiny New Yorkers during rush hour.

Even after her meditation, she still felt antsy. Journal writing usually calmed her nerves. She returned to the tent and grabbed her little leather journal and a pen. On the way to a park bench she'd discovered earlier, she heard Storm's voice coming from the interview spot. Eavesdropping on him wasn't right, but her curiosity won over her better judgment. Crouching, she hid on the other side of her tent and listened.

"You stated you want to start an organic farm," the female interviewer said. "Why is that business so important?"

"For the past five years, I've worked with organic farmers. I love the idea of using the gifts of nature to produce delicious and hearty plants. Now, I have a daughter to care for. Her mother is leaving for South America in January. She won't sign off on granting me full custody if I can't provide a permanent home for our daughter. The prize money will allow me to buy farmland and build a house."

Still hidden, Colleen held her breath. She had no idea about the obstacles Storm faced to gain custody of Harper.

"What are your plans if you don't win?"

Storm cleared his throat. "Not winning has never been an option because I've put everything into this competition. If I don't win, I won't have enough time to find a good paying job and establish a home before Valerie leaves. Then, my daughter will go live with her grandparents in New York City."

"How tragic. Would you move there to be with her?"

"My mother struggles with mental illness, and she's working hard to get healthy. I'd have to stay in

Liberty Ridge, at least for a while. A move at this point would mean changing doctors, which would hamper her progress. So, you see why I'm motivated to win. I really have no other option."

"Well, best of luck to you. I'd hate for you to become separated from your daughter."

At the sound of shuffling feet moving in her direction, she ran back to the quiet spot on the bench. Guilt brewed in her gut. She shouldn't have eavesdropped on Storm's interview. What was she supposed to do now? If she won, Storm and Harper would be separated. Having seen Storm glow when talking about his daughter, she knew he'd be devastated.

A scream of frustration rose inside her, and she craved to release it into the barren expanse of the desert. At this point in the competition, she shouldn't question her desire to win. How could go on, knowing how much Storm had riding on the prize money?

"Hey," Storm said, coming up from behind.

She jumped, and her heart leaped into her throat. "Good grief, you almost scared me into the grave."

"I got you nervous, huh?" He sat and nudged her lightly with his elbow.

"Not nerves." *Guilt.* She didn't want to stand between him and a life with his daughter.

"We'll be done after today, and then our lives can go back to normal."

Storm smiled, but underneath Colleen saw tension. The fine lines between his eyebrows were deeper, and the normal warm brown color of his eyes darkened to deep pools. "Do you want to return to normal between us?" She wrung her hands. "I don't want to go back to you hating me." Whatever his true feelings, once they'd completed the competition, she'd work to mend their relationship.

"I really never hated you. Actually, just the opposite." He combed back his shaggy hair with his fingers. "You've always provoked strong feelings from me. Actually, you seem to have that effect on a lot of people."

"Hey." She whacked him on the chest. A chest hardened by years of manual labor. *Sigh.* Why did little Stormy have to grow up to be such a hottie? Back in the fourth grade, she'd never guessed the scrawny boy would evolve into a swoon-worthy, hunky man.

"Just remember, we agreed in the beginning that winner takes all." Storm's grin widened.

In reaction, she felt a fluttering in her chest. Whatever the results of the competition, she knew one thing for certain—Storm had already won her heart.

****

At twelve-fifteen, thirty minutes after Colleen left, Storm grabbed his clue.

Head to Johnson's Marina in Salton City. Be prepared to get wet.

After getting into his car, he desperately scanned the map of California. Just to the south of Joshua Tree National Park lay the Salton Sea. He did a double take, not expecting a large lake in the middle of the California desert.

The drive south was relatively short, compared to some of the other long hauls. When he pulled into the parking lot of Johnson's Marina, he saw Colleen's car. Whatever the challenge, she hadn't completed it yet. *Good.*

As he exited the car, he was hit with the scent of rotten fish. He didn't consider himself sensitive to bad smells, but the odor was gag-inducing. Ignoring the churning of his stomach, he ran toward the red flag and grabbed the lone envelope.

Your next clue is floating somewhere on the Salton Sea. Take a personal watercraft to search for the red buoy.

Storm stripped off his shirt, put on a life vest, and then climbed aboard the only personal watercraft parked by the dock. After taking a moment to figure out how the machine worked, he decided the watercraft used a throttle lever similar to an ATV. He turned the key, hit the throttle, and took off in a spray of salt water. Out in the distance, he noticed Colleen circling an area. He'd head in that direction in case she'd located the red buoy. He started toward her.

Colleen moved farther south. Then, she made a sharp U-turn and rocketed back to the dock.

He scanned his gaze over the water. Panic took root in his gut and grew. In order to win, he had to keep his cool. Just because Colleen might have found the clue didn't mean he couldn't easily overtake her. The choppy water made for a bumpy, wet ride. He continued in the direction she'd earlier occupied. Out of the corner of his eye, he detected a red flash. The flag bobbed about fifty yards to the south. He increased his speed until he reached the buoy, and then ripped off the envelope. After stuffing it unopened in his life-vest, he raced back to shore.

By the time he arrived, Colleen was nowhere to be seen. He slipped back into his T-shirt and read.

The USS Midway is your destination.

Having never heard of the USS Midway, he asked the few people milling around. No luck. After spotting an older gentleman standing along the rocky shore, casting a line into the murky water, he decided to try one last person before taking off. He cleared his throat to announce his presence. "Excuse me, sir. Are you familiar with the USS Midway?"

"Son," he said, not taking his gaze off his fishing line. "I'm an old sea dog. Of course, I know the USS Midway."

Finally. "Can you tell me where the ship is docked?"

The old man made a deep throated—a pack of cigarettes a day—laugh. "San Diego, of course. They turned the ship into some sort of museum."

"Thanks." Storm ran to his car. San Diego was about a two-and-a-half-hour drive. If he was lucky, he'd catch Colleen. Maybe even pass her.

With his adrenaline pumping, he felt the drive pass in a blur. He arrived at the Navy Pier and parked, then ran in front of the giant Kissing Statue on his way toward the show's red flag. Once there, he grabbed the next clue.

Take an aerial combat ride. Test your skill on the Flight Simulator.

His stomach churned at the thought of being whipped around inside a giant hamster ball. He pushed down his anxiety and moved forward, onto the ship, and toward another obstacle set in the way of his prize.

****

"*Yeehaw.*" Colleen performed an aerial loop in the flight simulator. *What a rush!* She'd been afraid she'd get sick, but so far so good. After one last spin combo, her flight ended. Once she was released from the harness and her feet hit the ground, she accepted a red envelope.

Somewhere on this ship is your final clue. Keep your eyes sharp and your feet fast. You have a lot of ground to cover.

Colleen stepped aside as Storm approached with a touch of temper in his narrowed eyes. Well, he shouldn't get his boxers in a bunch. She wasn't very far ahead, and they both had an entire aircraft carrier to search.

Time to hustle. But where to start? She needed a plan. Pulling out a map of the ship, she reviewed the layout, deciding to start at the top and work her way down. If luck stayed by her side, she'd find the red flag hanging off one of the ship's huge gun turrets.

An hour later, she wanted to kick luck between the legs. No red flag and no clue in sight on the gigantic flight deck. Every so often, she'd catch a glimpse of Storm and perceived his frustration matched her own.

The time was almost four-thirty, and the ship would soon close. What then? Were they kicked off or given more time to search? She descended and wove her way through narrow halls. Finally, the blessed red flag came into view, tucked inside the Executive Officer's Quarters. Relief and excitement bubbled up. Grabbing the envelope housing the precious clue, she ran. The twists and turns of the halls weren't conducive for speed, but she made her way back to daylight without delay.

As her foot hit the main deck, she saw Storm barreling toward her. She thought about Harper and how much she needed her daddy in her life. A little voice of conscience whispered in her head. "Hey, Storm," she called. "The clue is on the lower deck, in the EXO's room. Go down the stairs and the room is to your left."

Already halfway descended, he spun back. "Why would you tell me where to find the clue?"

"I'm helping you, believe me or not." Colleen took off at a fast-paced jog. Despite assisting her competitor, she wouldn't concede defeat. Stepping off the ship, she let her anxiety blow away with the fresh air.

The sun hovered over the Pacific Ocean with a blast of pink and orange, and she took a few seconds to appreciate her surroundings. With her mind and body calmed, Colleen opened the next clue.

The bonfire on the beach is your final *stop. Take one last drive and go to the Crystal Pier. The first contestant to arrive is the winner of the Great American Scavenger Hunt!*

Every trial and challenge of the previous seventeen days boiled down to this moment. As long as she kept her composure and didn't waste time on the trip to Crystal Pier, she would be the winner. Excitement bubbled inside her as she pictured her final destination.

****

After wandering down narrow halls, Storm felt ready to scream. He spun in a circle, frantic to remember where he'd already searched. He'd been confident she'd given him wrong directions, so he'd started in the opposite route.

He strode down a tight hallway and after a few turns, he finally found the clue inside the ship's Post Office, not the EXO's room like she'd stated. Had she resorted to deceit in order to win?

He kicked himself for trusting her. How could he have thought they'd have a chance at a real romance? Their budding relationship was a made-for-TV scam. Storm grabbed the envelope and hurried topside. After reading the paper, he steadied himself as the ship underneath seemed to tilt. The last clue. He'd drive fast and hard to beat Colleen to their final destination.

After sprinting off the ship, he swung by the museum ticket booth to ask for directions. The Crystal Pier was close. Instead of meeting victory, he feared defeat waited at the finish line.

****

Colleen waited at a red light to turn onto the freeway and replayed Storm's interview in her head. She bit her lower lip, like the slight pain would be enough to distract her mind. He needed the money to keep his family together. If she won, would Harper live far away? Or would Storm leave his mom to stay with his daughter? Storm's calming presence in Rose's life was the reason for the improvement in her mental health. If he moved away again, she'd certainly spiral into the dark well of mental illness, having lost her reason to fight.

Maybe he'd find a way to keep everyone together. But most likely, not. Storm wasn't blessed with the money she'd been born into. He had no other resources. She did.

Her cause was important as well, though. If she accepted her dad's money, she'd hand over control to a man whose only interest was his own. In order for the retreat to be a success, she needed to run the program without interference.

Ugh. She pounded the steering wheel. What should

she do? Win, build her retreat, and start helping veterans, or let Storm arrive at the finish line first. Either choice left her unsatisfied.

When the light turned green, she pressed her foot on the gas, and guided her vehicle onto the freeway, heading north toward Crystal Pier. The closer Colleen drove to her destination, the greater she firmed her decision. She had a moral obligation to do the right thing. Otherwise, she could never live with herself.

Chapter Twenty-Five

Storm pulled his car into an open spot along a side road next to the beach. After slamming the transmission into Park, he didn't bother turning off the engine. He jumped out and sprinted toward the glow of firelight and production lights down on the beach.

He pushed away thoughts of Colleen already at the finish line. A singular motivation kept him running faster than he ever thought possible—Harper. Even if he didn't win, he'd finish for her, giving his best effort. Storm jumped down the wooden steps three at a time. The deep sand didn't slow his pace. He dug in, and the remaining strength pushed him along.

Ahead at the bonfire, Burt Blackstone waited. Burt's face held no emotion.

Storm halted to a stop on the red mat. Where was Colleen? As he stood by the fire and waited for judgment, he breathed in and out in deep gulps. Soon, he'd either be pronounced the winner or walk away under the weight of disappointment.

Burt's serious face brightened with a large grin. "Congratulations on finishing *The Great American Scavenger Hunt.*"

Three cameramen stepped closer.

Exhaustion and nerves trembled through his body.

"And also on being the first to arrive. You are the winner." Grinning, Burt extended his arm and shook

Storm's hand.

The ground underneath his feet tipped and spun. Had he heard right? How had he beaten Colleen? Was he really the winner, or just the victim of a cruel joke? Storm vaguely felt Burt slap his back. He blinked, clearing his vision. *This moment is real. I've just won one million dollars.* His dream of owning land for a farm would come true.

Placing his hands on his knees for support, he bent over and closed his eyes. The sound of rushing blood in his ears muffled all other noise. He needed time to calm the whirl of emotions before forming words.

"Congratulations," a feminine voice sounded.

He instinctively pulled Colleen into his arms, needing a connection to something real and familiar. The wonderful sensation of her arms wrapped tightly around his neck sent his heart soaring. After several long seconds, he regained rational thought and released his hold.

She stepped away and toward Burt.

"Colleen, you have arrived in second place," Burt announced. "Congratulations on finishing *The Great American Scavenger Hunt.*"

"Thank you." Smiling, she gave Storm a kiss on the cheek then walked back to the small team of crew members assembled by the dunes.

His heart soared in victory, but while he watched Colleen leave, a small part of him grieved for what he had lost.

****

Colleen didn't regret her decision—not after watching Storm win and become overwhelmed with emotion.

On the way to the beach, she'd driven in the slow lane until she saw him pass by. Would the video from the camera in her car show her strategy that insured she'd lose? *Maybe*. When the show's producers put together the final episode, they might highlight her hesitation for added drama. But she really hoped not. Storm deserved an unblemished win. He should believe he'd won, because he was a better player, not because Colleen had thrown the race.

After shaking hands with the cameramen and producers in the hotel lobby, she went to the room the show booked. A room with a view of the ocean. She took a long shower, and then sat on the patio and listened to the crashing waves. A small bottle of champagne chilled on the counter—a gift from the show. Colleen pulled the bottle out of the ice-bucket, popped the cork, and poured herself a glass, then another, and another. The bubbles tickled her mouth and throat with each sip. When she went back for a fourth refill, she found the bottle empty.

A loud knock on her room door sounded. Suppressing a yawn, she shuffled over and opened it. Storm stood on the other side, looking disheveled and very sexy.

"I want to know why?" He leaned in with a forearm resting on the door frame.

Colleen stepped aside. "What are you talking about?"

"Why you gave me bad directions on the ship?" He stood in the center of her room, arms folded across his chest.

Why the attitude? "Huh? I told you where to find the clue."

His scowl deepened. "No, you sent me on a wild goose chase."

"I told you the clue was in the Executive Quarters." She poked a finger into his chest. "And that's where I found it. So, what's the problem?"

Storm's eyes narrowed. "The clue wasn't in the Executive Quarters."

"You're kidding me, right?" Her buzz evaporated, and her temper flared. "You're accusing me of lying? I found my clue envelope in the EXO's room, and I assumed the second one was there, as well, although I didn't take the time to look. I should have kept my mouth shut and not helped you at all." She moved away. Why had the producers switched the rules for the clue location during the last challenge? Jerks.

"Yeah. You should have." His gaze dropped to her lips.

"Get out." Colleen pointed to the door. After everything she'd done to help him win, she still was accused of misdeeds. "When we get home, we can go back to avoiding each other."

"Fine." He marched out of her room and into the hall, before facing her again. "You had me fooled. I thought we had something real. I planned on asking you out. Guess falling for you makes me an idiot."

He couldn't have hurt her anymore if he'd slapped her. "Don't you dare act like I'm the bad guy. We were both competing. I gave you directions on the ship, because I honestly wanted to help you." She inhaled to steady her voice and said a quiet good-bye for any hope of a relationship. "I understood how much winning meant for you and Harper, and I felt something growing between us, too. But relationships take trust, and your accusations just killed any hope."

Storm opened his mouth but then closed it before speaking. Shaking his head, he marched across the hall and closed the door to his room.

With him out of sight, Colleen leaned against the wall. Fat tears rolled down her cheeks. How could he accuse her of purposely misleading him? He still thought she was the same mean girl she'd been in school.

After a build-up of courage, she'd shown her true heart, and he'd ripped it to shreds. She remained an insecure girl, desperately searching for unconditional love. Neither her dad nor Storm found her worthy. Did a man exist who'd ever give her such a treasured gift?

Totally drained and with a splitting headache to boot, Colleen slipped on an old T-shirt and climbed into bed. A mattress, sheets, and a blanket had never felt so good. Tomorrow, she'd conduct her final show interview and head home—back to Liberty Ridge.

She'd lost the competition and, in doing so, didn't gain the money to start her retreat. Her choice was an act of love for a man who refused to see her value.

Move on.

She'd find a new way to finance her dream, which would take longer. Despite the setback, she'd see her retreat become a reality, one way or another.

****

Storm's plane ride back to Austin was quiet. He ignored Colleen, and her matching avoidance made her feelings about him clear.

Before leaving San Diego, he'd signed an affidavit, stating he wouldn't disclose the results of *The Great American Scavenger Hunt* until after the finale aired.

How could he keep silent for two months about one of the biggest moments of his life?

Luckily, the show's producers planned on fast editing, and the first episode would air without much delay. By the time Val left for Brazil, he'd have a big fat check deposited in his bank account, assuring her Harper would be well taken care of without breaking the confidentiality agreement.

Across the aisle, Colleen closed her paperback book and slipped it into her purse.

He still hadn't concluded if she'd purposely mislead him on the ship. Up until that challenge, all the clues were hidden in the same spot. Why would the show change the set-up at the end? Then again, he'd learned enough about manufactured TV drama to have no doubt the producers were capable of anything.

The fact she'd left the ship before him but arrived at the Crystal Pier afterward also confused him. She wasn't the type to get lost. Not Colleen Gardner, super-planner. Well, maybe the one time she got turned around in New Mexico but to be fair, driving across dark, unmarked roads had been the culprit.

A week ago, in the middle of the competition, he believed she was different from the girl he'd known in school. Colleen acted like she'd cared about him, about his mom, and his daughter. In her career, she was devoted to helping veterans struggling with PTSD. Was her caring attitude all an act? A strategy to win? Wasn't he just as guilty of doing the same?

The plane jolted as its wheels touched the ground. At the sight of familiar landscape outside the window, Storm relaxed, his tension easing. He was back in Texas. The Austin skyline in the distance welcomed him home. What happened between Colleen and him during their time away was a creation built for a TV show. Time to face reality.

He powered up his cell, which had been returned after the completion of filming, and checked his email to verify his driver had arrived. Once back in Liberty Ridge, he'd go to the psychiatric hospital and inquire about discharging his mom. Since he'd been out of communication for several weeks, he hoped she hadn't already left on her own.

Then, he'd take her home. Soon, he'd build a large house on the perfect plot of farmland he'd found, with enough room for Harper and his mom to live comfortably. Harper wouldn't grow up with the stigma he'd endured. Thinking about his baby girl calmed his jittery emotions. Soon, he'd have her back in the safety of his arms.

While Colleen exited the plane, Storm remained in his seat. Obviously, they both found simply ignoring one another easier than attempting another conversation. Since they lived in Liberty Ridge, someday he'd deal with the drama between them. But not today.

Today, he'd savor victory.

****

The driver from the car service Colleen hired made good time from Austin to Liberty Ridge. After he dropped her off at her lonely apartment, Colleen tossed her suitcase inside then drove out to True Horizon Ranch. When she rolled down the gravel drive, she noticed Grace standing on the front porch of the white farmhouse. Resting on Grace's hip was baby John, a chubby version of the infant Colleen had seen only a few weeks ago.

Colleen exited her car and stepped onto the porch. "He's gotten so big. What are you feeding him?"

"Hello." Grace pulled Colleen into a hug, and then pointed to the rocking chairs set out on the porch. "He's such a little chunk. I told Heath to ask his buddy, Reagan Harrison, for football pointers. Our little John might grow up to be a lineman someday."

"I'm so happy to be home." Colleen inhaled a lungful of fresh, country air. Ever since she and Grace became friends, True Horizon felt like an extension of home.

"So, spill." Grace set down John on a blue blanket spread out on the porch.

The little boy started hitting two plastic blocks on the wood-plank floor.

"Tell me as much as you can." She rubbed her hands together. "I still can't believe you actually competed on a TV reality show."

Colleen angled her body to face her friend. "I had the experience of a lifetime and saw parts of the country I'd likely never visit otherwise. During the competition, we took two flights and one bus ride, otherwise, I drove the remainder of the time." She wanted to say more but bit her tongue. Keeping quiet about the details was tricky.

"You must be exhausted." Grace rested her head on the back of the rocking chair and blew out a breath.

"I'll take off tomorrow before jumping back into work. Dr. Ertle was kind enough to cover for me while I was gone, but I need to return to my clinic schedule."

"How did you and Storm get along?" Grace's mouth formed into a grin.

Storm—the one person she couldn't get out of her head. "Let's just say our interactions were interesting. Some things changed, and others will always stay the same."

"Like how much he loves you?" Leaning forward, Grace handed a fussy John a rattle, which he then stuck into his mouth.

"I'm positive love is not the emotion he's carried for me all these years." A tight lump formed in her chest, and she folded her arms over her body. She would not allow her unreturned feelings turn her into a gooey mess—again. "I wish I could take back every mean thing I did and said when we were younger."

"Hey, he was no angel either." Grace pressed together her lips and frowned. "I might have been a few years younger in high school, but I could tell he cared about you. All the pranks he played were to get your attention. Why do you think the guys teased him so much? He was mooning for you—a girl far out of his league."

A tingling sensation across her skin caused her to shiver. "Storm used to hang around the water fountain by my locker, but I never gave it much thought." Colleen blinked. Along with the multitude of times he walked past the bleachers during every cheer practice. *Holy cow.* Storm hadn't hated her. Was his gruff behavior, both then and now, simply a way of protecting his heart?

"You didn't know?" Grace smiled. "But then again, why would you? You two didn't exactly hang out in the same circles."

"Storm didn't hang out in any circle." Why hadn't she paid more attention to all the people outside the popular group she'd called her friends? She bent over and held her head in her hands. "I'm a horrible person. I was so awful."

"Give yourself a break. You were a teenage girl." Grace patted her back. "We all had our differences in high school and still found a way to forgive and forget. I'm sure you and Storm can make amends, too. Especially after you spent so much time together during the competition."

As pain rippled in her heart, Colleen straightened in her chair. "I stupidly fell in love with him."

"That's great." Grace's eyes brightened. "I'll start planning the wedding."

With soft laughter, she shook her head. "No one is getting married. Especially not myself and Storm. He'll always think the worst of me, and I'm done making amends. He can hold his grudge forever. I don't care." In reality, she did care—very much. Her pain felt too deep to share.

"Storm's a stubborn fool." Grace reached down to wiggle one of John's chubby toes. "He doesn't deserve you, then."

She gazed off into the distance, at the herd of Longhorn cattle munching in the field. Throughout school, Colleen acted mean to Grace, and Grace found a way to forgive and move one. Over the last year, they'd become good friends. Colleen confided in Grace about her childhood, her mother's death, and her alcoholic father. Grace told her that one day, she'd find the courage to forgive herself.

During the competition, Colleen discovered an inner strength she hadn't known existed. She'd learned forgiveness didn't come with a price tag. No one could force her to pay for things she didn't owe. Storm's issues were his own, and Dad numbing his grief with alcoholism was his responsibility alone. She was done feeling badly for other people's actions.

A new fire lit in her heart. Moving forward, her veterans' retreat would take every ounce of her attention. She would raise the remaining money to open the doors and work her tail off to make sure the date was soon.

Chapter Twenty-Six

Two months later, Storm cuddled with his daughter on a worn-out recliner, while his mom rested in her rocking chair. He hit the remote to power on his small television. *Here goes nothing.* Across the screen flashed the title of the show—*The Great American Scavenger Hunt*. An image of Storm standing in a field played during the opening credits. At the sight of himself on TV, he recoiled.

"Oh." Rose gazed over with a wide smile. "You look so handsome."

"Daddy." Harper's plump hands clapped together as she bounced on his knee.

The increased weight of his baby girl surprised him. She'd grown so much since he'd seen her last. The time between visits had been too long. Very soon, though, he'd have her with him permanently. Everything was coming together. He'd have the prize money before Valerie left for Brazil.

Since the competition ended, he'd secured a temporary job on a ranch outside of town. They'd needed help clearing their fields for the winter, and he had to earn some cash until the prize money landed in his bank account. Beside the occasional Colleen-sighting around town, his life here was almost perfect. He kept his distance from her. Around town, the buzz of gossip about them and the show grew daily. No need adding to the volume.

Like a ghost summoned, Colleen's face flashed on to the screen. Her enticing smile lit up the television.

"There's Colleen." Rose pointed to the TV. "I can't wait to see what happens between the two of you. With the way you've sulked around the apartment since coming back, I wonder if sparks did fly."

Enough sparks to light a fire hot enough to burn them both. "Colleen hasn't spoken to me since we returned home."

"Who could blame her?" Rose pulled up a rainbow-colored blanket to cover her lap. "You're so crabby all the time."

"I'm not crabby." Okay—maybe a little. Due to his bad behavior at the end of the competition, he missed Colleen's presence in his life.

"Shhhh." Rose waved a hand. "The show's starting."

He watched the entire cast of contestants stand on the steps of the Capitol Building. He remembered the nervous excitement of that moment, when he had no idea what adventures lie ahead.

After a wide shot of the entire group, the camera panned the row of contestants. As a group, the contestants opened their first clue, and chaos ensued. People ran in all directions, while Storm followed Colleen. Good grief—he'd looked to her lead like a loyal dog from the very beginning.

Having grown bored with the TV, Harper wiggled off his lap and found her crayons and a coloring sheet.

As the show progressed, Storm watched the scene in the Metro station. *Great.* The first of many times Colleen stepped in and helped him. He relived the panic he'd felt buying a ticket for the Metro train. At the time, he'd been perturbed Colleen swooped in and guided him through the jungle of the terminal to the right train. He'd been so angry and unwilling to accept her goodwill. Even though, she'd pushed past his ego and, in doing so, helped him save face in front of the TV camera.

"I think you owe Colleen a cup of coffee for helping you," Rose said with a laugh as she pointed toward the TV. "Looks like you'd still be wandering around DC without her."

"Thanks for the vote of confidence." Storm suppressed his smile.

His mom sighed. "Colleen is a wonderful person. I wish you two could put the past behind and find a way to be friends again."

His love for Colleen crushed his heart too many times to recover. If he could stop thinking about her and dreaming about her now, he might heal. But no matter how hard he tried to forget her, he couldn't let go of the hope he'd someday be a good enough man to earn her love.

****

A round of applause sounded as Colleen switched off the television. Grace's brother, Alex, hosted a *Great American Scavenger Hunt* party at his restaurant, The Desert Rose. The place was packed. Many residents from town showed up to watch the show along with her.

Of course, Storm declined Alex's invitation. She'd hoped to see him tonight and relive those crazy moments at the beginning of the competition. They'd both looked so wide-eyed and confused.

Despite constant attempts to harvest information from the attendees about the show's outcome, she'd done a good job of keeping her lips sealed. They'd have to watch another nine episodes until the finale aired, and then everyone would learn Storm was a millionaire. Hopefully, no one would ever discover she'd thrown the race and let him win. Once the restaurant cleared, Colleen helped clean. She didn't want to go back home.

"I can tell from the first episode that you and Storm enjoyed competing against each other." Grace walked by, holding a tray of dirty glasses. "I mean, you're both still alive, so I know neither of you killed the other. I noticed Storm did not want to accept your help at the Metro Station."

Yeah! She could finally talk about her experiences on the show, or at least what happened in the first episode. "Storm didn't trust me, which he made very obvious for the camera." Tonight's show spent a lot of time focused on the two of them. The knot of worry in her gut tightened. Would the producers keep the focus on the drama and tension between her and Storm for the rest of the episodes? If so, Liberty Ridge would be all set with good gossip for the next nine weeks. Probably longer. Colleen moved around the restaurant, picking up dirty plates and silverware. "I had fun tonight, watching the show with a good group of people. I love living in Liberty Ridge."

"We should make getting together here to watch the show a weekly ritual." Grace set down the tray of glasses on a table with a melody of clinks. "I can't wait to see what happens next week."

"I don't know about watching each show with a large group from the town. Things might get awkward."

What if they used the clip of her and Storm kissing at the motel in Albuquerque, or when they shared the same cabin at Custer State Park? Talk about uncomfortable.

Grace tilted her head and smiled. "Awkward? Like when the kissing starts?"

"Who said anything about kissing?" Heat bloomed on her cheeks.

"Please tell me there's kissing." Grace's eyes sparkled, and she set a few more dirty glasses on the tray and hiked it back onto her shoulder.

"My contract forbids me from saying." She shrugged and pressed her lips together in a tight line, preventing any impulsive confessions.

"Yeah, right." Grace hip-bumped the swinging door to the kitchen. "That's okay. I'm patient. I'll eventually find out why you and Storm haven't said two words to each other since you've been back." She disappeared into the kitchen.

Colleen followed with hands full of dirty dishes. After setting them into the sink, she headed back into the restaurant to collect more.

Grace appeared through the swinging doors. "The bus staff will finish up in the morning. Let me tell Alex I'm leaving, and we can head out. I need to get home for John's feeding."

After saying their good-byes, Colleen and Grace walked out the front door. Downtown Liberty Ridge looked rolled up for the day. Besides the streetlights and the glow from inside the restaurant, the night had fully taken over.

"Have either you or Heath talked to Storm lately?" Colleen dared to ask. "I saw him yesterday with Harper.

I hope everything has worked out regarding custody."

"Heath had a beer with him over at the Damn Yankee Bar last weekend. I guess he's doing really well. The Whitmans hired him temporarily to help on their ranch, and Valerie agreed to sign over full custody while she's out of the country."

"That's good news." She often thought about Storm and Harper and now rejoiced at the news he'd raise his daughter like he'd dreamed. During her return to Liberty Ridge, she'd accepted her feeling wouldn't recede. She was stuck in a riptide of emotion. One day, when the drama from the show died down, she'd force Storm to talk over what happened between them. After pushing back against the current, she might find her way to shore and return both feet to solid ground.

****

The Great American Scavenger Hunt was the talk of Liberty Ridge. So far, five episodes had aired, meaning the public had seen half the season. Storm couldn't go anywhere in town without being stared at or, even worse, stopped and pestered with annoying questions.

"Did all that driving make you tired?"

"Weren't you scared kayaking through alligator-infested waters?"

"Are you in love with Colleen Gardner?"

As tonight's episode ended, he clicked off the television. He hadn't known Colleen ran out of gas on her way to Denver. On that trip, he'd taken off without her, breaking their alliance and making him look like a jerk. Of course, she'd come out smelling like a rose. Poor Colleen was left all alone, stranded at the side of the road—hoping not to end up some axe murderer's next meal.

To date, he'd watched every episode in the relative safety of his home. Besides his mom and Harper, no one was around to witness his flushed face every time the camera zoomed in on his intense gazes at Colleen. He hadn't realized how obvious he'd made his attraction.

If Rose picked up on the romantic tension, she hadn't said so. His mom still struggled under the haze of her antipsychotic drug treatment, but she had a new awareness in regard to Storm. She didn't pester and didn't judge. Rose simply loved and supported him, just as he did her.

He wished he'd had this new version of Rose while growing up. In appreciation of the gift he'd been given, he let go of his resentment. Harper would be living with both a father and grandmother who loved her fiercely. Hopefully, their love would soothe some of the sting of missing her mother.

"Well, that was a fun episode. Denver is such a pretty city. I've always wanted to visit someday." Rose gripped the arms of her rocking chair and stood. "I'm heading to bed. See you in the morning."

"Sleep tight." His mom spent more time in bed than usual. Her doctor mentioned the new medication might make her drowsy. The meds helped stabilize her erratic behavior but, unfortunately, dulled some of her spunk—part of what made her so special.

If she continued improving, she'd someday hold a job. Or instead, work happily with him on his farm. Regardless, she'd again embrace life.

He checked the time. Only nine o'clock. Too early to turn in, and he was restless. Watching himself act a fool on TV left him with a need to blow off steam.

So far, the show showed Colleen as kind and supportive of everyone, including Storm, while he acted obnoxiously unfriendly. During one of her interview segments, she spoke about her love for helping veterans and her goal of opening a retreat. Colleen was the show's sweetheart. Time and again, she stepped up to assist him, even when he pushed her away.

Doubt gnawed his gut. What if she meant to help at their final clue, and he accused her of deceitfulness?

Storm grabbed a hoodie and headed out for a walk. He needed answers and knew exactly where to find them.

****

The Damn Yankee Bar was packed for a weeknight. On Thursdays, the bar ran a dollar draft special, leaving no seat empty. She moved around the room, her legs felt like lead weights. Her feet hurt. Her back ached. Looking at the neon clock above the bar, she groaned. Another hour until the end of her shift.

A practicing psychiatrist waitressing tables at a bar was a strange sight. She needed the extra money, though, and every single dollar of her tips went toward her veterans' retreat trust fund. Over the past month, between her side job at the bar, fundraising efforts, and grants, her account grew to the halfway point. By this time next year, she hoped to have enough to break ground.

A shout from the other side of the bar grabbed her attention. She looked toward the crowd and noticed Storm enter through the front door.

After shaking a few hands of the ever-present fans of the show, he glanced her way. He strode to the bar then took a seat on a recently emptied stool.

Colleen approached with caution, like a cat would a sleeping dog. "What can I get you?"

"A minute of your time." His gaze traveled up and down her body. "I never pegged you as the barmaid."

She spread her hands wide, palms up. "A bar is a shrink's playground. I think of serving in a bar as research."

Storm smiled. "A congregation for head cases."

Despite her nerves, she laughed. "If you don't need a drink then I should get back to waiting tables." She needed distance between them. He pulled at her heart and warmed her body.

"Wait up." He took hold of her hand before she moved too far. "Take a break. Will you give me a few minutes?"

She looked around—tables needed clearing, people lingering for their bills, a few newcomers appeared ready to order. They could wait another minute. She untied her apron and motioned for Storm to follow her toward a side door. The air outside was chilly, causing her to shiver.

He unzipped his hoodie and wrapped it around her shoulders. "We should clear the air."

Without any easy reply, she stood quietly and stared at the dry leaf pile swirling with the wind.

Storm stuffed his hands into the front pockets of his jeans and rocked back on his heels. "Did you purposely mislead me on the ship?"

She shrugged. "You won't believe me no matter what I say. You always think the worst."

"Months ago, yes, but not now." He stepped toward her, staring into her eyes. "Was I wrong?"

"Colleen," the bartender called from the doorway. "I'm gettin' overrun in here. Say what ya gotta and get back inside."

"Sorry." She returned her attention to Storm. "I have to go. If I'm out here, I don't get tips."

"You can't possibly need the money?" His brown-eyed gaze studied her.

"My veterans' retreat does. All my income from bartending is deposited into the fund. So as you can see, I have to go." She knew this conversation needed to happen at some point, but not now. She'd already sacrificed a lot for him, and she couldn't afford more.

He grabbed her elbow. "I'm sorry for not trusting you. I wish you'd trust me with the truth."

With a jerk of her arm, she pulled out of his hold. "Trust you?" She sniffled back tears. Pausing, she gathered emotional strength. "If you knew me at all...the version standing here right now...you'd already know the truth."

Back in the safety of the bar, she realized she still wore Storm's hoodie. Taking off the sweatshirt, she lifted the fabric to her nose and inhaled his scent, quickening her pulse. She missed the smell of him, herbal and fresh, like he'd rolled around in a pile of dried mint and rosemary.

He'd come here for answers, but she hadn't felt much in the giving spirit. Nothing she'd say would change his heart. Only Storm had the power to break down the barrier he'd built.

Chapter Twenty-Seven

"Oh, my." Rose's hand fluttered over her chest. "Please tell me you were giving that girl CPR."

Heat filled Storm's body. Not only was his mom a witness to his lip lock with Colleen inside the motel room in New Mexico, but so were approximately seven million other people. "I kissed her...so what?"

Her blue eyes sparkled. "I know firecrackers when I see them. And yet, here you are, spending every evening home with me."

"I kissed her in a moment of weakness. We were tired and stressed out. Neither of us showed very good judgment that night." He stood, heart thumping, and paced the room.

No need to watch the action on TV because he'd lived it. The memory of his kiss with Colleen still taunted him. He'd never gotten such a hot spark with merely a simple touch of lips. The chemistry between them was intense. No denying that truth.

Because of the friendship they'd shared as children, she held a special place in his heart. Besides his mom and Harper, Colleen was the only other person he'd truly loved.

Tonight's episode ended with scenes from next week's episode, which included hiking down the Grand Canyon. More of Storm and Colleen, working together with long looks shared between them. Even he couldn't deny the cameras captured something special. Now, he lived with the knowledge he was one-hundred-percent at fault for the destruction of their relationship.

"Are you going out tonight?" Rose grabbed the remote and changed the channel to a nature show.

He snorted out a laugh. "After that episode, I can't show my face around town."

"Maybe the time has come to finally grow up and face your feelings like a man." She spoke without taking her gaze off the TV.

"What?" Such a snippy comment from his laid-back mom raised his defenses.

"You've been living in Liberty Ridge for six months. Yet, you hide out in this apartment, afraid to open yourself to the people of this town."

"I've gone out a few times with Heath Carter." In Heath, Storm found a kindred spirit. But Heath was busy running his ranch, along with spending time with his wife and baby son.

Rose waved her hand at his words. "If you plan on raising your daughter here, as well as operate a business, then you need to become part of this community. Did you know Colleen is holding a fundraising dinner on the night the last episode of your show airs?"

He'd been invited to attend but of course had declined. Storm's lingering regret wasn't strong enough to change his mind. "Someone mentioned it."

"You better plan on going. Her foundation is a good cause, and she's struggling to raise enough money to open. Since you can't tell me who won, I'll have to wait for another three weeks. All I know for certain is Colleen's working hard to raise money to help her veterans."

"Are you rooting for Colleen to win instead of your own son?" *Man, that hurt.* Had his own mother turned against him?

"I wish you'd find a way to both come out winners. Even if the prize is only true love." She stood and pulled him into a strong embrace.

"Oh, for crying out loud." He allowed his mom to say her peace and get in her hug. Once she released her bear hold, he stepped away.

Rose rubbed his shoulder. "I love you. Think about what I said, okay? I might be crazy but I know love when I see it, and you've loved Colleen since your first day of kindergarten. I can tell she cares an awful lot for you. Not many people get the chance to experience such a deep devotion. Don't close your eyes to the gift you've been given."

Hollowness expanded in his chest. He'd opened his eyes to the amazing person Colleen was, and regrettably, he'd seen the truth too late.

****

Colleen sat in a large leather chair in her dad's home office, as still as an ice sculpture and just as cold.

"Take the money." Clive extended his manicured hand, which held a check written with a large sum.

"I don't want your money, not if it comes with conditions." She stiffened her spine, imagining the many strings attached to the check.

"Of course, I'll want to oversee my investment. I'm only asking for a spot on the board of directors not to run the place." Clive reclined in his large office chair. He pressed his fingers together, forming a triangle with his hands. "Are you saying you don't need the money? Did you win on that asinine television show?"

"Save your money. I'll run my charitable organization without your interference." Colleen clenched her fists.

"You know how small-minded and cheap the people are in this town." He lifted a highball glass of amber liquor and took a long drink. "You'll never raise enough funds holding local bake sales and raffles."

"Why do you do that?" She narrowed her eyes. How many times had she sat in this very chair, listening to her father either belittle her or someone else?

"Do what?" He set his glass on the desk and spun in his chair, reaching for the half-full crystal decanter on the bookshelf.

"Put down the people who live in Liberty Ridge."

"Because they're a bunch of hicks." He lifted off the teardrop-shaped top and poured. "Especially the man kissing you on TV. Storm, is that his name? He's not good enough for you. None of these people are."

"How would you know?" Filled with a raging anger, she jumped to her feet. "You're too drunk most of the time to notice anything but the booze in your hand."

"Now, see here." He bolted from his chair, swaying with the sudden movement. "You should know better than anyone why I drink. Your mother—"

Colleen pounded her fist on his desk, cutting off his words. "Mom's death was hard on me, too. I practically raised myself. I had no one to show me right from wrong or how to be a good person. For years, I emulated you. I wanted your attention. I blamed myself for Mom's death, for your drinking, and for not being a good enough girl."

Clive stared back, his face flushed a deep red, and sweat dripped from his brow. "I read the police statement from the accident. Catherine was distracted by your temper tantrum, and that's why she crashed."

"I was seven years old!" she screamed, a release of years of pent-up anger. "Just a child. How dare you lay that all at my feet."

He stumbled back into his chair, hung his head, and released a long sigh. After glancing sideways at the glass of alcohol sitting on his desk, he closed his eyes.

"I paid as high a price as you did." Colleen's voice lowered to a whisper, her throat scratchy and raw. "I would give anything to have Mom here, but neither of us can change the past. All we can do is work for a better future."

"I'm too old and tired, Colleen. This is who I am." He motioned with one hand around his office. The room was filled with business awards and golf trophies, pictures with famous people and politicians. "I'm a terrible dad. I'm sorry. Take the check, and allow me to redeem myself."

Colleen shook her head. "You can't buy me like a politician. I will build this retreat without your money. If ever a time comes when you fully support my mission, please feel free to make an anonymous donation." Walking out of the office, she shed the weight of years of guilt. Dad made his own choices, and she prayed they wouldn't kill him.

An hour later, she sat in her office, preparing for Heath's session. She shouldn't have favorites, but Heath was one of the best, as well as her toughest case. When Heath first came to her office, he'd struggled with debilitating PTSD. In him, she'd identified something she deeply admired—a fighter's spirit.

Heath entered her office wearing a huge grin. "Hey, Doc."

She was tired, emotionally drained, and needed a good cry but smiled and motioned for him to take a seat. He leaned in with a conspiratorial gleam in his hazel eyes.

"Before we get started, I have something to tell you. Off the record."

"I'm not a reporter." Colleen chuckled.

"Here's the deal. My new buddy, Storm Thompson, is driving me crazy…making me sick. I don't know how much more I can take."

From what she knew of Heath, he got along with everybody. She lost her smile. "I'm not on speaking terms with Storm. What do you expect from me?"

Under his beard, Heath bore a large smile. "Put the poor dude out of his misery. Tell him you love him…that you've always loved him. Kiss him 'til he can't see straight. Come on, Doc. I'll die if I have to listen to his sob story one more time."

"Oh, please." Colleen reached across and swatted his tattooed arm. "He's not dropping tears into his beer over me."

"Yes he is, Doc. If you don't do something about his heartbreak, then I will. But trust me, my solution won't be as pleasant."

Warmth rose up her neck and filled her face. "Enough talk about Storm. Let's officially begin your session."

Heath winked, resting his elbows on the chair arms. Propping his foot on the opposite knee, he picked off a few pieces of hay from his pant leg.

She ignored him while reading over her latest notes in his file. As she raised her gaze to meet his, she noticed Heath's smirk. Who did he think he was— Cupid? She imagined the ideas of happy-ever-after Heath might have put in Storm's head, and her stomach tightened. A provocative prospect or an alarming attempt—only time would tell.

****

"I'll be takin' bets 'til Thursday at five p.m.," the bartender at the Damn Yankee Bar shouted to the patrons who lingered after the evening rush.

"Rick, you know betting is illegal, right?" Colleen made her way behind the bar. Glancing over at the white board hung by the restrooms, she shuddered. A week ago, a few people started talking about betting on *The Great American Scavenger Hunt*. Now, the odds were on everyone's lips. With the finale set to air in two days, she couldn't wait for the train-wreck show to be over.

"I'm not concerned about the Texas State Gaming Commission shutting down my little office pool." Rick towel-dried a beer mug. "Don't worry, Doc, my money's on you."

Not a wise bet, but Colleen couldn't share that information with Rick. After last week's episode, only four contestants remained. On the whiteboard, someone had written the winning odds for Storm, Colleen, Tammy, and Lenny. Good grief, she felt like a racehorse at Churchill Downs.

Keeping her expression neutral, Colleen sidestepped over to the tap and pulled a pale ale for a guy at the bar. If the odds of winning weren't bad enough, someone became clever and placed odds on Storm and Colleen's relationship status, as well as if they kissed during the final episode.

She guessed most of the town was in on the action. People on the street pumped her for information. She even caught someone taking frequent walks past her apartment, in an attempt to catch her and Storm together. The whole situation was ridiculous.

"I think Ms. Colleen and Storm are holding out." The guy at the end of the bar stood and swayed on his feet. "Everyone in town knows you two pranked one another back in the day. If that's not a sign of true love, then I don't know what is." He downed the remaining beer from his mug and grabbed his leather jacket from the back of the stool. "Call me a cab, Rick. Time to head home."

In reply, she simply smiled. Good service meant good tips. "You shouldn't waste your money betting on a reality TV show."

"Don't be such a spoil sport." Rick rested his heavy frame against the bar. His large, rough palm tapped the wooded top. "I plan on giving your foundation my winnings."

"I can't take illegal gambling winnings." What in the world was happening to this town? Everybody had reality-show fever.

After calling for a cab, Rick walked around the bar, holding a plastic tub and began collecting empty bottles and mugs. "You and Storm have us all guessing. I know you two had a thing for each other since you carried lunch boxes to school. Young love that strong doesn't just go away."

"Sure, whatever you say." She'd learned from

countless conversations regarding the TV show not to argue. *Let it go*. They'd find out soon enough. She and Storm would never see eye to eye, let alone be involved in a romantic relationship, despite the sizzling attraction highlighted on the show week after week.

Colleen counted out her tips. Fifty bucks—not bad for a week night. The money would go straight into the charity trust fund. Not the fastest way to earn the funds, but she'd eventually reach her goal.

After punching out for the night, she strolled a half-mile home. The air was pleasantly chilly and quiet. Since she wasn't speaking with her father, she spent most weekends at Grace and Heath's place. Baby John and his cute antics kept her spirits lifted.

Now, loneliness crept in and settled in her heart. Each footstep grew heavier. Would she ever enjoy love? Or marry or have kids? Maybe her destiny rested with her career, working with her new foundation and retreat. She wished for a magic mirror and a glimpse into the future.

Right now, she wanted to curl up beside Storm's warm body and fall asleep in his arms. She thought of Harper's sweet face and her strawberry blonde piggy tails, and smiled, picturing herself a member of his family—a part of Harper's life.

She entered her apartment and tossed her purse and keys on the side table by the door. What she needed was a really long vacation, away from Storm and Liberty Ridge. Tomorrow, she'd research a January tropical vacation.

Tonight, she'd escape into her favorite dream, where Storm waited at home with a smile and a kiss.

Chapter Twenty-Eight

Two weeks later, Colleen accepted two tickets from an elderly couple at the front door. "Thanks for supporting our veterans. Enjoy the show." For the past hour, she'd worked the hostess station at the Desert Rose restaurant. They held a fundraising dinner, with all profits donated to the veterans' retreat trust fund. For a typical similar fundraising event, she'd expect a light crowd, but tonight, multiple flat screens hung on the wall for viewing *The Great American Scavenger Hunt* finale. The added bonus for the attendees was watching alongside Colleen, one of the contestants. Alex, the restaurant owner, pulled in people not only from Texas, but as far away as Florida.

"We have about thirty minutes until the show starts." Alex approached from behind. "I told the chefs to have the pre-selected meals ready to serve. Everything should be in place when we dim the lights for tonight's feature presentation."

She turned to face him and touched his hand. "Thanks, Alex, for putting on the event. Any help raising money is deeply appreciated." The fundraiser, at one-hundred-fifty dollars a plate times two-hundred plates sold, would net a large deposit in the retreat's account, especially since Alex had donated both the use of the restaurant and food.

"No problem. Oh, hey." Alex moved closer and

lowered his voice. "Storm called this afternoon and mentioned he might stop by. Just thought I'd give you a heads up."

"Thanks." Her pulse quickened at the news. Good to know. She'd steel her heart before seeing him.

As Alex left, she saw two familiar faces approach. Colleen squealed and embraced her dear friend. "Molly!"

Molly's husband, Drew, stood behind them, laughing. "Hey, Doc. You didn't think we'd miss your grand finale?"

Not only was Drew a good friend, he'd also been her patient. "I'm so happy you're both here." She broke from Molly to hug Drew. "Just surprised you could come on a weekday."

"Well, Drew's on break from school, and I took some vacation time." Molly held Drew's hand. "I'm glad we're back home, even for a little while."

"Grace and Heath are sitting over there." Colleen pointed. "Go squeeze in at their table."

Molly stood still while her gaze scanned the room, which then rested on the whiteboard propped underneath one of the TV screens. "Is someone taking bets on the outcome of the show?"

She cringed at the thought of her law enforcement friend's disapproval. "Someone's idea of a joke." A bad one, in her biased opinion.

Molly approached the board and read the odds listed. "You know betting on the results of a TV show is illegal, right?"

She shrugged, heat rising in her face. "Like I said, it's just a joke. Think of it as a raffle for a charitable organization."

Drew looked over Molly's shoulder. "What are these lines about?" He pointed to the ones listing Colleen and Storm. "Are you two romantically involved?"

"No." *From bad to worse*. Colleen shrugged. "People have a strange sense of humor, I guess."

"Drew hasn't watched the show, but I have. Things are getting really hot between them." Molly's face glowed with a huge smile. "Who's taking the money? I'll bet we'll return for a wedding next summer."

"What?" Colleen's jaw dropped.

"Has anyone started a line on guessing a wedding date?" Molly shouted to the crowd.

"Hey, that's a good one," Rick hollered from across the restaurant. He'd closed down the Damn Yankee Bar for the night so he could attend. "Come see me, and I'll hook you up."

With a sigh of resignation, Colleen returned to the hostess station at the front of the restaurant. No hiding from embarrassment tonight.

If Storm did appear, the crowd would really get their money's worth. Too bad they wouldn't see any romance in tonight's final episode. The people who'd bet money on them ending the competition as a couple would go home very disappointed. Colleen would leave saddened as well. She remembered a time during the middle of the competition she'd hoped they might find their way back to one another.

About one minute until show time, someone dimmed the restaurant lights and turned on the TV screens. Guess Storm was a no-show, which filled her with a mixture of relief and disappointment.

When the opening credits appeared, the buzz of

conversation stopped. The first scene showed the four contestants arriving at Joshua Tree National Park. The cameras followed Storm because he'd been the first to arrive.

All ticket holders had arrived, so she left her post and sat on a bar stool toward the front of the dining room. As she watched Storm wander around the desert in Joshua Tree National Park, growing visibly frustrated, Colleen stifled a laugh.

"That wasn't funny," a deep voice drawled from behind.

She bit back a laugh and turned to see Storm, who must have sneaked inside.

He held Harper in his arms. A half grin highlighted his scruffy face.

Her heart hitched at the sight of him.

"I enjoy seeing everything I missed during the competition," he said. "I was so focused on my own tasks, I wasn't aware of the other dramas unfolding."

"Like when Tammy and Amy got into a shouting match descending into the Grand Canyon?" Colleen quietly chuckled. "I knew they both made it out alive, but I couldn't help but worry one of them would push the other off the ledge."

Storm pulled up another barstool and set Harper on his lap.

"Down, Daddy."

"You have to stay with me, or I'll take you home to Grandma." Storm rubbed a hand over Harper's blonde curls. "I'm still not sure my mom's capable of watching her alone. But I wanted to come tonight."

Harper arched her back and wiggled like a fish caught in a net. Colleen reached out and touched her small hand. "I'm happy you're here. Let me get her a snack. She might sit still with something to eat." She stood then she stepped back as Harper's slight arms reached out. "Honey, stay with Daddy. I'll be right back."

"She can go with you." Storm released his hold and set Harper's feet in the ground. "Just don't let her sweet talk you into ice cream."

"Really?" Stunned, she watched Harper place her small hand inside her own. The soft warmth of her skin produced an instinctual feeling of protectiveness. Did he really trust her with his daughter?

"Yes." He smiled. "Hustle before the commercial break is over."

She led the little girl to the snack table and, after some intense negotiations, brought back Harper with crackers and cheese. "Is this snack okay?" Colleen asked Storm. "I said no to the cookies, even though her pouty lip almost broke my heart."

Storm nodded. "Don't be fooled. She knows how irresistible she can be." He kissed Harper's cheek.

The commercials ended, and the show resumed.

Every so often, Storm glanced over and smiled. "You're good with her."

The feeling of Harper resting securely on her lap was heavenly. She swallowed a surprisingly large lump of emotion. "Thanks."

An hour into the finale, Lenny and Tammy were eliminated. Only Storm and Colleen remained. The restaurant filled with excited energy. Questions of who would win buzzed in the air.

As an aerial picture of the Salton Sea glowed on the screen, she grimaced. "That lake was nasty."

Talking again with Storm did her heart good. Maybe they could find a way to regain their friendship.

"You know the Salton Sea used to be a big vacation spot for Hollywood types in the 40s, 50s, and 60s." He leaned in and whispered, "Sonny Bono and his set hung out there."

"No way." She'd vote the area least likely to attract the rich and powerful.

"The lake is drying up, now. The salt concentration is increasing, killing off the fish. All the white along the shore is not sand…it's ground-up fish bones."

"Ew." Colleen crinkled her nose. "No wonder the lake was so stinky."

"Pesticide run-off is another culprit." He lifted his chin. "I've worked on promoting natural alternatives to farmers, but for most, chemicals are easier and cheaper."

His passion for organic farming came through loud and clear. She'd done the right thing at the end of the competition, but her confidence didn't loosen the tangle of nerves building in her gut. Would the show expose her secret or the footage edited to illustrate a true race to the finish line for added drama?

Behind her back, she crossed her fingers. No one, most of all Storm, could ever learn the truth.

****

Sitting beside him, Colleen looked as tightly wound as a newly sprouted plant. She'd set her shoulders so high, they almost touched her ears. He itched to reach over and massage her strained muscles. If he touched her, though, he wouldn't stop.

During the latest commercial break, Heath stopped nearby. "Man, I can't believe you two are duking it out for first place. I won't confess which of you I placed money on, but I'm hoping for a win." He smiled broadly.

"You'll find out the winner very soon." Storm took a drink of ice water.

Heath turned his attention to Colleen. "So, Doc, you make a nice, little family over here. Tell me the wedding date, and I'll place a wager for a sure win."

Colleen's face turned as red as a strawberry.

Wedding date? His stomach clenched. Should he be worried? "What are you talking about?"

"You don't know? A group is betting on who can pick the date closest to the wedding."

Storm scratched his head. "Whose wedding?" As soon as the words left his mouth, he understood and shivered.

"The Gardner-Thompson wedding, of course." Heath leaned close. "So, tell me…June, July, August. Give me a hint."

"Go back to your wife, Heath." Colleen swatted his arm. "Or I'll charge you triple for your next session."

"Okay, okay." He raised his hands, palms facing them. "I can take a hint. Catch you two later." Heath winked then strode back to his table before the TV show resumed.

"What else are they betting on?" He studied her face, which had blushed pink. Did he really want to know?

"Everything their devious minds can think up." She handed Harper a piece of cheese. "I'm surprised they haven't started on how many kids we'll have."

"Don't give them any ideas." Three sounded nice. He glanced around at the crowded restaurant. Everyone appeared totally engrossed in the action playing out on the television.

The screen displayed a clip of Colleen driving to San Diego, and then Storm behind the wheel. The infamous ship scene was up next. Maybe he should leave and avoid embarrassment. Soon, the whole town would witness how Colleen had helped him locate the last clue, and he'd totally lost his cool.

In preparation for Harper living with him full-time, he'd put in a lot of effort toward letting go of past grudges and pain. His mom was right about him becoming a part of the community. Finding his way back to Colleen would fully settle his soul. He needed her in his life. Only, after the way he'd acted, he wondered if she held enough forgiveness in her heart. Somehow, he'd earn her trust, no matter how long or hard the road. She fit him like no other woman ever had. Colleen Gardner was worth the fight.

Another commercial break began, and he felt the sharp glances of disapproval thrown his way. With only ten minutes left in the show, he felt his anticipation grow. Soon, he'd close the door on the latest chapter and, with any luck, move forward with Colleen. With firm determination, he reached across to hold Colleen's hand.

She stiffened at first, and then relaxed.

He sat connected with her and watched Colleen race off the ship first, followed by himself. During the drive to the final stop, the dramatic music grew louder. The muscles in Colleen's hand turned rigid, but he didn't release his hold. He needed the physical connection with the one person who deep down, really understood him.

Storm watched the footage of Colleen driving to the Crystal Pier. At first, nothing unusual caught his attention. But soon, he noticed the other cars on the freeway moving swiftly past her as she tootled along in the far right lane. Was she driving under the speed limit? From what he remembered, Colleen drove carefully but never slow.

As he watched the clip of himself speed down the road, he fully comprehended how he'd won. His chest squeezed tight, and he struggled to breathe. Storm's gaze met Colleen's wide blue eyes. "You let me win."

****

Colleen trembled as her heart pounded inside her chest. No one else appeared to have caught on, but Storm knew her better. Without warning, he pulled her toward the front door. She held on to Harper and followed him outside. Through the restaurant window, she saw on the TV screen Storm streak across the beach to a waiting Burt Blackstone.

"Why?" he choked out. "Of all the dumb things you could have done, why let me win?"

Harper lowered her head and buried her face in Colleen's shirt.

She opened her mouth then closed it. With palms sweating, she wasn't sure if she should admit or deny.

"I'm right, aren't I? You drove slowly so I'd pass you. You should have been the first to arrive at the beach." Storm stood frozen. His breath misted in the cold air.

"I—" She forced out then faltered. Colleen pulled Harper close to her body to keep the child warm. "I couldn't live with myself if I'd won the money you needed to keep Harper. I just couldn't do it." Pressure

277

built behind her eyes, followed by the release of tears. She sniffled and blinked fast.

"I don't know what to say." He rubbed a hand down his face. "I really don't."

"What I did was my choice." She inhaled the sweet smell of the little girl's hair, relishing her nearness. "In the end, you needed the win more."

"But look at you." He pointed to her then down the street toward the bar. "Slopping drinks at a bar to raise money for your retreat. If you won, you'd be set."

Holding Harper in her arms, she understood the deep love that drove Storm during the weeks of the competition. "Your daughter needs you now. Consider the win an offer of settlement."

Storm hunched his shoulders. "I am so sorry for acting like the world's biggest jerk. Will you please forgive me?"

For a second, she held her breath, almost not believing his words then she nodded.

He leaned in, crushing his lips against hers. His arms wrapped tightly around her waist.

She'd never let anyone or anything separate them again.

Harper, who was propped on Colleen's hip, reacted in a fit of giggles.

When he pulled his mouth off hers, he peered down at Colleen and smiled. "My heart has always belonged to you." He stepped back to cup her face in both of his hands. "I've loved you Colleen Gardner since our first day of kindergarten. I loved you through high school and every year after I left town. But the wonderful woman you are today is who I love most."

A soul deep calm flowed through her. She inhaled

his words, sweeter than pure syrup. The lump in her throat loosened. Her emotional dam broke, and hot tears flowed down her cheeks.

Storm wiped away the dampness with his thumb. "Will you give me a chance to be worthy of you?"

"You have always been worthy, Stormy. I love you," she choked out in between sobs. With her free hand, she pulled out a red-cellophane-wrapped candy from her pants pocket and handed it to him. "Please share strawberry candies with me…again."

Eyes gleaming, he tipped back his head and laughed. "I thought you'd never ask."

A low rumble sounded from behind, and she turned to face the restaurant. Everyone inside was crammed against the front windows, watching with intense interest.

"Kiss her again," shouted a man from the crowd.

"Didn't I tell you they'd end up a couple?" A woman poked the arm of the man on her left. "You owe me twenty dollars."

Heath opened the door, sporting a giant grin. "Looks like my work is done."

"You're just a regular matchmaker." Molly bumped him with her hip, wearing a deadpan expression.

"Hey, don't knock my skills. I brought you and Drew together, too."

Molly huffed, smiled, and then walked away.

Colleen, still secure in Storm's arms, visually soaked in every detail of his face—the fine lines around his brown eyes, the way his lips curled up at the ends when he smiled, and the earthy smell of his skin.

He leaned down to kiss her again, earning a round

of applause from their audience.

Before they went back inside, she had one more thing to say. "When you said I let you win, you were wrong. I had my sights set on a bigger prize."

Storm grinned. "Our deal was winner takes all but looks like we both won something more precious than money."

Colleen lifted their linked hands, along with Harper's sandwiched inside, and pressed them against her heart. "We found love. The greatest win of all."

Epilogue

"Is everything ready for this afternoon?" Colleen hopped into the cab of Storm's old pick-up truck. She leaned around Harper, who sat in a booster seat between them, and gave her husband a kiss on the cheek.

"Everything's set. The ribbon is up, I tested the microphone, and I even remembered to bring the big scissors you bought." He turned the key in the ignition, and the timeworn engine rumbled to life.

"Perfect. Let's go home and change." The little buzzing inside her stomach turned into a swarm of bees. Today, she celebrated the ribbon cutting for the Liberty Foundation Veterans' Retreat, built on the grounds of the Liberty Harvest Organic Farm.

With his winnings from the show, Storm bought the prime piece of farmland they'd both wanted. A few months later, work began on a house, and his farm thrived like a seedling planted in warm soil.

For the year, Colleen stood by his side as first his girlfriend, then fiancé, and finally as his wife.

As an engagement gift, Storm set aside ten acres for the veterans' retreat. He also donated enough money so she could break ground. His farm and her retreat were dreams now fulfilled.

Storm parked next to their two-story farmhouse and unbuckled Harper from her seat. Once her little feet hit the ground, she ran straight on to the porch and toward her puppy, whom she'd ironically named Kitty.

"Kitty want to go inside." She petted the tan fur covering the pup.

Storm unclipped Kitty's collar from the rope keeping her on the porch, and then opened the front door.

The dog scampered inside.

"Let's get you changed into your pretty dress." He lifted his daughter.

Harper waved with arms, accidently smacking him in the face.

Once Harper was changed, Storm and Colleen left her playing in her room while they moved into their bedroom to get ready.

Pushing the door closed with his foot, he pulled Colleen into his arms. "I'm proud of you," Storm said in between kisses. "The people you'll help are so lucky to have you fighting in their corner."

"We did this together, don't forget." Instead of competing against each other, she and her love were now a solid team. Storm's farm would be an integral part of the retreat. The animals would serve as therapy, and the veterans could work out in the fields, if they wished.

Two hours later, Colleen stood before the large crowd gathered before the steps of the retreat's main building. A bee hive of nerves buzzed in her stomach. She scanned her gaze over the hundreds of people who'd shown up in support. The Mayor, Police Chief, and even the Austin and Dallas/Fort Worth media were present. Both Rose and Clive were there. Colleen still hadn't fully reconciled with her dad, but they were at least talking, which was a start. She saw Heath, Grace, Molly, and Drew. Heath and Drew gave her a salute—a silent message of a job well done.

Storm and Harper stood at her side. An overwhelming swell of love flowed through her veins. She was the luckiest girl in the world. Colleen felt a tug on the hem on her skirt and looked down.

Harper smiled with hands lifted high.

She picked up the little girl, who weighed heavy in her arms, and stepped up to the microphone. All her carefully planned words flew from her mind. Instead, she let her celebratory speech flow from her heart.

She spoke about Storm's passion for growing food naturally from the earth and her desire to help the country's brave veterans find life after war. Together, they built a home with respect and love as the foundation.

Applause sounded after her concluding remarks, breaking through her shaking reserve. Tears flooded her eyes, and love filled her heart. She thought back to earlier in the day, when she stood alone in the bathroom, and smiled. The little white stick showing two lines signaled a wonderful change in their lives.

Stepping back, she eased Storm's hand to her abdomen and placed her lips next to his ear. "Darling, we're in for a very bountiful year."

Laurie Winter

Enjoy the first scene from the last book in the Warriors of the Heart series, *Know You by Heart*:

When Alice Liddell chose her legal name at the age of eighteen, she meant it as a symbol of her new life. Like Alice in Wonderland, she'd visited strange lands, met distrustful people, and barely survived a brush with death. She'd been afforded more than one second chance, something she was grateful for every day.

Now, she straightened her spine and stepped through the walkway, toward a 747 bound for Texas.

The attendant escorted her to a large, leather seat at the front of the plane.

Her first-class accommodations were definitely an upgrade from the military cargo planes and assault helicopters she'd grown accustomed to traveling in. Physically spent after the long walk through the airport, Alice breathed a sigh of relief. For the next several hours, she could sit and relax.

As she limped over to her window seat, she winced at the sudden muscle cramp in her right leg. She eased herself down and used her strong fingers to knead out the ache, just as her physical therapist instructed. After a minute, the cramp subsided, and she sat upright, begging her body to cooperate for the remainder of the flight and resist any more bursts of pain.

People walked by and down the aisle, rolling small suitcases and carrying bags, travel pillows, and children. One woman wearing a purple pantsuit clutched a designer bag in her hands while whispering words of comfort to the small dog tucked inside. Outside the window, baggage carts hurried around the tarmac.

She hoped both her suitcases would arrive in Austin. Her so-called vacation would transform from bothersome to aggravating if she had to spend the week wearing the same outfit.

"Excuse me." A deep voice sounded from the aisle. "Would you mind if we switched seats? I prefer to sit on the inside, away from the aisle."

She turned her attention from the action outside to the man speaking, and her gaze moved up the length of his athletic body, finally settling on a striking pair of brown eyes. After several seconds of flipping through her recently unreliable memory bank, she placed a name with the face. He had the look of a young Keanu Reeves, circa *Point Break*. Despite the fact she recognized him, she wouldn't give Micah Palmer the satisfaction.

Why did he want the interior seat? Maybe to hide from obsessive sports fans, which she was, but neither of him nor his team. "Sure." *Why not?* As long as she remained in first-class, the location of her seat didn't matter. She stood and shuffled out into the aisle.

He was tall, beating her by a few inches, and his hands were large. She imagined he had no trouble keeping a tight grip on a football. Micah was the star quarterback of the Timber Lake Warriors, or more accurately, the former star. After last year, his standing with the team and its fans dropped.

"Thanks." He smiled and stepped back to make room. He moved his gaze from her face to her lower half. "Is your leg okay?"

Forcing her face to remain relaxed, she blocked out the pain radiating from the entire right side of her body. "I'm fine. It's just stiff."

Once Micah was in her old spot, Alice settled herself into the aisle seat and the ache in her leg subsided. At least in her new location, she could stretch her leg into the aisle every so often.

Curious, she subtly peeked at her new neighbor. He was more handsome close-up than on TV. Most people would be thrilled to sit beside a professional football star, but not her. Or, at least, not when the star was Micah Palmer. First, she was a huge fan of the Arizona Scorpions, the Warrior's biggest rival. Second, Micah Palmer missed most of last season due to a torn ACL. Third and most important, she'd read reports about his excessive partying and alleged drug use.

The flow of boarding passengers trickled to a final few people.

She reclined her head on the chair's soft headrest and closed her eyes, listening to the sounds of the attendant preparing for take-off mixed with passengers' chit chat. A phone chimed beside her, and she lifted her eyelids to peer over.

Micah cleared his throat. "Hey…I'm on the plane and need to shut off my phone. What do you need?" After a brief pause, he rubbed his face. "I told you I'll be out of reach for the next two weeks." Another pause. "No, I can't have any guests while I'm there…I got to go…bye."

His groan of obvious frustration made her smile. Alice heard enough through the phone's speaker to concur the caller had been a female admirer. *Poor guy.* All he wanted was two weeks of peace. His phone chimed again, and Alice almost rolled her eyes.

"Ana, I'm so glad you called. I wanted to let you know where I'm staying." He straightened in his chair.

"Oh, okay." He paused. "That's fine. I should get off my phone anyways, so I'll talk to you soon. Maybe tonight after I get settled in." Micah picked at some lint on his khaki shorts. "Sure, I forgot you're leaving with Ray. Have a good trip…bye."

Another female caller, but she'd received the gold-star treatment. Alice turned her head to gaze upon the seemingly most popular man in the world.

He clicked off his phone. "Sorry about that." He grinned and shrugged. "You know how it is…people need to reach you every second of the day."

"No…I don't know how it is." She returned the smile then mentally slapped the grin off her face. Don't want him thinking she was another flirty, star-struck girl. From what she'd read in news reports, his ego didn't need any more stroking. "I'm lucky if I get a call once a month." Her circle of friends was small and tight. Most of her Army Cultural Support Team sisters were either deployed or busy with their civilian jobs. Her only family was her cousin—a newlywed. Kate had other things on her mind.

"Consider yourself lucky. I'm unplugging these next two weeks. Get off the grid so to speak." Micah slipped his phone into his carry-on bag then showed her his empty palms. "If you see me pull out my phone during the flight, feel free to slap me."

Alice laughed at the invitation. During previous football seasons, she would have loved to do just that. Especially during the game when Micah threw a touchdown pass with eight seconds left for the win, knocking her beloved Scorpions out of the playoffs. "You'll be safe with me. My fighting days are over."

The plane bumped with sudden movement, and

then glided away from the gate.

Alice jolted with an increasing tempo in her pulse, either the result of the stress of flying or the nearness of Micah Palmer. So what if he was cute? Good looks weren't necessarily a reflection of a good soul.

She'd brought along a book about helping women in third-world countries become business owners. She opened it in an attempt to read through a couple chapters.

After about fifteen minutes, she gave up, unable to concentrate on the typed words on the page. She had a bad case of the jitters and couldn't calm her over-analytical mind. Flying normally didn't make her nervous. She'd jumped out of planes with nothing but a parachute strapped to her back. Maybe, she'd feel better after a nap.

Alice closed her eyes and visualized her destination—a veterans' retreat. She had no idea what to expect. Her friend, former Special Ops soldier Heath Carter, helped start it, and she attended at his invitation. She'd gotten to know Heath when she'd served alongside him in Afghanistan. He was a good man and soldier—actually, the best.

She'd never made a secret of her injuries as a result of an IED and how she still suffered. Heath traveled to visit while she was at Walter Reed and witnessed firsthand the wounds marking her body. He hadn't needed a PhD to understand the damage done to her mind.

Two of her soldier brothers lost their lives to the same IED. Yet, she was still breathing, with a few scars to show as souvenirs.

After only two weeks at the retreat, she had no

illusions that she'd learn the answer to the question keeping her wide awake at nights—why had she lived?

A word about the author…

Laurie Winter is a true warrior of the heart. Inspired by her dreams, she creates authentic characters who overcome the odds and find true love.

She keeps her life balanced with regular yoga practice and running. When not pounding the pavement or the keyboard, she's enjoying time with her family, who are scattered in Wisconsin and Michigan. Laurie has three kids and one fantastic husband, who all inspire her to chase her dreams.

http://lauriewinter.com

~

Titles by This Author
available from The Wild Rose Press, Inc.

The Warriors of the Heart Series:
Home Field
True Horizon
After All
Winner Takes All
Know You by Heart